Falling for Theo

KYLE COFFMAN

The Library of Congress

ISBN: 9798218934149

Cover design by Sebastian Films Unlimited.
Editing by Greg King.

Falling for Theo is a work of fiction. Names, characters, businesses, organizations, places, events, and incidents are either the product of the author's imagination or used in a fictitious manner. Any resemblance to actual persons, living or dead, or to actual businesses or locations, is purely coincidental.

For the one who refused to let this story fade and never let me give up. Gregg, this is all because of you. It's finally complete.

Author's Note

The idea for *Falling for Theo* originally came to me in a dream. The moment I woke up, I jumped out of bed and ran to my computer to document the dream before it faded from my memory.

In the dream, I was observing two men lying in bed. One appeared to be around 30 years old, the other in his late 30s. One was Caucasian, the other Latin. They were both shirtless, wearing only pajama bottoms, their legs tangled together like pretzels, holding each other tightly.

I could feel the intense connection between them, their desire to stay in that bed, in that moment, together for a lifetime. But I also sensed that the world wouldn't allow it. They knew they only had this brief window of time, wrapped in each other's arms and legs, to fully enjoy their togetherness.

The connection between them was so powerful, it filled

the entire room. It was the kind of love that makes your chest ache, the kind of love that, if made public, would come at a cost. And underneath it all, there was a lingering feeling that one of them belonged to someone else.

That dream became the seed that grew into *Falling for Theo.* Over the next several months, I began crafting the story, outlining each chapter and developing three unforgettable characters: Cameron, Theo, and Daniel.

My ultimate goal in writing this novel, the question I leave with you, the reader, is this:

What if you married the love of your life… Then you met your soulmate?

What would you do?

It's not as easy an answer as one might think.

-Kyle Coffman

Chapter 1

Life truly began for me the night I met the love of my life. Sometimes, when I think about it, it feels like it was just yesterday. Not everyone can remember their first kiss or even who they lost their virginity to, but I think we can all agree that we never forget our first love. Whether that love broke our heart, or we married them, we all remember the first one.

My name is Cameron Taylor, and I was lucky enough to meet my first love when I was just 20 years old. I'm from a small town outside of Philadelphia, Pennsylvania, called Collingswood, New Jersey. Separated by a bridge, Collingswood is home to about 14,000 people.

After graduating from Collingswood High School, I was accepted into Penn State's College of Communications to study communications and film. I've always been a writer, and I wanted to continue exploring my craft through visual art. Studying film turned out to be one of the best decisions I've ever made, it opened up a world of opportunities for me, but that's a story for later.

The day I met the love of my life was at the very end of my sophomore year. My best friend, Donna, had just graduated with a degree in communications. She and a few of her sorority sisters hosted a graduation party at one of their friend's houses.

I didn't drink much at 20, mainly because I couldn't legally get alcohol, but also because I didn't like the taste of it. Beer made my stomach feel like it was going to explode, and red wine tasted like the smell of dirty feet to me. But on that night, I was drinking rum punch someone had made. It was Donna's big night, after all. Surprisingly, I couldn't taste the rum, just a sweet punch with a hint of coconut.

Donna had graduated from Penn State and was moving to Chicago for a broadcasting job she had landed through an internship. It's also worth mentioning that Donna had been a huge partier during college and could really hold her own when it came to alcohol. I had seen men twice her size pass out before she did, or vomit, and she only weighed 120 pounds.

Donna had straight blonde hair that she always wore down. She was more of a guy's girl than a girly girl, jeans and T-shirts were her usual uniform, with the occasional flannel thrown in just to throw guys off, assuming she was a lesbian. She wasn't, though. Come to think of it, I remember hearing some sorority stories about her experimenting, but I'm not sure how much truth there was to that.

I met Donna halfway through my freshman year. I was struggling with a statistics class, and she was tutoring to make extra cash for drinking money. After three tutoring sessions, we started hanging out. We're both huge fans of horror movies, so every Thursday night we would host movie marathons in our dorm rooms and watch anything scary. Most of the time, they were cheesy B-rated flicks with bad actors, poor cinematography, and off-sounding audio. But for every three bad movies, there was always that one dark and amazing gem.

I should probably mention that I'm gay. I came out at the end of my senior year of high school, finally embracing the attraction I'd felt for the same sex my entire life. My parents were hardworking Democrats, so I expected them to be okay with it. My brother, Tyler, who was two years older than me, used to make gay jokes growing up, classic stuff like "smear the queer" when we played tackle football or calling someone a "homo" because they didn't share his misogynistic views. I figured he wouldn't take the news badly, thinking he'd just been teasing for the sake of being "tough."

I came out to my family one Saturday morning during breakfast. I remember it like it was yesterday.

"I'm gay," I blurted out right after Tyler took a bite of his banana and nearly choked.

My mom and dad exchanged a glance and nodded like they already knew and had been waiting for me to say it.

"It changes nothing, sweetie," my mom said. "Your father and I still love you."

Then Tyler, who was in his second year at Philadelphia University, suddenly had this brilliant idea that, because I was gay, that somehow made him a minority and that he could apply for a scholarship. He tried, but of course, it didn't work.

Back to Donna's party. The house was packed with partiers who were mostly graduates and their friends. A banner hanging from the ceiling read *Congratulations*

Alumni! which was ironic since it wasn't even in Penn State's school colors. It was pink with red text, probably from the drama department's set collection for some play about graduates.

Donna was wearing only a white bra and blue jeans, chugging a beer from a funnel surrounded by four guys cheering her on. What did I say? She was *one of the guys.* That's one of the things I admired most about her. She was fearless and didn't conform to gender roles.

When Donna finished the funnel, she stood up and belched like a man. The four guys cheered, and each of them took off their shirts. I'm pretty sure they were playing some sort of drinking-strip game, but I didn't mind. Two of them were cute and had the bodies of Olympic swimmers. They must have been on the swim team.

I sat on the couch sipping my rum punch from a red Solo cup. Suddenly, a guy joined me, holding a beer.

"Mind if I sit here?" he asked.

I glanced over, unmoved at first, but when I locked eyes with him, I immediately straightened up.

"Sure," I said.

He flashed a beautiful smile. He was definitely my type, olive skin of an Italian lover, or what I would think the complexion of an Italian lover would have. He had dark hair and sported a five o'clock shadow. He looked older than the rest of us. If I had to guess, I'd say he was in his late 20s.

He extended his hand. "I'm Daniel," he said. "I was told by *her* I should talk to you." He pointed at Donna.

We shook hands, and I noticed how warm his hand was.

"I'm Cameron," I replied.

He smiled, and we both leaned back on the couch.

"You don't look like you're having as much fun as

they are," he said, nodding toward Donna and her friends. One of them was removing his jeans and stripping down to his boxers after failing to chug a beer from the funnel.

"I could never keep up with them," I shouted politely, the music blaring even louder now.

Daniel eyed my red cup. "What are you drinking?" he asked.

"Rum punch, I think. Or whatever they put in the punch," I said.

Daniel laughed and took a sip of his beer. "You're cute," he said, still chuckling.

Cute? That caught me completely off guard. What was this handsome guy doing talking to me and calling me cute? Am I really this lucky? Was he gay too? He had to be, right? All these thoughts flooded my head at once.

We ended up chatting for about half an hour. The conversation was easy, natural.

Later that night, Daniel and I moved to the front porch and sat on the wooden patio swing. The living room was packed with people now, and the noise was unbearable. We wanted a place where we could actually hear each other.

It was a perfect East Coast night. The air was crisp and fresh. As it turned out, Daniel knew Donna's older brother, Brian, and had come to the party to meet me. He was in town for work. I learned that Daniel had graduated from Penn State's College of Business and was ten years older than me. He had just turned 30, and yes, he was gay.

As we sat on the porch swing, Daniel's hand accidentally brushed mine, and I felt butterflies in my stomach. I had never felt this nervous around a guy before. To be honest, I had only had one boyfriend before, back in freshman year, but that had been a disaster. He was a serial dater, and I'd thought we were exclusive. But with Daniel, everything felt different. He was mature, confident, and that's what attracted me to him the most.

"What are you studying in school?" Daniel asked.

"Film. I'm focusing on screenwriting," I said.

Daniel took a swig of his beer. "A writer. That's impressive," he said, clearly fascinated.

"What do you do?" I asked.

"I'm a junior executive at a consulting firm in New York City."

"Wow. Do you like it?" I asked, now I'm impressed.

"I like the money, but not so much the hours. What about you? What are you writing?"

"I'm actually working on an action script right now, but I typically like to write mysteries."

"That's so cool. I don't think I've ever met a writer before. I'd love to read some of your work," Daniel said.

I nod. *Of course you can read my work*. I didn't know what it was about him, but he was so easy to talk to. We talked for five hours on that porch swing. By the end of the night, I found myself resting my head on his shoulder, his arm around me. I could hear his heart beating through his chest, and for the first time in my life, I felt complete.

Chapter 2

We went on our first date two nights after Donna's party. Since I was out of school for the summer, my schedule was free, and Daniel was in town for three more nights. I didn't have any expectations with Daniel because I knew he lived in New York City, and I didn't think anything would come of us. But I enjoyed his company so much on that porch swing that I thought it couldn't hurt to hang out with him a couple of times before he went back home to New York. Plus, he was really cute, so that was a bonus.

Daniel picked me up at my parents' house, where I was staying over summer break. He drove a black luxury SUV with leather interior. I can still smell that leather when I entered the vehicle; it smelled like expensive candy, like black licorice. Collingswood was 96 miles from New York City, so if a relationship happened to develop, it wouldn't be long-distance, really.

Once I sat in the passenger seat, the smell of his cologne hit me, and my heart dropped into my stomach. He smelled so good, and that made me nervous.

He smiled at me when I got into his car and said, "Hello, handsome."

This, of course, made me blush. Even though we hadn't seen each other since Donna's party, we had talked on the phone for an hour each night for the past two nights, getting to know one another.

"Hi there," I responded, sending a smile back.

We had decided the night before that we would go to the movies and then dinner. Donna had once told me that whenever you go on a dinner-and-movie date with someone new, always make sure you go to the movie first, then dinner. That way, if you don't have anything to talk about, you can talk about the movie.

When I first told Daniel about this idea, he laughed. "Cameron, we talked on that porch for five hours and have talked every night since. I don't think we'll run out of things to talk about."

We chose to see a horror movie, mainly because I love scary movies, but also because there were a bunch of superhero movies playing, and neither of us was a fan of that genre. The movie was a classic supernatural thriller, featuring eerie music, unpredictable jump scares, and some very intense moments. I knew Daniel was comfortable halfway through the movie because he laid his hand on my lap. At first, I jumped, not from the hand, but because he did it right at the moment a scary scene happened. My eyes immediately darted left and right to make sure no one saw. And no one did. Everyone's eyes were glued to the screen. I wasn't used to public displays of affection, but it felt nice, so I picked up his hand from my lap and placed it in my own. I scooted closer to him, and our shoulders brushed against each other. He was so warm.

Daniel was right. We didn't run out of things to talk about at dinner. In fact, we had way too much to talk about. We went to an Italian restaurant, and Daniel introduced me to a sweet red wine. This certainly didn't taste like the smell of dirty feet. I liked it. Daniel told me that wine is an acquired taste, and the more I experimented with it alongside food, the more I would like it. Then he promised to take me to a winery where I could get better educated on wine and be a total wine snob by the end of the tour.

The date ended with Daniel dropping me off at my parents' house. Just like in those romantic movies, we kissed. It was an amazing first kiss that lasted about two minutes, which I might add, is an exceptional amount of time for a kiss. That could even graduate to the "making out" level. I felt like I was floating on a cloud the entire time we kissed. His tongue massaging against mine was the most incredible feeling I had ever experienced.

On our second date, Daniel took me to a winery outside of Philadelphia, in Chester County. I wasn't quite 21 yet, but Daniel knew the owners of the winery, so they pretended not to notice when they checked my I.D.'s date of birth. Since Daniel knew I wasn't a big fan of wine, he arranged a special tasting just for me, full of the winery's sweetest wines. We tried a Riesling first, which was very sweet, and I liked it. Then we moved on to a Moscato, and finished with a sweet white called Tanners, which was the winery's signature white. It tasted like a crisp apple. We moved on to the red wines next, starting with a sweet red, which tasted a bit bitter to me, but I was told by the employee that my palate was used to the sugary whites. We then tried a Pinot Noir, Cabernet, and ended with a Merlot, which was incredibly dry and bitter. It literally took my breath away.

"How do people drink this stuff?" I asked as I spat the Merlot into a bucket the winery's employee had at her bar.

"It's an acquired taste," Daniel said, taking the last sip of his Merlot.

The winery's tasting bar was rather small. It had five wooden stools, and Daniel and I were occupying the last two stools on the right side.

The employee, Martha, was in her 50s and had curly brown hair. She told us she had worked at the winery for 15 years and couldn't be happier with her job. Plus, she got a 20% discount on all wines and free tastings when she was off duty.

"I tell you what," Martha said. "I have a nice Riesling from a harvest three years ago in the back. Why don't I get you boys a bottle and two glasses, and you can take it and walk the vineyard?"

"That sounds perfect," Daniel said, pulling out his wallet.

Martha smiled and headed for the back room. I started to pull out my wallet, too, but Daniel put his hand on top of mine and insisted I put it back in my pocket.

"My treat," he said.

Martha returned with the Riesling in a shiny blue bottle and uncorked it for us. She set down two wine glasses and rang up the wine.

The vineyard was absolutely beautiful acres upon acres of lush greenery. Daniel and I walked through the vineyard, sipping on the wine, and continued to get to know one another.

We stopped at an old wooden bench in the middle of the vineyard. It was engraved with a gold plaque that read: IN LOVING MEMORY OF DAVID AND WILMA HAMILTON. HAPPY 65TH ANNIVERSARY!

"Wow," I said as we both took a seat. "That's a long time to be married."

Daniel nodded in agreement. He set the half-empty bottle on the ground after pouring each of us another glass.

"Yes, it is," he said, staring into my eyes. "You are so adorable, you know that?"

My face reddened, of course. He leaned in, and we kissed.

"Thank you for such a romantic second date," I said to him.

He kissed me again and put his arm around me, pulling me closer.

"You're so welcome," he said.

It was at this moment that I realized I was starting to develop strong feelings for Daniel. I knew it was absurd because it was only our second date, but I felt like I knew him so well already. With the number of hours we'd spent on the phone, this might as well have been our tenth, eleventh, or even twelfth date.

"When do you have to go back to New York?" I asked, not really wanting to know the answer. I wanted to stay in this moment, with him, for the rest of my life.

"Tomorrow," he replied. "I have to get things ready for work on Monday."

My stomach ached suddenly. I didn't want him to go back to New York. I wanted him to stay right here with me. Then, this idea popped into my head.

"What if I came to see you next weekend?" I asked him. He let go of me and smiled.

"Yeah?"

"I haven't been to New York since I was a kid, I could always use another tour of Manhattan."

Daniel laughed. "I would like that," he said. "I can give you a tour. It's an amazing city. So much to do."

"Then it's a date," I said. "Our third date, in fact. A date weekend."

Daniel's eyes suddenly lit up. "You can meet my friends," he said. "We're getting together for dinner next Saturday night. Something we try to do once a month."

That made me nervous. Meeting his friends already? What if they didn't like me? Or what if they thought I was too young for Daniel? These thoughts had crossed my mind before. When I told my parents I was casually seeing Daniel and getting to know him, they were less than thrilled to learn he was 30 years old. My mom immediately said he was too old for me and that I should get to know guys my own age. I had to assume if I was hearing this, then he was probably hearing that I was too young for him. But I didn't want to ask him, in case I was right. I didn't want to know. I really liked Daniel, and I didn't want to put the idea in his head in case someone else hadn't. Plus, I knew I was starting school in the fall, so I didn't think whatever we were doing would last longer than the summer anyway.

Daniel and I kissed again just as the sun started to set. This whole thing started to feel like a romance novel. How did I get so lucky so young? Or did I?

Chapter 3

Our third date went just as planned. I took the train from Philadelphia to Penn Station in New York City, where Daniel met me on the platform.

"How was the ride?" he asked.

"Good," I replied. I'd only brought one bag with me, just enough for two nights. I didn't need much.

We immediately left Penn Station, and Daniel hailed a cab for us. A yellow cab quickly pulled over, and we got in.

"East 51st and 2nd," Daniel told the driver, who immediately turned on the meter.

"Where are we going?" I asked.

"Well, I figured we could stop by my place first so you can drop off your bag, then meet my friends at an Irish pub around the corner. They've got great wings."

I swallowed hard. I was nervous about meeting Daniel's friends, mostly because I had no idea what he'd told them about me.

We stopped at Daniel's apartment. He lived in a very small one-bedroom, *and I mean very small.* His kitchen consisted of a tiny refrigerator, a long counter, and a stove with only two burners. There was a small table with room for just two chairs, and his living room couch was practically in the same room as the kitchen.

The bedroom was a bit larger than I expected for an apartment this size. It led to the only bathroom.

"Did you want to take a shower or anything?" he asked. Was he asking if I wanted to shower with him, or just if I wanted to take one by myself? I was so nervous that I couldn't tell.

"There are fresh towels under the sink if you want. We have a bit of time," he added.

"I'm good," I told him, setting my bag on the bed. He smiled broadly.

"It's so cool to have you here," he said, pushing me gently onto the bed. He climbed on top of me and kissed me. He sniffed my neck. "You smell so good." Thank goodness I sprayed on that cologne this morning. And yes, I sprayed it on my neck, too. Donna always said that's the first place a man's nose goes when he's close to a woman. I wasn't sure if it was just a hetero thing, but I figured it couldn't hurt to spray there, too. Turns out, it's just a man thing in general.

He felt good on top of me, and I could feel that he was getting excited. We kissed again and continued making out for a while until his phone rang.

"Ahh," he groaned, rolling off the bed to answer it. Strangely, my nervousness started to fade. Maybe it was because I'd felt his excitement earlier, or maybe it was because he had made me feel more comfortable. Either way, I was finally relaxed.

"They're meeting us in half an hour," Daniel said, hanging up his phone.

"Okay," I replied. Maybe I would take him up on that shower, just by myself, for now.

We arrived at the Irish pub right on time. The city was buzzing on this Friday night, and the pub was packed to capacity.

Daniel and I muscled our way through the crowd, him leading the way, parting people like the Red Sea, and me following closely behind.

There was a table in the back corner with four people sitting and two empty chairs next to each other. Daniel pointed to the table, signaling me that that's where we were heading.

Once we arrived, I noticed two full pitchers of beer, one light and one auburn-colored, four empty shot glasses with clear liquid residue, and a basket of cheese fries.

"You guys started without us," Daniel shouted, pointing to the shots.

The four friends laughed. There were two men and two women.

"Everyone, this is Cameron," Daniel said, pulling out a chair for me.

"Hey, hi!" the four of them greeted me in unison.

I took the seat, feeling shy. "Hello," I said softly.

"You old enough to drink beer?" one of the guys asked. He was built like a football player, with a short crew cut. "I'm Ian," he added, handing me an empty beer glass.

"My ID says I'm old enough," I said and allowed Ian to pour my beer. Everyone laughed, including Daniel. Although he seemed surprised to hear of my fake ID. I wish I could take credit for it, but that was all Donna. She had one made for me so I could get into a rave concert with her. They carded pretty hard, so she arranged for me to go with her, fake I.D. in hand.

"I'm Sherry, Ian's wife," one of the women said to me. She had long, straight brown hair and freckles, wearing a pretty low-cut top that revealed some cleavage.

"And this is Brian and Marcy," Daniel said, pointing to the other man and woman. "They're not married."

Daniel and Marcy cracked up. "College friends," Marcy added.

Brian was really cute. He wore a black tank top that showed off his well-defined biceps. Marcy looked more like Velma from *Scooby-Doo*; she had black glasses and kept her brown hair cut short, just to her chin.

Our waitress arrived and pulled out her notepad. "What can I get for you guys?" she asked.

"Another round and two more shots for these two," Ian said, pointing to Daniel and me.

She glanced at Daniel and scribbled on her pad. When her eyes rested on me, she asked, "I.D.?"

Everyone laughed. "He's a pup!" Brian said.

I pulled out my wallet and handed her my fake I.D. She barely looked at it, didn't even seem to care if I was old enough. Hell, she didn't even look old enough herself.

"I'll be back. Any food?" she asked.

"Dozen wings!" Daniel shouted, raising his voice to be heard over the noise. "The spicier, the better."

"No," Thelma moaned. "Mild."

Daniel shook his head. "Spicy," he said, winking at the waitress. She smirked and walked away.

The next hour went much better than I'd anticipated. I only caught a few playful jabs at Daniel about me, but he defended himself well. I also learned a lot about Ian.

He had dated someone much younger than him, and she turned out to be a total psycho. Well, that's how they described her, at least. Daniel should be pleased to know that I'm not a psycho.

"Did you guys see the Dow dropped 1,000 points today?" Ian said, stuffing fries into his mouth.

Everyone nodded, concerned, so I nodded too. What the hell is the Dow, and why were they worried it dropped? My youth and inexperience were getting the best of me, but I couldn't let any of them know that.

I placed my hand on Daniel's lap. He jumped a little, clearly startled by the move. He eyed me for a second, then smiled and placed his hand on top of mine.

More shots were consumed, more laughter followed, and in that moment, it seemed like I was making a good impression with his friends.

Ian and Brian got into a debate about how many protein shakes one should have while following a workout regimen. Meanwhile, Sherry and Marcy talked to Daniel and me about the law firm they worked at when Daniel took my hand and slid it toward his crotch.

I immediately got warm, maybe it was from the shots, or maybe it was because his female friends were having a conversation with us not knowing that my hand was resting on Daniel's crotch under the table.

I thought about jerking it away, but I was feeling pretty good courtesy of the alcohol, so I decided to play along. Obediently, I left my hand on his crotch and began to rub it. Moments later, I started to feel it grow.

The conversation continued with Sherry and Marcy, but Daniel leaned in and kissed my neck. The girls smiled at one another and started to converse with themselves allowing our exit.

Daniel leaned in my ear, "Wanna get out of here?"

"What? Why?" I asked.

He whispered so only I could hear him, "Because I want to take you back to my apartment and take this shirt off you, then your pants, and get you naked. I want to give you the best massage of your life. And when I have you completely relaxed, I want to make love to you all night long." And with that he bit the tip of my ear.

I froze and immediately got excited myself. My heart was beating so rapidly I thought it was going to bounce out of my chest.

I finished the last quarter of my beer and nodded at him.

"Guys, it's been fun!" Daniel shouted as we both rose.

"What? Dude, you're leaving?" Ian asked.

"Oh yeah," Daniel said wrapping his arm around me giving me a kiss on the cheek.

Sherry and Marcy caught on right away. They knew why we were leaving. Ian and Brian would need it explained to them.

"So nice to meet you, Cameron," Sherry said.

"It was nice to meet all of you," I responded. Everyone waved and Daniel and I fought our way through the crowd to leave.

That night Daniel and I made love for the first time. Three times to be exact and it was amazing. I had only been with one other guy before Daniel, that serial boyfriend who wasn't exclusively dating me, even though I was exclusively dating him. Daniel was so much better, and experienced in the bedroom. I didn't know I could feel that good for that long.

The next morning, we woke up in each other's arms completely naked. We were only covered by the sheet on his bed. The sun shined in warming our faces. I kissed him on the lips and he smiled.

"Good morning, babe," he said returning the kiss and rolling on top of me.

"How'd you sleep?" I asked.

He started to kiss my neck. "I didn't get much sleep," he said now kissing my chest, then down to my stomach until his mouth found my... and then I stretched my arms hitting the headboard. This was something I could really get used to in the mornings.

After I had another incredible orgasm, I returned the favor giving Daniel one too. We laid in the bed for what seemed like hours talking about a future we may have together. Daniel asked me how I liked his friends and I told him they were great. Then we moved on to figuring out how we would see each other when I went back to Penn State in the fall.

It was at this point that Daniel and I decided to take the leap and enter into a relationship, and what soon would become a long-distance relationship come that fall. I hesitated because I'd always heard long-distance relationships never worked. But Daniel reminded me that it is different for us because we can see each other however often we wanted to on our laptop's webcam or video call. I agreed and we began officially seeing each other, exclusively as boyfriends. This time the exclusivity was mutual.

Chapter 4

Over the next two years, Daniel and I became very close. My parents finally got over the 10-year age difference between us. I had always considered myself more mature than my peers, so the age gap didn't bother me, and it certainly didn't bother Daniel.

I graduated from Penn State's College of Communications with a degree in Film. That day also happened to mark Daniel and my second anniversary. Daniel took me out for a celebratory dinner that night and presented me with a key to his apartment and an invitation to move in with him in New York City. With my fresh degree and no job prospects, I had the freedom to relocate anywhere I wanted, and I definitely wanted to be with Daniel.

His one-bedroom apartment was small for the two of

us, but we made it work for a couple of months while I searched for a decent job. When I say small, I mean very small. The day I moved in, the apartment was packed wall-to-wall with boxes and furniture.

I landed my first job by answering an ad on a New York City website looking for production assistants. The pay was minimum wage, which barely covered living expenses in the city, but I needed the experience. The job turned out to be a success because it was on a low-budget independent film. One of the producers and I hit it off, and he referred me to a daytime talk show that was looking for a production assistant. I applied and got the job the following week.

Not long after, Daniel was promoted to a better management position at his firm, and the money began to flow in. We moved into a larger one-bedroom apartment in Manhattan.

About a year later, I received a promotion and started producing my own segments for the daytime show. One of the directors was kind enough to float one of my screenplays around, and I received a call from a literary agent who told me that, with the right critiques, he was confident he could sell my script to a smaller studio.

On our fifth anniversary, we were celebrating three things. The first, of course, was our anniversary; the second was the sale of my first script for $200,000; and the third celebratory event came when Daniel got down on one knee at the restaurant and proposed. It was completely unexpected, and the entire restaurant erupted in applause when I said yes. We drank two bottles of champagne that night and made love until the sun rose.

We had a long engagement, three years, to be exact. So much had changed during those three years, which kept delaying the wedding. Daniel's career continued to flourish, and by the time he was 36, he had been promoted to vice president at his firm, making him one of the youngest VPs in the company.

My literary agent sold another script I had written and suggested I move to Los Angeles to continue my writing. He had a small agency and connected me with a talent agent named Michael Corday, who worked with most of the big studios in Hollywood.

I flew to Los Angeles, all expenses paid by The Corday Group, and fell in love with the City of Angels. Everything in LA moved at a slower pace than I was used to in New York, and I really liked the weather.

The relocation conversation with Daniel didn't go well. He suspected the request was coming when I told him that The Corday Group wanted to meet with me in Los Angeles.

"Why can't you write from New York and sell your work to them from here?" Daniel asked.

"It doesn't work like that. If you want to be in the business, you have to be where the business is," I explained. That's essentially what Michael Corday had told me when he pitched the idea of moving to LA, but Daniel didn't need to know that. He only needed to know that it was the right move. After all, I had moved to New York City for him.

"Our lives are here, Cameron. We built our lives here," Daniel said, shutting down the conversation. That infuriated me. I had always supported his career; why couldn't he support mine now?

Daniel's stubbornness put a real strain on our relationship. I wasn't the same anymore because I felt like he was being incredibly selfish. I didn't expect him to say yes immediately, but he wouldn't even consider the idea.

It took two months before Daniel spoke of the relocation again. He knew how much I wanted it. He came home one night with two plane tickets to Los

Angeles.

"I was able to get a few days off next week," he said, presenting the tickets to me. "I'm willing to see what you want me to see."

I nearly jumped on top of him I was so excited. I knew that once Daniel saw the beautiful city full of palm trees, he wouldn't want to come back to New York either. Of course, that didn't happen.

We stayed at a small boutique hotel in West Hollywood, which featured a rooftop Jacuzzi and pool. We quickly realized the gay scene in Los Angeles was very different from New York City. It's hard to explain, but it felt like night and day. New York had the better gay scene, and it was less judgmental. Strike one against LA in Daniel's book. But I didn't let him hold onto that, since we rarely went to local gay bars in New York anymore.

Daniel loved the weather. What's not to love? It's freezing in New York during the winter, and we took our trip in March. The beaches weren't as warm as we thought they would be. Apparently, Los Angeles isn't a constant 85 degrees as many of us on the East Coast believe.

It was cheaper, not by much, but cheaper to live in Los Angeles than in Manhattan. Daniel and I agreed that if we were going to make the move, we would invest in a house rather than rent. The fact that Daniel was considering buying a house showed me he was finally open to the idea of relocating.

When we returned to New York, Daniel and I went to a nice Italian restaurant on the Upper East Side. The place had about 20 tables, and every one of them was filled. The music played softly overhead, and the dim lighting created a mood as if we were dining in Naples.

I had acquired a taste for red wine by then. Chianti, and only Chianti. Daniel and I were finishing off our first glass when the waiter poured us another from the open bottle.

"So, let's talk about Los Angeles," Daniel blurted out. He was one glass of wine in, so this was a good sign.

The very mention of Los Angeles excited me. "Let's," I said eagerly, leaning in.

"I talked to Rich about relocating to LA," Daniel said. Rich was his boss. "I didn't want to say anything to you before, but there was a reason I suggested we visit LA last month."

Now I was curious. "Go on," I said.

"He's going to put me in for a transfer to the LA office."

"What!" I said, utterly excited. "Seriously?" I couldn't have been more thrilled. This was so unexpected.

Daniel reached over and placed his hand on mine. "There's a catch," he said. "It's not a permanent transfer. I'll work out of the LA office, but my home base is still in New York, so I'll have to fly back and forth. I'll spend most of my work week in New York."

"Oh, okay," I said, taking a sip of my wine. This wasn't exactly what I had in mind, but it was progress. Three months ago, Daniel wouldn't even entertain the idea of moving across the country. Now he was willing to be a bi-coastal employee.

"And how do you feel about it?" I asked.

He shrugged and took a large sip of his wine. "You made some good points. You moved here for me, and your writing career has really taken off," Daniel said. "Just remember that my work is still in New York. Luckily, Rich said I can use one of our corporate apartments when I'm in New York, so we won't have to rent apartments in both cities."

I was so happy. Sure, there would be sacrifices, but this was really going to happen. Daniel had actually agreed to move to Los Angeles.

The move went smoothly. Our one-bedroom apartment in New York was rented within two hours of listing it. Daniel's new office in LA was eagerly anticipating his arrival. I was the happiest person on the planet because I was finally going to start living my dream. My agent started shopping around an action-drama screenplay I had just finished revising. He saw great potential for it in the indie market.

The first thing we did when we arrived in Los Angeles was look for a home. The housing market was so different in LA compared to New York, far less competitive. We toured a few homes: one in the Hollywood Hills, one in Studio City, and then one in West Hollywood. I immediately fell in love with the West Hollywood home. It was a brand-new "McMansion," a large house that replaced a smaller one on the property, too large to match the neighborhood's aesthetic.

The home had all the bells and whistles: a two-story modern facade with an attached two-car garage, a ten-foot oak front door, charcoal marble tiles in the foyer, and a large open staircase. To the left was a den, perfect for my writing room, as Daniel pointed out.

Down the hall was a massive sunken living room with a beautiful fireplace and beige marble mantle. White built-in shelves lined the walls, and Daniel suggested a flat-screen TV would look perfect over the mantle.

To the right was an enormous kitchen, big enough for a restaurant, with black granite countertops, stainless steel appliances, and a checkered black-and-white glass tile backsplash. A large kitchen island sat in the center, and the refrigerator was so large it made our entire New York bathroom look tiny. Beyond the kitchen was a small eating area with a large window overlooking the backyard and a built-in swimming pool.

Upstairs, we found three spacious bedrooms, and the master suite faced the front of the house. What sold me was the master bathroom. It was so large it could have been another bedroom. With a Jacuzzi and a separate shower stall large enough to fit five people, plus three shower nozzles, it was perfect.

The price tag was above our range, but we decided to splurge and put in an offer. Since the house had been sitting vacant for months, our real estate agent thought we had bargaining power. After some negotiations, we agreed on a price, and 30 days later, we closed the deal. And that's how we landed in the City of Angels.

Chapter 5

My phone vibrates on the nightstand, waking me up. The drapes are drawn, making the room nearly dark, but I can see a ray of sunlight shining through a crack. I slowly open my eyes as the vibration continues. Glancing over, I see Daniel, nestled under the covers, fast asleep on his right side. I pick up the vibrating phone. The screen reads: *Michael Corday Calling.*

My agent is calling me at, wait, what time is it? The phone's clock reads 7:28 a.m. in the upper right corner. What on earth is Michael calling me at 7:28 in the morning on a Saturday for? This is very unusual.

"Hello?" I whisper into the phone. I pull the covers off and rise from the bed, so I won't disturb Daniel.

"Good morning, Cameron," Michael says. "I'm really sorry to call you so early on a Saturday, but I have some rather interesting news."

I creep to the bathroom and close the door behind me to avoid waking Daniel. "It's no problem, Michael. What's up?"

"Well, I think you're going to want to sit down for this."

I'm immediately intrigued. "Okay," I say, sitting on the edge of the Jacuzzi. "I'm sitting."

"I found a buyer for your screenplay *Hold Up*."

"That's great," I say. *Hold Up* is the action-drama script Michael has been trying to sell for me since we moved to Los Angeles. Michael believes the script would be a better fit for the independent film market, but its action sequences have made it difficult to find a buyer due to the budget the sequences would require.

"There's a catch, though."

"Okay…"

"They want to attach their lead actor to it, and he'll also be co-producing."

"Okay… Sounds like a plan to me. Who is the lead?"

"I'm sure you've heard of him. Up-and-coming movie star, Theo Diaz."

For a split second, my heart stops. This is real. This will be my first screenplay to actually go into production. My first real movie.

"Cameron?"

"Yes, I'm here. I don't know what to say. The Theo Diaz?" I'm nearly speechless. It's been almost two years since I finished *Hold Up*, and now there's actually a buyer lined up, and they want Theo Diaz to star in my movie.

Theo Diaz is a television actor who has starred in a hit show called *Crooked Lies* for the past seven seasons. He's a well-built and very toned Latin actor who's been gracing Hollywood for a few years now. If I remember correctly, he's 36 years old and a Gemini. Last year, a popular magazine named him an up-and-coming star of the year.

Crooked Lies is a raw, gritty prison drama where Theo Diaz plays one of the supporting roles. His character, Diego, was originally meant to die in season one, but the writers and fans loved his performance so much that they kept him around. By season 3, he was a series regular. This was also around the time his very public divorce from Amanda Preston hit every tabloid. Amanda, another television actress, had just starred in a romantic comedy that grossed over $300 million, making her an overnight Hollywood star.

The divorce was messy, with rumors of Theo's infidelity with female extras on *Crooked Lies* and supermodels around Hollywood. He even made headlines for being kicked out of nightclubs for fistfights. This helped him gain the reputation of Hollywood's bad boy, which, in turn, boosted the show's ratings. Eventually, they reconciled, and the media moved on to a new scandal.

Last year, Theo co-starred in the summer blockbuster *Charge Man*, a superhero film that made nearly $80 million on its opening weekend. Theo played the villain, Daunter Man. It ended up being the second highest-grossing movie of the year. Theo Diaz is definitely a rising star, and I still can't figure out why he wants to do this independent action film I wrote.

"They want to go into production soon. In fact, it's going to be the studio's next film," Michael tells me.

"And he wants to be in *my* movie?" I ask, still dumbfounded.

"Well, yes, but he's also putting up some of the financing."

I smile, amazed. "Wow, I figured he'd go on to bigger budget films after *Charge Man* did so well."

"Never underestimate small projects, Cameron. Those are often the ones that snag Golden Globe and Oscar nominations. Plus, this role is very emotional for him, so he's probably looking for that challenge. Anyway, he wants to meet with you for lunch today."

"What? Why?" I gulp.

"He said he wants to meet with the writer. The studio's scrambling to find a director this weekend, so he wants to pick your brain. Remember, he's coming from TV, where writers run the show." In Hollywood, directors typically have the final say in movies, but in TV, writers usually call the shots.

"Yeah, okay. Great," I say, nervously.

"I'll have Charlotte set it up for you. How about noon?" Michael asks. Charlotte is his assistant, who takes care of all the work Michael doesn't want to deal with.

"Yes, text me the details." I hang up and lean forward, resting my elbows on my knees. I'm actually nervous to meet Theo Diaz, which is odd, because I've never been starstruck before. Of course, I've never met a TV or movie star before, but this will be my first time. I once saw Julia Roberts at a grocery store and Hugh Jackman at a movie theater, but I never spoke to them.

I open the shower stall and turn on the water, but my excitement gets the best of me. I run back into the bedroom to wake up Daniel.

"Daniel, Daniel, wake up," I say as I run to the bed and shake him. Then I realize my body pillow is under the covers where Daniel usually sleeps. I pull the sheets back and confirm my mistake. Daniel isn't even here. I completely forgot he's not home right now. I frequently use the body pillow when Daniel's away because it gives me comfort, as though he's lying next to me. But I've never mistaken the pillow for him. How much wine did I drink last night?

I run back to the bathroom and grab my phone to call him. I'm so excited I can feel my voice about to squeal.

"Hey, you," Daniel says when he answers.

Excitement takes over, and I can't even say hello. Instead, I blurt out, "You are never going to believe this, Michael might have sold my script *Hold Up*."

"Really? Finally?" Daniel responds, not quite the enthusiasm I was hoping for.

"Daniel, I told you it's not an easy script to sell." Silence on his end. I know he's waiting for me to continue, so I do. "But they found a lead actor too. Theo Diaz. He's going to produce it as well."

Still silence. Does he really not know who Theo Diaz is?

"Theo Diaz? The guy from *Crooked Lies*," I explain.

"Cameron, you know I don't watch that crap," Daniel says. "Do I hear running water?"

Oh, right. The shower. I'd forgotten I turned it on, but got too excited to shower and wanted to call Daniel first. I open the shower stall and turn the water off.

"I was going to take a shower, but wanted to call you with this exciting news," I say, wiping water off my hand.

"Congratulations, babe. I know you've been wanting this one to sell for a while," he says. I can actually hear his smile.

"Now maybe you'll find the time to read it?" I tease.

"I don't want to spoil it for myself. I'll see it when it's made," Daniel replies.

Classic response from him. He doesn't really have time to read my work anymore. To be honest, I spend more time writing than actually finishing a story. He used to read my work all the time, but ever since he became a bi-coastal VP at his firm, I'm lucky if I get him to have dinner with me three nights in a row, let alone read my scripts.

"We still on for dinner tonight?" I ask.

"We are, hopefully," he responds. Uh-oh. That means maybe I'll be on a plane later today, or maybe I won't, depending on how the morning goes. Clients are 24/7 at Daniel's firm, so weekends don't exist for them. If he can make his flight, he should be landing at LAX around 5:00 p.m. Fingers crossed.

"I'll keep you posted. Love you," he tells me, and we say our goodbyes.

My lunch with Theo floods my thoughts again. Now I have to decide what to wear. What does a screenwriter wear to a meeting with a TV star?

Chapter 6

I hop onto my neon green Japanese made Phantom 360XR, one of the sleekest crotch rockets on the market today. I fell in love with the color after seeing someone riding it on the 405. Something about that neon green just stuck with me. Daniel bought me one for my 30th birthday. I call it *the Phantom.*

Back when we lived in New York City, I had a blue scooter that was incredibly helpful for navigating traffic. Daniel's father used to ride motorcycles and taught Daniel how to ride. Later, Daniel taught me how to ride the Phantom safely in L.A., even though I already had some experience on two wheels thanks to my scooter days in New York.

I love the Phantom, not just for its speed, but because it makes weaving through traffic in Los Angeles so much easier and faster.

The freeway still scares me, though. That need for speed on two wheels just isn't my thing. But I love riding it on non-freeway streets. There's something about the wind in my face that clears my mind and makes space for fresh, new ideas. The life of a writer, I suppose.

I arrive a few minutes early at the Beverly Hills Café. I had a hard time finding the right outfit. After much deliberation, I settled on a red polo shirt and blue jeans. It's a step up from just a T-shirt, and I feel like I'll look a bit more professional.

The restaurant is small, with plenty of patio seating in the front. The hostess podium is stationed outside, right in front of the door. She greets me as I approach.

"Hi, table for one?" she asks with a smile.

"No, I'm actually meeting someone. We have a reservation under Taylor," I inform her.

She pecks away at a computer screen and then grabs two menus.

"Right this way, please," she says, leading me to a table a few seats away. I take a seat, and she places the menus, one in front of me and the other in front of the empty chair across from me.

"Your server will be right with you," she says, then walks away. A busboy approaches and fills two glasses with water from the pitcher he's holding.

I take a sip of the water when someone catches my eye. Approaching the hostess station is Theo Diaz, and he looks even better in person than on his movie posters and TV screens. He's wearing blue jeans, a blue shirt, and a leather jacket. Black sunglasses rest on top of his head. His short black hair is styled in a clean cut.

I notice he and the hostess exchange a few pleasantries, and she escorts him to our table. She seems incredibly happy and almost jittery now. As they approach, I stand.

"Cameron?" Theo asks.

I nod and extend my hand. We shake briefly.

"Nice to meet you," I say, and we take our seats.

"I just love your show," the hostess says, grinning from ear to ear. Theo smiles at her, flashing perfectly straight, white teeth.

"Thank you very much," he responds, then grabs her hand and kisses the top of it. She nearly stumbles into his lap when he lets go, making a funny noise as she hurries away, running into a couple of chairs behind her.

Theo slides off his leather jacket, revealing toned, defined biceps and an array of tattoos on both arms. For a split second, I feel like I'm caught in a trance. This guy is beautiful, and I don't typically use the word "beautiful" to describe men, but in this case, it seems fitting.

"Ever been here before?" he asks.

Quickly, I snap out of my trance. "No," I reply, hoping he didn't notice me staring at his arms. "My agent recommended it."

Theo picks up his menu and starts flipping through it. I follow suit, becoming engrossed in the options. There's an awkward silence as we both occasionally glance up at one another.

"Not one for small talk, huh?" Theo asks, acknowledging the awkward silence. How embarrassing.

"I'm sorry, I didn't realize…" I trail off, fumbling for words. Come on, Cameron, get it together. I've never been starstruck before, and I don't know what's going on with me.

"You seem nervous. Are you nervous?" Theo asks, eyeing me with amusement.

"Maybe, a little," I admit.

"Don't be nervous. I should be nervous. Your script is fantastic," he says.

That's music to my ears. "Thank you," I respond proudly. "I was happy to hear you wanted the role."

"Are you kidding me? It's been a long time since I've read such a developed character."

Our server arrives to take our order. She's a young, model-like type, probably in her early twenties, and I can't help but assume she's yet another hopeful who moved to Hollywood aiming for fame. Or maybe I'm just being judgmental, assuming anyone young and pretty is a potential Hollywood candidate.

"Are you gentlemen ready to order?" she asks politely.

Theo glances at me for approval, and I nod, signaling that I'm ready too.

"Yes, may I have the grilled chicken sandwich with the potato salad?" Theo asks.

"And for you?" she asks, turning to me.

"Salmon salad," I reply. "Light dressing." I've always hated how restaurants drown salads in too much dressing.

She smiles, collecting our menus, and leaves. I notice that as she passes the hostess station, both girls nearly squeal.

"So, what else do you write about?" Theo asks, placing his napkin on his lap.

"What do you mean?"

"Do you have any other scripts in production? How did you get into the business?"

I'm not used to anyone taking this much interest in my work, other than my agent and his lawyers. I have to admit, it's nice to be asked by a stranger. Theo Diaz is actually asking about me, and he seems genuinely interested.

"No other projects in production," I say. "After I graduated film school, I worked for a small production company in New York City that eventually found me my agent. He insisted I move to L.A., so I did, along with my husband."

Theo looks up, surprised. "Husband?"

"Yes. His name is Daniel." I'm not sure how to read Theo's expression at this moment. He seems caught off guard by the fact that I have a husband. It's not uncommon in Hollywood for someone to be gay, but it's clear that he wasn't expecting me to mention it.

"And what does Daniel think of your script?" Theo asks.

I take a sip of my water. "He's a marketing V.P., bi-coastal, between here and New York City. He doesn't have much time to read screenplays."

"Well, that's his loss for not reading great work," Theo says with a smile. "So the reason I wanted to sit down with you is to ask some questions about Baldwin. You, being the writer, know him better than anyone, so I wanted to get some of your feedback."

I lean forward, impressed. Granted, I'm a relatively new screenwriter in Hollywood, but I'm incredibly flattered that Theo is taking the character more seriously than I expected. He actually cares.

"Wow, um, okay. Shoot," I say.

Our server brings a basket of fresh-baked bread to the table. Theo immediately grabs a couple of pieces and slathers butter on them.

"I have an intense workout after this," he says, stuffing a piece of bread into his mouth. "Gotta carb up."

He smiles, and I smile too. I feel very at ease with him.

"So, Baldwin is going through this horrific grief from the murder of his family, and his revenge seems to be focused only on that. But is he feeling betrayed by Richard for giving the mob the location of his wife?" Theo asks.

I think for a moment. *Hold Up* centers around

Baldwin, a man on a quest for revenge against the organization responsible for his family's deaths, which he views as punishment. While I recognize this plot may not be the most unique in the action genre, I'm pleased to know that it is going to be sold. I'm also grateful that Theo has invested this effort into further developing the character.

"Well, you could look at it like that, but if it wasn't Richard, the mob would've gotten the information from someone else. Baldwin knew that." I say.

"So, there's no animosity toward Richard?" Theo asks, chewing thoughtfully.

I shake my head. This is actually fun, answering questions about my characters. "Although Baldwin feels completely isolated after the murder of his family. If you need to play him with bad feelings toward Richard, then by all means, you can do that."

Theo nods in agreement. Then, "Do you have plans tonight?" he asks suddenly.

I place my napkin in my lap and pick up a piece of bread. "Yes," I respond. "Daniel and I are supposed to go to that new Bohemian restaurant that opened on Melrose."

"There's this thing they're throwing for the cast and crew of *Crooked Lies* tonight at The Monastery in West Hollywood. It's kind of a post-wrap party," Theo says. When a movie or TV show finishes production, they usually throw a wrap party for the cast and crew.

"Oh yeah?" I respond.

"It's mostly a thank-you for the crew, since they've been working on the show for seven years. But I'm told all the actors are coming too. If you wanted to swing by for a drink after dinner, with Daniel, you should come."

Daniel's never been a fan of anything Hollywood-related. He always called it a fantasy land of artists, and not in a positive way. I respond, "Daniel's not really into the Hollywood scene."

"He's into drinks, though, right?" Theo asks, not letting me off the hook.

I laugh politely. "Yes, he drinks."

"Then he can have a drink. There just happens to be other Hollywood people there, if that's okay with Daniel."

Theo winks at me conspiratorially as he says Daniel's name. I suspect he may be a little annoyed by my comment about Daniel not being into the Hollywood scene.

"I'm sorry, he's not that bad," I recover. "I'm making him sound worse than he is."

"Nah, I get it. Some people just aren't into the scene. But I promise it'll be low-key."

"We'll see," I say. The truth is, I haven't seen Daniel in over a week. He's been in New York City working at their firm. Our phone calls have even been limited because of the time difference between Los Angeles and New York. Daniel's plane lands later this afternoon, and I'm excited to finally see him.

"Or you can always send him home after dinner," Theo says, smirking. "Okay, enough about that. I have another question about my character."

As Theo continues to ask his questions, I lean back in my chair and just listen. I can now see why he wanted the part of Baldwin in *Hold Up*. He sees something in the project that I don't see. That's the beauty of books and screenplays, their meaning can change for each person.

Chapter 7

I arrive home and park my motorcycle in the side driveway. The gate closes behind me as I enter through the kitchen's side door. My phone chimes with a text message from Daniel.

Daniel: *Hey babe, looks like I'm not going to make it back to L.A. until tomorrow. Last-minute client meeting.*

I roll my eyes and respond.

Cameron: *No problem. See you tomorrow.*

I set my phone on the counter. I figured this would happen. It seems we spend more time rescheduling dinner reservations than we actually spend dining out.

I decided to treat myself to a hot bath. I fill the Jacuzzi tub with hot water and bubbles from an overpriced bubble bottle I bought at a Beverly Hills spa for my 30th birthday.

As I soak in the bathtub, my meeting with Theo Diaz keeps replaying in my mind. Theo Diaz wants to be in my movie. Theo Diaz actually took the time to meet with me, the writer, to learn more about his character. Theo Diaz, oh, those arms. They are perfectly toned, and those tattoos... Then I shake my head, trying to refocus. Theo Diaz wants to co-produce my movie.

I get out of the tub and dry myself off, realizing I'm starting to get hungry.

I head downstairs to the kitchen and open the refrigerator. Daniel and I aren't exactly chefs, so nothing looks appetizing. I see some take-out from a Chinese restaurant I ordered a few nights ago, but that doesn't sound good either.

I open the freezer and find a frozen dinner. *Salisbury steak and mashed potatoes*, the label reads. The picture looks like something out of a magazine. This will do. I open the box, pull the black tray out, and remove the clear film. The food looks like a frozen brown-and-white blob. Once cooked, this definitely won't look like the picture.

I heat the frozen dinner in the toaster oven for twenty minutes, just as the box instructed. When I pull it out, I toss it onto the counter, pull back the film again, and think it will pair nicely with red wine. I open the wine cooler under the kitchen island and pull out a bottle of Chianti.

I sit in the living room, having just finished my frozen dinner. As expected, it didn't look anything like the photo on the box, and it certainly didn't taste as good as I imagined. The wine, however, went well with it.

I flip through the channels on the large flat-screen TV mounted above the fireplace, hoping to find something to entertain me. I hate being in one of these moods, nothing sounds good to watch, and I don't have the attention span for a two-hour movie tonight.

I take the last sip of my wine, glance at the bottle sitting on the coffee table, and see it's only a quarter empty. I could have another glass… then another… and I'd probably just end up going to bed. It's Saturday night, after all.

I grab my phone and text Daniel.

Cameron: *You still up?*

I pour more wine into my glass. Moments later, my phone chimes.

Daniel: *In bed already.*

I roll my eyes and toss my phone back onto the coffee table with a frustrated sigh. Thanks for calling me to say goodnight.

I take another sip of my wine, flip through more channels, and still can't find anything decent to watch. Annoyed, I turn off the TV. We subscribe to more than six streaming services, yet I can't find a single thing to watch.

I grab my phone again and stare at the black screen. I hit a button, and the time appears: 8:15 p.m. Then I remember Theo's invitation to the wrap party tonight at The Monastery.

I take another sip of my wine. Should I go? What else am I going to do tonight? Finish this bottle of wine and go to bed early? But it's Saturday night.

Screw it. I haven't been out in a while.

I race upstairs and enter my master bedroom's closet. It's massive, with rows of men's clothes on each side. Daniel's side, on the left, features suits, collared shirts, ties, and jackets. My side, on the right, has colorful shirts, jeans, and other casual clothes. Business executive versus screenwriter.

I strip off my shirt and pants and survey my side of the closet. Standing in only my boxers, I select a blue polo and put it on. I open the built-in drawers and grab a pair of jeans. Then I head to the bathroom to brush my teeth.

The Monastery is a restaurant and bar located in West Hollywood. Though it usually attracts a gay crowd, the restaurant is world-famous due to some talentless socialites who've made their mark on reality TV, using the venue as a backdrop. Plus, their weekend brunch is amazing.

I step out of an Uber, thanking the driver. The Monastery has a large patio seating area in front of its doors, with neon lights illuminating a few stationary water fountains. The patio is packed with people eating, drinking, laughing, and having a great time.

I approach the patio and follow a black carpet to the host station near the entrance. Once I arrive, I notice a red rope blocking the inside of the restaurant, with a security guard standing watch. A sign reads: *PRIVATE PARTY.*

The host stands behind his station. He's a flamboyant man in his early 20s, wearing a black button-up shirt with The Monastery's logo embroidered above his right pocket. Above his left pocket is a nametag that says *PETE*. He forces a smile.

"Welcome to The Monastery. We're full tonight. Do you have a reservation?" he says with a hint of attitude. *Gays and West Hollywood.*

I peer beyond the red rope and spot Theo chatting with a group at the bar, holding a beer.

"Actually, I was invited by Theo Diaz," I tell Pete, leading his eyes behind the rope.

Pete raises an eyebrow. "Of course you were, dear," he says dryly. "Name?"

"Cameron Taylor."

Pete speaks into a small microphone attached to his collar, then adjusts his earpiece. Seconds later, his demeanor completely changes.

"Right this way, Mr. Taylor," he says, his full smile on display. *Bitchy to pleasant in less than three seconds. Oh, L.A.*

Pete nods to the security guard, who pulls back part of the red rope, allowing us to enter. Pete escorts me to the party.

Inside, The Monastery isn't very large, but it's crowded tonight. A long bar sits on the right side, with tables scattered around. On the left side, a buffet is set up with chicken and vegetable kabobs, salmon, pasta, and desserts. It smells amazing.

"All the food and drinks are included for the party tonight," Pete says as I follow him. "Have a nice time." He winks and turns back toward the host station.

I walk toward the bar where I spotted Theo moments earlier. He's drinking with a few guys and taking shots. Once they slam their glasses down in triumph, the bartender pours another round. Theo notices me as I join them.

"Dude, you made it," he says.

The three guys look at me. They're in their mid to late 40s. Theo wraps his arm around me, pulling me closer to the bar.

"This man makes the best lemon drop in the entire state of California," Theo says, pointing to the bartender. The bartender, a handsome man in his late 30s and clearly flattered, smiles and pours a beer. "Another round!"

Theo's three pals shake their heads. The bartender laughs and continues making drinks.

The three guys look at me. Theo introduces them. "This is John, Hank, and Tom," he says. We all shake hands. "And this is Cameron Taylor. He's a screenwriter. He wrote the indie I'm shooting next month."

Everyone offers pleasantries, and Theo looks around quickly.

"You come alone?" he asks, shouting to be heard over

the noise.

"I did, wasn't sure who to invite on such short notice," I shout back.

The bartender slides two shots to Theo and me. Theo grabs one and hands me the other. "To us," he says, raising his shot.

We clink glasses, and I follow his lead, downing the shot. Theo takes his like a champ. I, however, nearly gag on mine, it tastes like rubbing alcohol. I've never actually tasted rubbing alcohol, but if I had, I imagine this is what it would taste like. I slowly set the glass down, making a sour face.

"Guess it takes some getting used to," Theo says, laughing.

John, Hank, and Tom move on to mingle with other people. I look around and spot a banner that reads: *THANK YOU FOR 7 GREAT SEASONS*. Another banner reads: *CROOKED LIES WILL MISS OUR CREW!*

"Great turnout," I say.

Theo nods. "Yeah, I'm glad everyone came. Even our stars, Janice Preston and Bradley Whitney, were here."

Janice Preston started on *Crooked Lies* as a nobody. After winning her first Emmy for the role, her career blew up, and now she's one of Hollywood's A-listers. Her last two movies each grossed over $100 million at the box office.

"That's great she came. She's a big star now," I say.

"She must have a better agent than I do," Theo giggles. "Want a beer? I'm done with shots."

"Sure," I laugh at Theo's agent joke.

Theo signals to the bartender, and moments later, two beers slide to us. Theo slaps a $100 bill onto the bar as a tip. The bartender smirks.

"For you, my man," Theo says, handing the bartender

the bill. Then he wraps his arm around me again. "Come on, I'll introduce you to some people from the show."

A couple of hours later, The Monastery starts to empty out. Very few customers remain, and the employees are tearing down the buffet. I'm sitting at a table with Theo, John, Hank, and Tom. There are several empty shot glasses and beer bottles, but we're all still drinking. I haven't had this much to drink in a long time, and I have to admit, I'm having a great time. Theo is in the middle of a story.

"Then Tom here says he thinks it'll be funny if we shoot the scene without my stuntman," Theo says. "But have me perform the actual stunt."

I take a swig of my beer, and for some reason, I can't get the taste of the last shot of tequila out of my mouth. "And the studio let you do this?" I ask. I can't imagine any studio's insurance policy allowing an actor to do a stunt they haven't trained for.

"Hello, no," Tom laughs. "They nearly lost their shit when they found out Theo Diaz was the one who jumped off a forty-foot building."

Theo and his pals explode in laughter. Everyone is clearly drunk. "Dude, if I wasn't high as a kite, I would have never had the balls to do it," Theo says.

"So what happened to the actual stuntman?" I ask.

John immediately jumps in after slamming his empty beer bottle on the table. "He was pissed because he didn't get paid."

The table laughs again. Theo is grinning ear to ear. "The studio was so pissed," Theo says. "They called my agent and said if I ever pulled a 'stunt' like that again, I was done." Everyone laughs at Theo's use of the word "stunt."

As the mood starts to settle, Hank rises from his chair.

"Well, guys, I'm calling it a night," he says. "I need to

get home."

John and Tom rise as well. "Thanks for coming out tonight, Theo," Tom says, hugging him briefly.

John and Theo hug too. John shakes my hand. "Good luck with your movie," he says to me.

"Thank you," I reply.

Theo's three pals lay down a wad of cash, and the server races over to clear the empty beer bottles and collect his generous tip. All that remains is one full shot.

"One more. Want it?" Theo asks.

"No, I'm already going to regret this in the morning," I say. I look around the empty restaurant and see Theo and I are the last customers. Employees have cleared the tables, placed the chairs on top, and are sweeping and mopping the floor. The bartender is drying glasses behind the bar.

Theo takes the shot.

"I think they're closing and want us to go home," I say.

Theo looks around and agrees. He waves at the bartender, who smiles and waves back.

"Wanna share a cab?" Theo asks.

"Sure."

We leave The Monastery and sit on the sidewalk. Theo orders a cab through his smartphone app.

"Three minutes away," Theo says, his shoulders leaning against mine to keep himself upright. His eyes are drooping.

"I want you to know I think it's cool you came out here tonight," Theo slurs.

"I'm glad I did. It was fun," I say.

"Next time, do me a favor?"

"What's that?" I ask.

"Don't let me do so many shots," Theo smiles, flashing his perfectly white teeth.

I laugh, and Theo nudges me with his shoulder. I wonder if he'll remember this in the morning. Then the yellow cab pulls up to the curb. We both stand.

Theo opens the back door and hops in. "Hi, two stops," he says, and I follow behind, sliding into the back seat with him.

Chapter 8

The next morning, the sun greets me, casting powerful UV rays straight into my eyes. Apparently, I didn't pull the curtains closed before passing out in my bed, so now I know how a vampire must feel when the sun attacks him.

I shield my eyes as I slowly regain consciousness. My head hurts, but not nearly as badly as I expected, given how much I drank last night. Fortunately, I have enough wisdom from my 30 years to know to drink two tall glasses of water and take four aspirins before bed. It's not guaranteed, but it usually helps alleviate a hangover.

I roll over so my hand can reach the nightstand and grab the half-empty water bottle. I open the cap and gulp down the remaining water just as Daniel enters the bedroom from the hallway, still wearing yesterday's suit.

"Morning, babe," he says, loosening his yellow tie.

"Hey, babe," I reply, smiling. "I thought you weren't coming home until tonight."

"Took an early flight," Daniel says. He removes his suit jacket and unbuttons his collar. Then, he unbuckles his belt, unbuttons his pants, and removes them too. Once he's standing in his red boxers, it takes everything in me not to throw him on the bed and ravage him. What's gotten into me?

Daniel slides off his boxers and tosses them in the hamper before walking into the master bathroom. I slowly rise from the bed and stretch. I glance down and notice that I'm excited this morning.

"Great, so we have the day," I say, following him into the bathroom.

Daniel has turned on the shower and is holding his hand to the nozzle, waiting for the water to heat up.

"Nope," he says. "After I shower, I'm going to get a couple of hours of sleep, then I have to go into the office."

The water reaches his desired temperature, and he steps in. I immediately slip out of my boxers and join him.

Daniel begins lathering his loofah with body wash just as I close the shower stall behind me.

"But you just got home, and it's Sunday," I say.

"Doesn't matter," Daniel replies. "We've got a huge client we're about to sign. You know how it is, Cameron." He hands me his loofah to wash his back. I obey. We used to do this all the time when we were younger and showered together. "What did you do last night?" he asks.

"I went to this thing at The Monastery." I hand him the loofah and turn around so he can wash my back. He does. "And I think I'm hungover."

"What?" he asks, his voice muffled under the sound of the water.

"I think I'm…" I pause, realizing his head is directly under the water, deafening any sound.

"I can't hear a word you're saying," Daniel says, as he starts rinsing his hair.

I take the opportunity to make things more interesting. I start to touch him, stroking him casually when…

"Cameron, stop. I told you I need to get a couple of hours of sleep," he says, beginning to rinse out the shampoo.

Defeated, I roll my eyes. Daniel and I haven't been great in the lovemaking department for quite some time.

"Whatever," I mutter, starting to apply shampoo to my own hair. Daniel surprises me by kissing me on the cheek.

"Maybe later this week?" he asks.

I nod, but deep down, I know *later* probably won't happen this week. Our lives are too busy to plan for later.

Later that morning, I sit at the kitchen island, sipping a cup of coffee. Daniel enters the kitchen, fully dressed in black slacks and a blue button-up shirt.

"Morning, babe," he says, pouring coffee into his portable mug.

"Morning. Sleep well?"

He nods and takes a sip, cautious not to burn his tongue. "I did. I don't know when I'll be home, but it'll probably be late." He walks behind me, wraps his arms around me, and kisses me on the cheek. "I'm sorry, babe. Things should settle down after this month."

I nod, playing along, but he always says that. Once this month is over, things will be different. And when I remind him that he said the same thing last month, his usual response is, *Well, you're the one who wanted to move to L.A. and knew it would mean more work for me.*

"What are your plans today?" he asks, snapping me out of my mental argument.

"Nothing," I reply.

Daniel grabs his briefcase from the side door where it's been sitting all morning. "Why don't you call up some friends and go paddleboarding? It's a beautiful day."

"I just might do that," I say, though I'm not sure I'm in the mood to paddleboard. I feel much better now than when I first woke up. Thank you, H2O and aspirin.

"Bye, babe. I love you," he says, walking out the side door, briefcase in hand.

"Love you too," I shout back as the door closes behind him.

I take another sip of my coffee and pick up my phone. I open the photo gallery app and slide through the photos from last night. I see a selfie I took with Theo at the bar, then a picture of Theo and his pals chugging a beer to see who could finish faster, and finally, a photo Tom took of Theo and me doing the same. I can't help but smile. I had a lot of fun last night. In fact, it was probably the most fun I've had all year. I can almost feel a sense of spontaneity I've been missing. I felt *seen* last night with Theo and his work pals.

I sip my coffee again and open the contacts app. I scroll down to find Theo Diaz's number, which I saved after our lunch yesterday. I wonder if he'd be up for paddleboarding. No, I can't call him. Technically, he's about to be my boss. But he's not my boss yet. He clearly showed signs of a work friendship by inviting me to his wrap party last night. I think for a moment. Ah, screw it. I'll call him.

The phone rings for what feels like forever before someone picks up. There's rustling, then, "Hello?" A very froggy voice says. If death had a voice, this would be it.

"Theo?" I ask.

"Uh-huh," he mumbles, clearly hungover.

"It's Cameron."

Silence, on the other line, except for the occasional breaths.

"What time is it?" Theo asks.

"It's after 11 in the morning."

I hear more rustling on his end.

"Oh," he pauses. "What's up?"

Suddenly, my paddleboarding idea doesn't sound so great. I should've known he'd be hungover based on his consumption last night. But it's too late now; he's on the line, waiting for me to respond.

"Have you ever been paddleboarding?" I ask.

"No, it's too early for this kind of talk." He sounds like he's smiling, and I laugh.

"You wanna go with me?"

"Go where?"

"Paddleboarding. In the ocean."

"I don't like water," Theo says, his voice hoarse.

"Then don't fall in," I tease.

He's silent for a moment. Then a long sigh, "Why did you let me drink so much last night?"

I laugh again. "You seemed to know what you were doing?" Or maybe not. He had a lot of shots. "So, you in? Paddleboarding?"

"Give me an hour, or two. Where?"

"Marina Del Rey. I'll see you in two hours," I say, figuring I might as well give him more time to hydrate, medicate, and feel better. We hang up, and I take another sip of my coffee, feeling pleased.

Chapter 9

Marina del Rey is a harbor in Los Angeles County that sits right on the ocean. With its close proximity to Venice Beach, it draws many tourists looking to sail or take boat rides along the waterfront. The sun shines boldly down on Marina del Rey Beach, where people are already enjoying activities in the water, such as kayaking, paddleboarding, and even swimming, despite the cold water.

I stand next to the paddleboard rental hut, waiting for Theo. The hut almost looks like a tiki bar, but instead of serving drinks, they rent paddleboards, snorkeling, and scuba equipment.

Theo arrives wearing white swim trunks and a green tank top. He's also sporting dark shades.

"Well, good afternoon," I say.

He half-smiles. "I don't care what time it is; it's still morning for me."

We each rent a paddleboard for $30 an hour and carry them to the water on the beach. I can't help but notice the bright sun shining on the beach, surrounding the marina that docks expensive boats and yachts. To my right, some people are picnicking on the sand, while others play volleyball to my left.

"You've never paddle-boarded before?" I ask Theo.

"Once. But I kept falling in the water," he replies.

Paddleboarding is a fun activity to do in Los Angeles. A paddleboard is about six and a half feet long, and the person stands on it, using a long paddle to propel themselves across the water. It requires great balance, otherwise, you'll fall in. Getting back onto the paddleboard also takes some decent upper-body strength.

We walk knee-deep into the water. As usual, the Pacific Ocean is as cold as a fisherman's ice chest. I hop onto my paddleboard, and Theo does the same. We both rise to stand and begin paddling through the marina. There are several other paddleboarders in the distance ahead of us.

Theo's almost got the hang of it when he loses his balance and falls into the water. His head pops up from the surface.

"Oh my God, it's cold!" he exclaims.

I laugh. He pulls himself back onto the paddleboard. I can't help but notice his amazing body as he does this. There's something about how water enhances muscles, and his are clearly defined as he pulls himself back onto the board.

I keep laughing as he slowly stands back up, cautious not to fall in again. Once he's standing with more confidence, he looks at me and smirks. Then, he leans his upper body onto his paddleboard and pushes it into mine, knocking me off and straight into the water.

I plunge into the frigid water and quickly realize Theo wasn't exaggerating, it's freezing. I almost forget to breathe as my head emerges from the water. I hear Theo laughing as I grab my paddleboard to climb back up.

"Oh my God, it *is* cold," I say, pulling myself back onto my board.

"Told ya," Theo says. "That's what you get for laughing."

Now that I'm back on my feet and holding my paddle in my right hand, I feel safe again and begin to paddle, with Theo following my lead.

We paddle out of the marina, initially concentrating hard to avoid falling again. But soon, we start making small talk.

Before long, we're just outside the harbor and decide it's a good spot to rest. The ocean stretches out before us, not a boat or piece of land in sight. The afternoon sun beams on our faces, warming us up.

I sit down on my paddleboard by getting on my knees first, then sitting cross-legged. Theo kneels too, but sits on his butt, spreading his legs so they dangle in the water, straddling his paddleboard.

"Woo wee, it's cold," he says as his feet splash in the water. "But the cold will make my feet numb in a minute."

I nod in agreement but keep my feet out of the water. At this moment, I realize how completely silent everything is around us, except for the occasional seagull squawking as it hunts for food. The water is calm. I glance over at Theo and see that he's at peace with the view too.

"I love it out here," I say. "I mean, look at this view. Open water and nothing for hundreds of miles."

"It is nice," Theo admits.

"Peaceful. This is where I come to clear my head, and get ideas for my stories."

"How long have you been writing?"

"As long as I can remember," I say. The truth is, I remember being in seventh grade, writing short stories in my notebook. Then I'd go home and turn those stories into short books. It's amazing how a story can reveal itself to you and take on a life of its own.

"That's cool. I always have ideas in my head, but I don't know how to get them on paper. How did you know you wanted to be a screenwriter?" Theo asks.

"I've always been passionate about movies. When I was looking for colleges, I wanted to pursue filmmaking, so I researched film schools and applied with an emphasis in screenwriting. I'd already written a couple of short books, so when I got accepted to Penn State, I wrote my first screenplay for a class."

"That's impressive, Cameron. Most people have no idea what they want to do after high school."

I gaze out at the open water. "What about you? When did you decide you wanted to pursue acting?"

"That came easy for me," he tells me. "I was obsessed with theater growing up. I'm from Brooklyn, and my mom worked in wardrobe for a lot of off-Broadway plays, so I was always around actors. I've never been great academically, so after high school, I moved to L.A. and took whatever jobs I could find until I landed my first agent. Many, many commercials later, I landed some great roles."

"*Crooked Lies*?" I ask.

Theo nods. "I was able to support myself for a while with the commercials. Most went nationwide, so the pay was great. But yes, my big break came with *Crooked Lies*." Theo pauses for a moment, then grins. "Want to know a secret?"

"Sure."

"The only reason I was hired as a series regular on *Crooked Lies* was because of the press covering my nasty divorce. My publicist knew it would get me hired on full-time, and she was right."

I nudge Theo, almost knocking him off his paddleboard. I didn't mean to do that. "Theo Diaz, are you telling me it was all a publicity stunt?"

"Not all of it. My publicist knew we were splitting up, and she thought a very public, nasty divorce, showcasing me as the bad guy, would help me get a better contract for the show. And it did."

I shake my head. Hollywood never ceases to amaze me. "And Amanda Preston was okay with this?"

"Are you kidding me? It jump-started Mandy's movie career. Everyone loved that she kicked me to the curb after my alleged affairs," Theo laughs. "So, our very public divorce boosted both our careers."

"Are you still friends?"

"I'd like to think so, but we don't speak anymore. If we ran into each other, I'm sure we'd reminisce. We married so young and wanted different things."

There's something about what Theo just said that makes me think. *We married so young and wanted different things.* I can't help but feel that way about Daniel and my marriage right now. We seem to be going in different directions, like two trains traveling to opposite sides of the country.

"What about you and…" Theo asks, pulling me away from my thoughts.

"Daniel," I remind him of my husband's name.

"Right, Daniel. How long have you two been married?" Theo asks.

"Two years, married. But ten years together."

Theo nods, impressed. "Isn't that a long time for the gay community?"

I can't help but laugh. Gay people have a reputation for being promiscuous and incapable of having long-term relationships. This is a myth started by homophobic conservatives decades ago. Gay people are just as capable of having long-term relationships as straight people. However, there are always exceptions, and gay people tend not to be as tied down in relationships because children aren't typically a factor.

"It is a long time. Daniel is ten years older than me."

"Ten years, wow. And he's cool with you doing the film thing? You mentioned he was in business."

"Yes, he's cool with it," I say. I have to admit things were much simpler when we lived in New York. We saw each other more often, and our relationship didn't feel so distant. I suppose that's my fault for insisting we move to Los Angeles, but I needed to do that for me, for my dream. It just seems like things were better when I was a low-paid production assistant and Daniel was a low-level manager at his firm. We seemed happier. I never thought about it until now. Is success bad for a relationship?

"You ever think that success can be a curse?" I blurt out.

Theo ponders for a moment. "I think it can be if you lose yourself in it. But ultimately, we are the masters of our own joy, happiness, and misery. We choose our paths."

Theo makes a good point. "I like that," I say. "Our own masters." How philosophical. I nudge his paddleboard again, but this time, he catches it, so I won't knock him off.

"I will not hesitate to push you in that water again," he warns, and I laugh.

"," I plead, extending my hand. "It's too cold."

Theo holds up his fist, and I do the same. We fist-pump to call a truce. Then Theo grins evilly, pulls my paddleboard up, and flips me off it and into the cold water. As I plunge in, I hear him laughing.

Chapter 10

I ride my motorcycle into the side yard. Dusk has arrived, and I'm exhausted from paddleboarding. After Theo knocked me into the water for the second time, we paddled two laps around the marina. I really enjoyed getting to know him today. I feel less star-struck around him now.

I enter the kitchen through the side door, and the smell of roasted garlic bread greets my nose. My stomach growls immediately. I hear Italian music playing softly in the background. I set my keys on the key table next to the door and find Daniel standing in front of the stove, stirring a pot of marinara sauce. Next to it, a pot of noodles is rapidly boiling. A fresh herb salad is prepared in a wooden bowl on the kitchen island.

Daniel pulls the wooden spoon from the sauce and

blows on it.

"What's all this?" I ask.

"You're just in time," he says. He holds the spoon under my nose and pushes it toward my mouth. "I'm cooking for you."

I blow on the spoon of red sauce and taste it. It's delicious, fresh tomatoes and basil. "Mmm, that's really good."

Daniel smiles, pleased. "Right?" He agrees. "A ton of fresh chopped basil from the garden out back. And garlic, of course."

I notice an open bottle of Chianti and two empty glasses on the kitchen table. I walk over and fill the glasses.

"I know it's been a rough couple of months with work and all," Daniel says, "so I decided to cook for you tonight."

"I'm not going to complain. It smells amazing." I hand him a glass of wine, and we share a brief kiss.

"Tastes like salt water," he says.

I laugh. That would be thanks to Theo making me fall into the ocean, twice. I sniff the air again.

"What you're smelling is garlic bread in the oven," Daniel tells me.

"Ooo, fresh or frozen?"

Daniel cackles. "Frozen, of course. I did work today."

We kiss again, then raise our glasses in a toast. My skin feels dry from the saltwater. "I'm going to get out of these clothes and take a shower. I smell like the ocean."

"Don't be too long. Dinner will be ready in fifteen minutes," Daniel says.

I leave the kitchen and walk through the foyer to the staircase when I hear Daniel's voice from the kitchen: "After dinner, I plan on giving you my own dessert."

I stop at the staircase and blush. I don't know what's

gotten into Daniel, but I like it. He hasn't been in one of these moods in a long time. I race upstairs to shower.

Later that night, Daniel and I lie in bed, naked. After dinner, we cleaned up the kitchen, raced upstairs, and made love, the first time in over two months, I might add. Daniel is now sleeping, and I lie wide awake. The clock on my nightstand reads 11:00 p.m. A Saturday night, and here we are, lying in bed for the night. It feels… sad.

My phone starts vibrating on the nightstand. I turn to my left side and pick it up. The screen reads: Theo Diaz Calling.

I hop out of bed and sprint to the bathroom to avoid waking Daniel. Once inside, I quietly close the door behind me and flick on the light.

"Hello?" I say.

"Cameron!" Theo shouts from the other end. I hear loud music thumping and laughter in the background.

"Theo, what's up?"

"What are you doing?" he shouts.

"I'm at home."

"What?" I can tell he can't hear me because I'm speaking softly, and his environment is far too loud for anyone to talk quietly on the other end.

I move deeper into the bathroom, farther from the door, so Daniel won't hear me. "I'm at home," I say a bit louder.

"It's barely 11. Are you kidding me?"

Thanks for the reminder, Theo. "Where are you?"

"I'll text you the address. It's a pretty cool club downtown. Hank and Tom are here, you met them at the wrap party. They don't think you'll come out."

I remember Hank and Tom. "I can't come out," I say. "Daniel's already in bed."

"So come out without him."

I sit on the edge of the Jacuzzi and sigh. "I can't."

"Come on, Cameron. Don't make me beg," Theo says. I can tell he's been drinking. "I went paddleboarding with you, hungover, I might add." He has a point. "Don't you want to see me?"

I snap my head up. Is he flirting with me? "What?" I ask, surprised.

"I mean us!" Theo corrects himself. I can hear his smile through the phone. I honestly can't tell if he's flirting with me or just joking around to get me to come out. It does sound fun, though. What's my other option? Crawling back into bed with Daniel and going to sleep for the night? No. Not tonight. "Text me the address," I tell him.

"Sweet," he says. "It's on its way."

"See you in 30 minutes."

"You've got 20." And with that, the line goes silent.

My Uber driver drops me off at the address Theo texted me. It's a large warehouse building in downtown Los Angeles. A line of people twists around the block, waiting to get into the club. There must be at least a hundred of them. Theo's text had already told me not to wait in line, but to give the security guards the password, and I'd be let in.

At the entrance, two very large men stand guard. One is Black, the other Latin, both wearing black shirts with the word "SECURITY" printed in white. They have earpieces and microphones clipped to their collars.

I approach the Latin security guard. He must be at least six-foot-five and built like a superhero. He looks at me, clearly annoyed, probably assuming I'm some schmuck trying to skip the line. But I say the password Theo texted me: "Lampshades are dusty."

He nods, steps aside, and lets me in. Strange

password, but it works. I hear the crowd behind me booing, assuming I cut in line. But I didn't cut, I've got a private invitation. The Black bouncer opens the door for me.

Inside, the club is packed to capacity. The dance floor is in the center of the warehouse, featuring dueling DJs. One DJ is to the left of the floor, the other to the right. Four bars surround the dance area. Neon lights pulse in time with the electronic music blasting from speakers as tall as my house.

To my left, an open staircase is blocked off with a velvet rope. A security guard stands at the entrance, and I notice a sign that reads: *VIP LOUNGE*. This security guard is another massive Latin man, wearing the same black shirt as the guards outside.

"Cameron!" I hear my name called. I look past the security guard and spot Theo trotting down the stairs from the VIP Lounge. The guard notices too and pulls the rope back for me to join Theo.

"Come on!" Theo shouts, and I follow him up the stairs.

Twenty steps later, we enter the VIP Lounge. The room is draped in purple velvet curtains that serve as walls. A railing overlooks the entire dance floor from this second story. I spot a half dozen women huddled around four men in suits sitting at a large table with bottle service. I wonder if the women are expensive call girls or mistresses, probably both. The women are in their twenties, the men in their forties, likely business executives spending their company's money on booze and sex.

Theo stops at a round table where Tom and Hank are sitting. We greet each other, and a couple of other guys in rock band T-shirts sit with them, also enjoying bottle service.

"Isn't this place insane?" Theo asks, pouring me a glass of champagne from one of the bottles.

I nod. It's very loud here, not as loud as the first floor, but still loud. I scan the table and see that Theo and his friends have already made a dent in two or three bottles of champagne.

An hour later, I'm three glasses in. Theo's friends in the rock band T-shirts are Canadians, in town for a reality singing competition they're hoping to win. They left about fifteen minutes ago to get some sleep before their audition in the morning. The four business executives and their six women have also left, so it's just our group remaining.

"Well, boys, I'm calling it a night," Hank says, standing up unsteadily.

"What are you talking about?" Theo asks. "It's early."

Tom rises too. "Maybe for you, Theo, but I've been drinking since noon. It's not early for me anymore."

A cocktail waitress in her early twenties, wearing a tight, sequined blue dress, brings us another bottle of champagne and pops the cork. She refills Theo's and my glasses.

"Later, guys," Hank says. Tom offers his goodbyes as well.

Now, it's just Theo and me in the VIP Lounge. I glance at my phone, it's almost 1:00 a.m.

"And then there were two," Theo says.

I glance over at the dance floor below. This dance floor feels more like a rave than a club. Shirtless men are dancing with women and other men. Girls are making out with other girls, and everyone is jumping to the thumping music. Strobe lights flash wildly over the crowd. It all seems surreal, women with men, men with men, women with women. For a moment, I can't believe my own eyes. This dance floor is completely judgment-free. No labels, no expectations, just pure freedom. The harsh security outside and the absence of paparazzi make it feel like anything goes here.

Theo taps my leg. "What's going on in that head of yours?" he asks.

I'm still staring at the dance floor. "It's so wild down there," I reply.

Theo turns to look to see the popping dance floor of ravers having the time of their lives. Then he removes a joint from his pocket and lights it up.

"What are you doing?" I ask, surprised by the lit joint.

"Smoking pot," he says, inhaling deeply. I eye him suspiciously as he exhales, then laughs. "Ever smoked a joint before?"

"Not since college," I say. The truth is, I smoked marijuana only once in my sophomore year, with Donna, of course. I never could inhale without coughing my head off.

Theo offers me the joint, but I shake my head. He takes another drag, holding it in. A few seconds later, he places both hands on my face and pulls me toward him. I forget to breathe. What is he doing? His lips hover close to mine. At this moment, I swear my heart is beating three times faster than normal. We lock eyes, barely an inch apart. Theo touches my lips with his finger, parting them, and blows smoke into my mouth. I instinctively inhale, keeping my eyes locked on his.

Theo smiles. "Shotgun," he says.

I slowly snap out of my trance. What the hell was that? I feel like I just left my body. Goosebumps run up my arms.

The cocktail waitress returns with two tall glasses of what looks like brown tea. She sets them down and leaves.

"Now this," Theo says, pointing to the drinks, "is

going to put some hair on your chest, Cameron Taylor." His finger touches my chest with three taps.

I'm still reeling from Theo's shotgun kiss. I grab the joint from him and take a puff. My heart is still racing, and now I have butterflies in my stomach. Theo hands me one of the glasses, and he takes the other.

"Don't sip it," he warns. "You've got to chug it."

"What is it?"

"Something my grandpa used to make," he says, raising his glass. "Cheers."

We clink our glasses and then chug. The taste is absolutely vile. It reminds me of the cleaning product I used to use on my wooden furniture.

"Oh my God," I say my face surely turned inside out. "That tasted like tar."

Theo laughs, taking another puff from his joint. "You've tasted tar?"

"No," I say, "but if I had, this is what it would taste like."

Theo laughs again, clearly amused by my reaction.

We lean back on the plush purple booth, high and buzzed, letting the electronic music from the dueling DJs wash over us. I can't help tapping my foot to the insane beats. My mind feels foggy, my body light as a feather. I feel like I'm floating.

"Let's dance," Theo says.

"What?" I blink, snapping out of my trance. "Why?"

Theo grabs a Los Angeles Dodgers cap from the edge of the table, puts it on backward, and then pulls me to my feet.

"It'll be fun," he says.

We leave the VIP Lounge and race down the stairs. Though it feels like I'm floating down them.

We push through the crowd on the dance floor until we find a spot. Theo and I face each other and start to dance. The energy of the floor is intoxicating. It feels like an out-of-body experience. The loud music, the strobe lights, neon colors flashing on everyone's faces, we're jumping, dancing, and existing in the moment.

A pretty girl with brown hair jumps between Theo and me, facing Theo. Theo grabs her lower back and pulls her close, grinding against her leg. I have to admit, it's hot watching him do this. Then Theo's eyes motion for me to join in. I laugh and move behind her, my chest pressing into her back. The girl goes wild, jumping up and down, screaming to the music.

Seconds later, she moves on, and someone starts grinding on me from behind. I glance at Theo for reassurance. He just smiles, gleaming his beautiful teeth. I decide to go for it and press back into the person behind me, letting them keep grinding. Theo laughs.

I turn my head to see it's a guy in his mid-twenties. He smiles at me. I smile back. The brown-haired girl returns, this time facing the guy behind me, pushing me forward into Theo.

I lose my balance and fall into his chest. His arms catch me. "You alright?" he asks, steadying me and reassuring me I'm still in control of my body.

I nod. We start dancing again, his hands on my hips. We lock eyes, and the rest of the world fades away. Nothing matters in this moment except Theo and me, swaying together in perfect sync. We stay like this, locked in a trance, until Theo suddenly pulls my arm, dragging me off the dance floor.

We rush into the men's restroom. The lights are dim, neon ropes illuminating the floor. Two of the stalls are occupied. I catch a glimpse of two men inside, snorting cocaine.

Theo pulls me into the third stall, the only empty one. He closes the door behind us and pushes me against the wall. The air in the stall is thick with the stale smell of men's cologne and sweat. We stare at each other for a moment. My heart races again. What is happening? Is this real? Was it the weed? The alcohol?

Theo holds my face in his hands, and we continue to gaze at each other.

"Hi," Theo says.

"Hi," I reply, my knees shaking. A sudden chill falls upon me. For the first time in my life, I have never felt more alive than I do in this very moment.

And then it happens. Theo lunges forward, kissing me. His tongue enters my mouth, and my body floats. He tastes so good. I wrap my legs around his waist, kissing him back. He leans into me, slamming my back into the wall, and I tighten my legs around him. I know it's too late to turn back now. It feels too good. He feels too good.

Boom! Boom! Boom!

We're snapped out of our trance by the pounding on the bathroom door.

"Come on, guys!" a deep voice sounds from the other side. "Get out of there!"

Theo and I pull apart, gasping. I look down and notice Theo has a raging hard-on, bulging through his pants. What the hell is happening? What the hell are we doing? He's straight. Was it the marijuana? The alcohol? Did he take something else before I arrived? Why is this straight guy kissing me? My mind clears, and suddenly, I'm flooded with questions. Theo is a fantasy. Perhaps it was the fog lifting, but it started to feel wrong.

"No, what are we doing?" I ask, loosening my legs from his waist. I push him back and, as surprised by his behavior as I am, unlock the stall door.

I bolt out of the bathroom, Theo adjusting himself and following behind. I run out of the club, gulping in the cool night air. Whatever sexual desire I felt on the dance floor stays there, because now all I feel is regret. Theo was an amazing dancer and an even better kisser, but I'm married. And he's straight. Why did I let him touch me like that? But more importantly, why did I enjoy it?

"Cameron!" Theo calls my name from behind me.

Just then, a yellow taxi pulls up, letting out three drunk girls.

Theo grabs my arm, stops me, and forces me to face him.

"Theo, I'm sorry," I say. "I have to go. It's late."

I jump into the cab just as the third drunk girl was about to close the door.

"Willoughby & Laurel," I instruct the driver.

As we pull away, I glance out the window. Theo stands on the sidewalk, hands behind his head, looking just as bewildered as I feel. What have we done?

Chapter 11

The next morning, I sit at the kitchen island sipping orange juice. Might as well pound as much vitamin C into my body as I can after the joint and drinks I had last night. Luckily, I'm not hungover today. I couldn't sleep when I got home last night, my nerves were going wild. I kept replaying the night in my head over and over.

The truth is, I'm still replaying it. I haven't felt that alive in my whole life. A flashback enters my mind: Theo shot gunning me in the VIP lounge. Then another flashback hits me, Theo grinding on that girl on the dance floor, but never taking his eyes off me. But the flashback that keeps repeating itself the most is when Theo lunged forward and kissed me in the bathroom stall. That moment still leaves me in awe... but also very confused.

I snap out of my thoughts when the doorbell rings. I

wasn't expecting anyone today, and Daniel certainly wouldn't ring the doorbell, so who could it be? A delivery? Maybe Daniel sent me flowers? Yeah, right. That'd be the day.

I walk to the foyer and open the front oak door. Standing there is Theo. He's wearing a gray hoodie and blue jeans. I spot his black Porsche parked in the street in front of my yard.

"Hey," I say, surprised.

"Are you alone?" He asks, keeping his head down.

I nod. "Yeah."

"Can we talk?"

I step aside and let him in. He closes the door behind him. "I remembered your address from when we shared a cab," Theo says.

I walk back to the kitchen, and Theo follows. I take another sip of my orange juice. "Would you like anything to drink?" I ask.

Theo eyes my glass of orange juice. "Is there any champagne in that?" He asks.

"There can be." I open the wine cooler and pull out a bottle of chilled champagne. I always keep one in there for impromptu special occasions. This is not one of them, but at least it's already chilled. I unravel the foil, and a moment later, pop! I pull out a glass, the same size as mine, fill it halfway with champagne, and then top it off with orange juice. I slide it to Theo. He takes a sip. We stand there in awkward silence.

"We don't have to talk about it, Theo," I say.

"No, I want to. We should," he replies, taking another sip of his mimosa.

"Why?" I take a sip of my orange juice.

"Because I liked it," he says.

Gulp. I nearly choke on my drink. "What?" I ask, confused.

"Last night was incredible. The dance floor. You. It was so hot in there." He looks at me with a mix of excitement and confusion.

Theo has me completely confused right now. He's straight. How can a straight man like kissing me, a gay man, if he is truly straight? I get that human sexuality can be complicated, but this is just too weird. Unless he isn't actually straight. Unless that was a lie.

"Aren't you straight?" I blurt out. He better not dance around this question.

Theo shoots the rest of his drink in one giant gulp and sets the glass down on the kitchen island. He shakes his head, no.

"Bi?" I ask. He shakes his head, no again.

"How can you be gay? You had a wife. Your divorce was public, all over the media. You slept with female extras on your show."

"Cameron, listen," Theo says, looking serious. "I tried to be something I wasn't when I was married to Amanda. She eventually got that too. It got bad, really bad. I started using drugs to numb myself, and it all went south from there."

I lean forward on the kitchen island, disbelief written on my face. This whole time, he was gay, knowing I was gay, but pretending he wasn't. I have to admit, I did not see this coming. "Who else knows?" I ask.

"My family knows. My very close friends, and my agent," he says, seeming ashamed of having hidden this from me. "Publicly, no one can know. Our society still isn't very accepting of actors coming out as gay, especially if they're playing badass roles." Theo slowly walks toward me. "That's why Amanda and I divorced. I eventually came clean with her, and it was our publicists' idea to make it a messy divorce. The truth is, she and I never did anything hurtful to each other. She told me I needed to find the right person, and so did she... since I wasn't it."

I decide to pour some champagne into my glass now too. I start to pour in orange juice, but then think, screw it. Champagne it is. I take a drink. Theo comes closer again, but I step back.

"It was wrong to kiss you," Theo says. "I know that, but I don't know how to explain the feeling I had with you last night."

"Theo, I can't," I say, hoping he'll just end this conversation and leave. Why do people feel the need to talk about everything? Why can't we just leave what happened at the club as a memory from last night?

"I know you can't," he says, "that's why I came to talk to you. I don't want there to be any awkwardness while we shoot our movie, but I wanted you to know, the truth about me. I owe that to you."

I finally smile. That was thoughtful. "I appreciate you clearing things up."

Theo nods and smiles too. He walks closer to me, but this time, I don't back up. He opens his arms for a hug. "No hard feelings? Hug it out?" he asks.

"No hard feelings," I say, and walk into his arms. He wraps his arms around me and holds me tight. Even though I don't want to admit it to myself, it feels good to be in his arms. I feel him sniff my hair and I pull away. This is wrong.

Theo backs off. "Okay, so I'll see you around," he says.

I nod again, and Theo walks toward the foyer. I can't let him leave like this. This is it. I have a choice to make right now, whether to let Theo walk out that door or not. I expected him to be honest with me, so it's only fair that I'm honest with him too.

"Wait," I say. Theo stops and turns toward me. "I liked it too."

"Say again?" He walks closer to me.

"When you kissed me. I liked it too. It felt good. It felt nice." We stare at each other for a moment. Theo seems surprised by my honesty. "Maybe just one more hug?"

I didn't know what I was thinking, but I did know I liked the way I felt in his arms.

Theo smiles, and we walk toward each other in the kitchen. We hug again, this time longer, tighter. I close my eyes. He smells so good.

Suddenly, I hear the front door open. "Cameron, you home?" Daniel calls from the foyer.

Theo and I leap apart just before Daniel enters the kitchen, carrying a couple of grocery bags. I quickly pull myself together.

"Hey, Daniel," I say.

Daniel sets the groceries on the counter and eyes Theo suspiciously. "Hi," Daniel says, glancing at Theo.

"Daniel, this is Theo. Theo Diaz."

The realization dawns on Daniel. "The actor?" he says. Daniel holds out his hand, and they shake.

"You have a great place here," Theo says, looking around the kitchen and living room. This must be his attempt to throw Daniel off.

"Thanks," Daniel says. I begin to occupy myself by emptying the groceries from the bags.

"Theo stopped by because he had some questions about the script," I say, alleviating any suspicion Daniel may have. He probably doesn't even suspect anything, but I'm being paranoid.

"I actually need to get going. Thanks for filling in the blanks, Cameron," Theo says. Daniel joins me in emptying the groceries.

"Nice to meet you," Daniel says.

"You too," Theo says and looks at me. "I'll see you

around, Cameron."

I smile and wave at him. Theo leaves. I hear the front door close behind him.

"Interesting guy," Daniel says. As Daniel continues to put the groceries away, I place my hands on the counter and stare for a moment, smiling. I notice Daniel pick up Theo's empty glass and see the open bottle of champagne.

"It's a little early to be drinking, don't you think?" Daniel asks.

I shrug. "It's gotta be 5:00 p.m. somewhere."

It's been a week since Theo and I last saw each other or communicated. That kiss definitely changed our new friendship, and his coming out to me changed the dynamic too. Things are different now. I needed this week to clear my head and think about what I was doing. I've decided I'm reckless with Theo, and that's for sure. His personality is the polar opposite of Daniel's, and I think I was drawn to that. But not anymore. I've had a lot of time to think. Daniel is my husband, and I love him. I think I just got so wrapped up in Theo because he's insanely attractive, has an amazing personality, and takes a genuine interest in me and my work. Daniel used to do that too, but it's been years since he and I connected that way. I know I'm guilty of it too. I used to take an interest in Daniel's work conversations, but after years together, they've become so redundant. The result never changes.

I sit in my study, staring at a blank screen on my laptop. Michael Corday contacted me earlier this morning to inform me that *Hold Up* has secured a director. His name is Marc Shepard, and his resume includes a few straight-to-streaming movies and a couple of made-for-TV network movies. He came at an affordable price, and his experience with TV movies, both action flicks, means he has knowledge of working with explosives. Production will begin in two months. Michael also informed me that Marc would like a table read once casting is complete, which is in the process right now. I'll attend the table read in case any changes to the script need to be made. *Hold Up* is no longer my baby; Marc now holds creative control as the director.

I've lined my study with several bookshelves that house my favorite books and the screenplays of my favorite movies. When I find myself developing writer's block, I often pull one of those screenplays out and read it. It's like watching the movie all over again in my head. Usually, this cures my writer's block.

I continue to stare at the blank screen, wondering what I should write next. I have a couple of ideas in my head, but I'm having a difficult time getting them onto the page. Whenever I develop a new idea, I free-write, meaning I take everything in my head and put it on the screen, then shuffle it around to make sense later. But today, it's not working for me. To be honest, nothing has worked for me this week. I still can't stop thinking about Theo. What has he done to me? I wonder what it would be like to sleep with him. He was such a great kisser, what would he be like as a lover? These thoughts are okay to have, even if I am married because that's all they are: thoughts. As long as I don't act on them, I'm giving myself permission to think about them.

My phone chimes, pulling me out of my daydream of Theo as a lover. I look down. It's a text from Daniel.

Daniel: *Hey babe, I'm coming home early. Let's do dinner on Melrose.*

This text makes me smile. It's exactly what I need right now, spending time with Daniel will get Theo out of my head.

I respond: *Sounds great.*

Later that night, Daniel and I came home after an amazing dinner at a new seafood restaurant. I ordered shrimp scampi, and Daniel ordered the salmon. We had a bottle of Sauvignon Blanc and decided to come home and drink more.

Throughout dinner, Daniel told me about a new client his firm helped land, one that will bring in millions in annual billing. He went on and on about business, and I didn't interrupt once. I decided to let him have his time, and when we got home, I'd tell him all about *Hold Up.*

We stand in the kitchen together. I retrieve a bottle of Chianti from the wine cooler, and Daniel puts the leftovers in the refrigerator.

"Guess what," I say, just as I'm pulling the cork out of the bottle.

"What, babe?" Daniel replies, pulling out two wine glasses from the cabinet.

"*Hold Up* hired a director."

"Cool," Daniel says dryly, setting the glasses on the kitchen island. I fill each glass with wine.

"Cool? Yes, it's very cool. We shoot in two months," I say, excited.

Daniel shrugs his shoulders. "Well, that's nice. Are you excited?"

He doesn't seem moved at all. "Yes, more excited than you, apparently."

He snaps his head up. "What does that mean?"

"Nothing. It just seems like you don't care."

Daniel takes a sip of his wine and rolls his eyes. "Cameron, stop. You know this movie stuff isn't a big deal to me."

"It's a big deal to me," I respond.

"I know, and I'm happy your movie is going to get made."

Happy? He is not seriously saying that to me right now when he looks less than thrilled. He's happy when the paychecks come in after I sell the scripts, but talking about character development, dramatic structure, or anything like that, he could care less.

"Why don't you read my work?" I blurt out.

"What?" He says defensively. I can tell this is going to turn into a fight, but I can't pull back now. I've had enough wine tonight that my courage is at full speed, and we're finally going to have this conversation, one I've buried for years. Theo has done a brilliant job of reminding me of it every time he asks about my scripts, while Daniel never does.

"Cameron, what are you doing right now?" Daniel asks.

"I'm just wondering why you don't ever read my work. It's important to me."

Daniel sets his wine glass down and marches to the living room to grab his briefcase from the mantle. He opens it, pulling out what looks like copy paper you'd buy at the store, except it's neatly bound with a cover design. He tosses it onto the kitchen island, and it makes a thud.

"This is a marketing packet for our new client," he says.

I pick up the bound packet and thumb through it. It's hundreds of pages of images, numbers, and legal jargon.

"This is what I read day in and day out, Cameron. My job. So, I'm sorry if the last thing I want to do when I come home is read a screenplay," he says. Something he said about the word *screenplay* stings. My eyes glance at his briefcase and I see another document fastened together. This one is half the size of the marketing packet.

"What's that?" I ask, pointing to it.

Daniel looks confused for a second, then sees the document I'm pointing at. "That's… That's nothing," he says. But I refuse to let it go. I march over to him and pull it from the briefcase.

If I had to guess, I'd say it's about 200 pages. It's hole-punched in three places and fastened with gold clasps, like a neat little book. The title reads: *A Year of Bliss.* Underneath the title: *Written By: Anna Parker.*

It's a manuscript. As I shuffle through the pages, I see it's double-spaced and clearly a novel of some sort.

"What is this? Who is Anna Parker?"

Daniel looks down, embarrassed. "She's the wife of a co-worker," he says.

"Is this a book? A novel?"

"Cameron," he says, as I step away from him, feeling betrayed. "Maxwell asked me to read it for her. On the flight to New York."

"For what?"

"He wants to know if it's worth her time to look for a publisher."

And then it hits me. Daniel's co-worker asked him to read his wife's novel. Daniel, who just proclaimed he doesn't have the desire to read fiction because of his marketing packets at work, has agreed to read Anna Parker's *A Year of Bliss.* Meanwhile, Daniel hasn't even read my sold screenplay, which is about to go into production, *Hold Up.* My stomach tightens, and I feel like I'm going to vomit.

"Cameron, I'm sorry. It's just that…"

I hold up my hand, silencing him, and do what any self-respecting writer would do at this moment. With all my might, I throw Anna Parker's manuscript across the room. The pages flutter like a fan before it lands on the floor.

"Cameron, really?" Daniel shouts, going to pick up the now-mangled manuscript.

"I can't believe you, Daniel," I shout back.

"You're acting like a child. Stop it," he scolds.

But I can't stop. I'm furious with Daniel. I feel completely betrayed. He doesn't care about my work or what I do. It's not legitimate to him, yet here's a novel from his co-worker's wife, and he's agreed to read it.

"I don't need this," Daniel says, heading up the stairs. I follow behind him. We enter the bedroom, and Daniel starts pulling his suitcase from the closet.

"I'm leaving for New York tomorrow morning, Cameron. Is this really how you want to spend our last night together?"

He begins packing. "Don't try to make me feel bad," I tell him. "I just want to know why you don't have time to read my work, but you can read Maxwell's wife's work."

Daniel stops and places his hands on my shoulders. "Cam, you're a sold writer. You're represented by a huge agency. Maxwell's wife is a housewife who wrote a book. That's it. It may not even be good. Why do you need me to read your work? I don't know what sells in Hollywood."

He starts packing again. He's right about that. He may be a Vice President at one of New York's finest marketing firms, but when it comes to screenplay sales and movie financing, he has zero clue of what's in or not. But it still burns. I feel like he doesn't care.

I take a deep breath and decide to let this conversation go. For now, at least. Daniel is leaving early tomorrow, and he's right: this isn't how I want to spend our last night together before his trip. I sit on the bed and watch him continue his predictable packing routine. He's gotten very good at it over the years. He's already packed his white undershirts, the exact number of boxer briefs for the exact days he'll be away, then moves on to his suits, followed by his shirts and matching ties. This routine has gone on for a long time now. I don't want to be in this routine anymore. I need something different. I need more.

And then it hits me. I need to see Theo.

"I'm going out," I say, rising from the bed. Daniel is still packing.

"Now?" he asks.

"Yes, now," I say, texting Theo to meet me out.

I see Daniel roll his eyes as he steps back into the closet. *Don't roll your eyes at me,* I want to scream. But I don't want to continue this fight.

"I just need to clear my head, you know?" I say, trying to ease the tension.

Daniel nods. "Maybe some fresh air will do you some good," he says, picking out the shirts I knew he would.

"Have a good trip," I say, walking out of the room. I hear him shout something back, like "Have a good week" or something like that. Normally, I'd ask him to repeat it, but my phone has chimed. Theo is returning my text.

Theo: *Staying in tonight. Come to my place. 1000 Ocean Ave, #802, Santa Monica.*

I head downstairs and grab my keys. Looks like I'm going to Theo's tonight.

Chapter 12

I ride my Phantom on this beautiful night. I'm a bit surprised he sent me his home address instead of suggesting we meet for a late drink or somewhere in public. Maybe he drank too much today and is hungover. I continued the text, telling him it is strictly a professional visit and that I wanted to talk about our new director. He agrees. I obviously lied. Who arranges business calls this late at night? The truth is, I want to see him. I know going to see Theo isn't a good idea, but I have so many thoughts swirling in my head after the fight with Daniel tonight. I couldn't even sleep if I tried right now.

I ride up the Pacific Coast Highway, heading toward Santa Monica with the beach to my left. Theo's address is in a high-rise right off Santa Monica Beach. Of course, he lives right on the beach. The bright moon shines down on the beautiful blue ocean.

I arrive at Theo's building, on Ocean Avenue, in Santa Monica. I park my Phantom in front of a meter. Standing before me is a ten-story condominium high-rise.

The elevator dings on the 8th floor. The concierge at the front desk was notified that I'd be stopping by, so he sent me up with his key card. Talk about great security, only key cardholders can use the elevator.

The doors open, and I step out, shifting my helmet under my arm. I walk down the long corridor. The walls are painted bright purple and gray, with matching carpet. I stop at the end of the hall in front of door number 801. I take a deep breath and knock three times.

The door opens, and Theo stands on the other side, shirtless, showing off his hard body. He has a clearly toned eight-pack and a tattoo of a circular tribal symbol just above his right pec. I knew his pecs would be perfect from the tight shirts he wears, but the eight-pack is a complete surprise. Tattoos cover his arms and spread onto his shoulders. I had just assumed they stopped at his biceps. He's wearing tight gray sweatpants that leave very little to the imagination, especially around the bulge in his pants. Though leaner and tighter than a bodybuilder, he obviously works out every single day to look like a chiseled Greek god.

Theo raises an eyebrow at my silence since he opened the door. It feels like it's been at least five minutes. I snap back to reality.

"Hi," I say, still admiring his physique.

"Hi," he replies. "Come in."

He steps aside, allowing my entry. Theo's living room features floor-to-ceiling windows offering a gorgeous view of the beach and the Pacific Ocean. The room is an open floor plan, with the living room, dining room, and kitchen seamlessly flowing together. A built-in wet bar is nestled into the wall opposite the windows in the living room. Four glass shelves sit fully stocked above it. A fireplace sits in the corner of the room. Above the fireplace, on a wooden mantle, I notice his two Emmy awards proudly displayed.

I see the script for *Hold Up* lying on the glass coffee table in front of the couch. The script is open to page thirty, with notes in the margins and highlighted dialogue for his character, Baldwin.

"I was working on the script, making notes for my character," Theo says, noticing my eyes on the script.

My gaze slides from the script back to Theo's shirtless self, then up to his eyes. "Would you mind putting on a shirt?" I ask, realizing I've probably been caught checking him out.

He smiles, flattered. "Sure," he says, disappearing down a small hall. He returns wearing a white tank top. His biceps are his best feature, I think. Why couldn't he have covered those up with a regular T-shirt? Unless he's deliberately trying to play with me. He sits on the couch and motions for me to join him. I sit down and place my motorcycle helmet in my lap.

"I'm sorry we haven't spoken since that day in my kitchen," I say.

"It's cool. I figured you weren't interested." I'm not sure what he means by *not interested.* I shift my helmet in my lap. "Here, set that down," he says, taking the helmet from me and setting it on the wet bar. Oh, the bar, where beverages are available to calm the nerves.

"Want a beer?" Theo asks as if reading my mind.

"Yes," I quickly say, too quickly. Theo opens the bottom cabinet of the wet bar, revealing a small refrigerator. He pulls out two bottles of beer and pops the tops. He hands me one and takes the other. We both drink. I notice he takes a generous gulp with his first sip.

He seems nervous, too.

"I feel like I owe you an explanation," I say.

"You don't," he replies.

"Especially since we're going into production soon and I'll be on set, and we'll see each other a lot." I take a generous gulp myself. Before I know it, we've both already drunk half our beers. Here it goes. I have to shut this down now, but why did I come to see him? "I'm married," I robotically blurt out. It just seemed like the right thing to say.

"I know."

I take another drink. "So, that's it," I say.

"Okay," he says, taking another sip. We don't take our eyes off each other.

"Okay then, we're clear."

"We are," he replies.

I decide now is the best time to chug the rest of my beer. It's already calming my nerves. I notice Theo does the same. Now we sit. Empty beers in hand, with an awkward silence between us.

"Okay, I guess we're good," I say. Theo nods and takes the empty bottles from my hands, setting them on the wet bar. I stand up and find myself standing directly in front of Theo, chest to chest. I gulp. Theo extends his hands and cups mine into his own. I begin to tremble.

"Except you liked it when I held you," he says in a soft voice, almost seductive.

"It was wrong," I admit. I've always heard that cliché about people getting weak in the knees when someone amazingly kisses them or holds them. I never thought it was true, just a bunch of fairy tale nonsense. Today, I stand corrected. My knees feel like they're about to give out. I have to stay strong.

"And you liked my tongue in your mouth," he says, even softer. I stand in silence, nearly falling into his arms.

He's right. I liked everything he was saying.

"It's not wrong to feel good," he whispers.

Without control, I begin to shake. I'm suddenly cold, or maybe my nerves are getting the best of me. I also feel nauseous. The beer is too heavy on my stomach. I feel it rising in the back of my throat, wanting to come back up. Theo notices my trembling, and his face shifts to concern.

"Come here," he says, pulling me into his arms. He wraps his arms around my lower back, pulling me closer to him. "Nothing has to happen. You're in charge," he whispers, reassuring me, but there is a bit of hesitation in his voice. Perhaps he's unsure what I need, I don't even know what I need a this point.

I suddenly feel my eyes swelling. What's happening to me? It's as though I have no control over my body. My knees finally fail me, and I fall into Theo's chest. He pulls me closer, and I hear his heart beating rapidly. Do I make him nervous? Everything floods into my mind, my feelings for Theo, the fight with Daniel, why we fought, and why I don't feel like Daniel and I are forever anymore. Why doesn't Daniel even bother to take an interest in me anymore? I can't help it, I start to cry.

I fall to my knees, and Theo gracefully falls with me, holding me, reassuring me.

"Shhhh," he says, kissing the top of my head as I sob. "Just let it out. I won't let you go." His hands gently move up and down my back calming me.

So I let it out. I sob harder, and Theo cradles me like a mother to a child. I don't know what it was, maybe it was his charm, or maybe it was just me, but I couldn't hold anything back anymore. For the first time in years, I couldn't control my emotions.

I look up at him and he gazes back at me. There's something in his eyes that soothes me. Like he never wants to let me go. Like he needs me. He pulls me in and hugs me tighter. I continue to sob.

And the realization hits me like a brick: I am lonely. I feel dead inside, but Theo makes me feel alive again.

Chapter 13

I wake up in Theo's bed, in his bedroom. Just like the living room, the bedroom features floor-to-ceiling windows. The curtains are drawn back, and the balcony's sliding glass door is cracked open, letting in the sound of the ocean waves. I'm lying on my right side. Theo's arm is around me, and I raise my head to get a better understanding of the situation. Theo lies next to me, sleeping. I carefully remove his arm from around me and sit up in the bed. I don't even remember coming in here. The last thing I remember is crying in the living room and losing myself in Theo's arms. He must have carried me in here, and we must have fallen asleep. I can't believe I cried like that. I don't know what's going on with me.

"You okay?" Theo asks. I glance over and see that his eyes are open. I must have woken him when I moved his arm. Embarrassed, I place my hands over my head.

"I can't believe I had a breakdown like that," I say. I begin to stand, but Theo pulls me back into the bed.

"You needed to let it out. People need other people sometimes. I guess I'm your person," he says.

"Huh?"

"Your crying buddy. When things get tough, you can cry on my shoulder," Theo says. "Oh Jesus, that sounds like such a cliché."

I roll my eyes politely and smile. It *does* sound like a cliché. "I'm hoping that breakdown was a one-time thing." Theo pulls me closer to him. We're both lying on our sides again. I feel him sniff the top of my head and let out a pleasant moan. He must like the smell of my shampoo. Wait, why is he moaning? I immediately sit up, pulling myself away from Theo's grasp.

"Theo, we can't do this."

Theo sits up too. "Nothing has to happen, Cameron," he says. Then, "unless you want it to."

"We can't."

"Why did you come here, then?" I sit back on the bed and turn to face Theo. It's a good question. Why *did* I come here?

"I honestly don't know," I say. "After my fight with Daniel, I could only think of you." Theo just stares at me until a small smile forms at the corners of his mouth.

"Only think of me, huh?" Theo says, nudging his knee against mine. "You need to decide what you want."

I rise from the bed again. This is all too frustrating. Why can't I just want a friend? Why can't Theo and I just be friends? Suddenly, a flashback of Theo and I making out in the bathroom floods my mind. Oh, right, that's why we can't just be friends. We're attracted to each other *too* much.

I step out onto the balcony that spans the entire length

of Theo's condo. The cool ocean breeze instantly cools my face. I lean over the railing, staring at the ocean waves hitting the beach. The sound is so peaceful. Theo steps out onto the balcony too and wraps his arms around me. Defeated, I place my hands on his forearms, which are wrapped around my chest. It's almost as if I can't stop him from touching me, some invisible force, like gravity, driving us together. I couldn't stop thinking about him before tonight. There's something about him that draws me in.

I turn to face Theo. We lock eyes. He has wide brown eyes. I slide my right hand from his bicep down to his forearm. His tattoos make him look even hotter in his tank top. Theo picks up my hand and kisses it, keeping my hand near his lips as he looks at me with pleading eyes. I move in closer to him, that same unseen force is pulling us together.

This is it. This is the moment. There comes a point in everyone's life when they arrive at the crossroads of right and wrong. They are forced to choose a path, and it's one of the most difficult decisions they'll ever make. Whatever is going on between Theo and me can't be controlled anymore. Eventually, the inevitable will win. So screw it.

Without hesitation, I kiss Theo, and he responds like a shark, devouring my mouth. We kiss for what feels like minutes, slowly moving back into the bedroom until we fall onto the bed.

Theo pulls off his tank top and leaps on top of me. We embrace, kissing deeply. I wrap my legs around his lower back as his lips travel to my neck. My calves can feel his tight back muscles and it excites me. The feel of his tongue tracing down to my right nipple sends a shiver through me. Goosebumps rise all over my body as he does the same to my left nipple. His tongue carefully circling each nipple.

My legs, still wrapped around him, push against his sweatpants. They get caught on his erection, so he helps me out, pulling them off completely. He isn't wearing underwear.

I can't help but stare at him, fully exposed, as he quickly removes my pants, leaving me in just my boxers. I remember the bulge I saw when I arrived earlier, now in front of me, standing as straight as a board, I see everything. He climbs back on top of me, and we kiss again, our bodies warm and pressed together.

My hand instinctively slides down, stroking him. His panting breaths fall close to my ear.

I decide to take charge. Flipping him onto his back, I straddle him, kissing him deeply as I move down his chest. When I reach his nipples, he arches his back, moaning softly.

Moments later, Theo flips me back onto my back again. He pulls my boxers off, leaving us both fully aroused. We continue to kiss.

I hear the dresser drawer screech open as Theo retrieves a bottle of lubricant. We continue kissing, the heat between us building, when I feel his finger slide inside me. My body tenses at first, but then I start to relax.

"Is this okay?" he asks, his voice soft.

I can't even speak, every sense in my body feels electrified. I nod, giving him permission, and he continues. Soon, I feel another finger enter. Each time I tense up, Theo compensates, his tongue delving deeper into my mouth, circling around mine, grounding me in the moment.

The dresser drawer closes, and Theo pauses to grab a red condom wrapper. He brings it to his mouth, tearing it open with his teeth. His voice drops low as he says, "You're so hot."

I watch him slide the condom on, his body glistening with sweat. The dim light enhances every contour of his muscles, heightening my already overwhelmed senses. He leans over me, his breath heavy, and slowly enters me.

He feels incredible.

Theo moves slowly at first, his body pressing against mine as we find a rhythm together. My legs wrap around his lower back, and our breathing falls in sync, constant and shallow. Our skin feels like it's on fire, every movement sending waves of pleasure through me.

His eyes stay locked on mine as we move in unison. The bed creaks beneath us, a reminder of the physicality of our connection. It feels like an electric surge has fused us together. There's no turning back now. It's too good to stop.

I feel like I'm going to explode, the sensation becoming nearly impossible to resist.

"Don't cum yet," Theo says, his voice strained, each breath measured.

I glance at him, confused but willing to comply.

"Cum with me," he says, his gaze piercing.

"Okay," I whisper, fighting off the incredible sensation that is nearly unavoidable.

We continue moving together, our eyes never leaving each other. Moments later, I see Theo's eyes squint, his expression contorting with pleasure. That's my cue. I let go, and we erupt together, moaning in unison as the tension releases. My toes curl, and I'm consumed with absolute pleasure.

Theo collapses on top of me, both of us panting heavily, our bodies drenched in sweat.

"You feel so good," he murmurs, catching his breath.

I don't want him to move, I don't want this moment to end. Our bodies stay pressed together, radiating heat as we recover.

"Again?" Theo asks, a hint of a smile playing on his lips.

I nod, and we begin all over again. It's incredible.

Chapter 14

The morning sun shines through the windows, waking me up. The curtains are completely open, so it's as bright as heaven in Theo's room. We both lie on our sides, Theo holding me like a lover should. The sun beams into my eyes, causing me to squint. I carefully remove Theo's arm without disturbing him and rise, rubbing my eyes. I look back at Theo, and he's sound asleep. My eyes scan the room and fall onto the trash can, which houses three empty red condom wrappers. A feeling of regret starts to cast over me.

I see my phone on the nightstand and pick it up. I press a button, and the screen lights up, reading: Daniel Missed Call (5)

Shit. I find my boxers in the corner of the room and slide them on. I take a moment to survey the room. My clothes are scattered about, and Theo's sweats are lying on the floor too. The bed looks like a wreck, with blankets disheveled, sheets pulled off the mattress, and the comforter in a heap on the floor.

I quietly close the bedroom door behind me and enter the living room. I hold the phone close to my ear and hit play on the first voicemail. They're all from Daniel.

"Hey, it's me. Call me back."

I move to the next message.

"Cameron, please call me back. I need to make sure you're okay." His voice sounded desperate.

I pull up the most recent voicemail's timestamp. It reads 5:23 a.m. I listen to it.

"It's me again," Daniel says, his voice sounding tired. "I know you're in Santa Monica. I tracked your phone, so I assume you're okay." There's a pause. "Cameron, I'm sorry. I know I can be a dick sometimes." Another pause. "I'm about to head to the airport to catch my flight to New York. I hate leaving things like this. I'll call you when I land. Please pick up when I do."

I set the phone on the coffee table and walk toward the windows. The ocean is crystal blue this morning. Flashbacks of Theo and I from last night fill my mind, and I can't help but grin.

"Morning, sexy," Theo says from behind me. I turn around, and he's leaning in the doorway of his bedroom, completely naked. His sexy body is ready for more. I flash him a smile.

"Morning."

"Come back to bed," he says. "I want to cuddle with you, and maybe..." He raises his eyebrows a couple of times.

I hesitate for a moment, but my phone is still in my hand, reminding me of the reality of the situation. "I should go," I say, walking past him into the bedroom to get dressed. Theo follows me.

"You're not going to be weird on me now, are you?" He asks, watching me pull up my pants.

"I have five missed calls from Daniel. Five voicemails," I reply, now fully dressed. I face him. "I had fun last night. It was..."

"Hot," he says, finishing my sentence for me, raising his right eyebrow as if waiting for my agreement. I half-smile.

"I have to figure out what I'm doing," I say, giving him a small peck on the lips. But Theo doesn't settle for that. He pulls me into him and gives me a real kiss. I feel his excitement against my leg.

"Okay, now you can go," he says, patting my butt. I smile again, heading for the door, but then I hear him shout, "But don't take too long to figure this out. I'd like to have sex with you again. Preferably tonight."

I shake my head, flattered, and grab my motorcycle helmet from the wet bar before heading out the door.

I arrive home forty-five minutes later and enter through the side door of the kitchen. The ride home was great for me because it gave me time to think about my actions last night and what I'm doing with Theo. I've determined that Theo is an unstoppable force in my life, and if I continue to see him, we'll have a purely physical relationship. I don't think Theo is interested in anything beyond that, anyway. With his looks and the way he pursued me, this is not his first go-around in getting what he wants. I know this, and I'm okay with it. What I haven't decided yet is if I want to see Theo again. I can't control myself around him. And then there's Daniel. Whatever has broken between the two of us needs to be dealt with, but I don't know how to fix it. I feel regret for sleeping with Theo last night, three times, but I also feel rejuvenated, like a sixteen-year-old boy who just lost his virginity. It feels good to feel a bit naughty.

My phone rings. Perfect timing. It's Daniel.

"Hello?" I say into the phone.

"Hey," Daniel says, his voice heavy with relief. I hear the city booming in the background, cabs honk and people chatter. He's outside.

"Hi."

We fall into silence for a moment, though his surroundings continue on as usual. "How are you?" he asks.

I don't know how to answer. Should I tell him I'm great because I had the best sex of my life last night, three times, in fact? Should I ask him how his flight was? I don't want to lie to him either, so I go for the most natural thing I can think of. "I'm good," I say.

Though I can't see him, I know he's nodding. "That's good," he says, and I nod to myself for guessing his next move. A few more seconds of silence. "Did you get my messages?"

"I did."

"As it turns out, I may be in New York for a couple of weeks. There's some stuff about to hit the fan. I don't know…"

"Daniel, it's okay," I say, reassuring him.

"I'm sorry about last night. I didn't realize you felt that way about me. About your writing." His voice sounds so sincere, and I'm suddenly flooded with emotion. "I'll try to do better in the future. Maybe we can schedule some time, and you can read me your work over wine or something."

My eyes well up, and a lump forms in my throat. "I'd like that," I manage to croak.

"Are we good?" he asks. I nod, but then I realize he can't see my nod.

"Yes, I'm sorry too."

"I'm about to get to the office, but I'll call you later?" Daniel says. He usually walks to the office from his corporate apartment. It's about four blocks, New York blocks, that is. That explains the hustle and bustle I hear in the background.

"Yes, sounds good," I reply, just about to hang up when…

"Hey."

"Yes?"

"Where did you stay last night? I left at 5:45 a.m., and you still weren't home." My heart stops. I honestly have no idea how to answer this. Think, Cameron, think. It's not like me to not come home, to stay at someone else's place, but he's right. I didn't come home last night, and he knows it.

"Santa Monica." I finally say.

I remember his voicemail. He tracked my location on my smartphone to make sure I was okay. He knew I was in Santa Monica. I need to turn that tracking software off in the future.

"I hung out with Theo," I blurt out. Oh shit. Why did I say that?

"Who?"

Too late now. "Theo."

Silence from him. He's probably trying to figure out who the hell Theo is, but I bet he's not imagining that I had sex with Theo last night. Or maybe he is, but why would he? I need to stop overthinking this.

"The actor?" he finally asks.

"Yes."

"Why?" Another question I don't know how to answer. Why didn't I prepare for questions like this on the ride home from Santa Monica? Then I would have been ready.

"I was upset," I say. "He told me before that he lived in Santa Monica and to call him if I ever wanted to hang out. We're going to be working together, you know." I wait for Daniel's response, hoping he buys the lie. It's so hard to tell since I can't see his face. It feels like hours of dead silence, hours of Daniel judging me from the other line, knowing I cheated on him last night. Three times.

"Oh, okay," he finally says. "Have a great day. I'll call you later. I love you."

My heart starts beating again, and I finally exhale. At least, from what I can tell, he bought it.

"Love you too," I say, quickly ending the call. I let out an enormous sigh. I think that's the first time I've ever lied to Daniel. Though, technically, I did hang out with Theo last night. The lie comes from not telling him what really happened.

Chapter 15

That evening, I sit in my study, staring at the screen in front of my computer. A blank document stares back, the cursor blinking as if to mock me. I'm trying to start a new screenplay, but all I can think about is Theo and the amazing night we had last night. How did I get here? What made me want this? I smirk.

I wanted this.

An idea suddenly pops into my head. I remember reading an article a long time ago about two fourteen-year-old teenagers who ran off and got married without their parents' permission. They rented a small house and had three kids before they turned 18. They found local jobs and supported themselves entirely. With my newfound physical feelings, I can understand how two teenagers, pumped full of hormones, would drop out of high school and run away together. It wouldn't have made sense to me before meeting Theo, but now it does. Attraction makes you do wild things. Impulsive things.

I decide to write a paragraph about these two teens, except, in my version, the boy is named Andrew, and the girl is Jamie. Suddenly, I'm typing feverishly, working out a treatment for the story. Andrew begins to take shape. He's not just the high school quarterback, no, scratch that. He's the star mechanic in his auto class. This skill will come in handy when he drops out of school. Jamie, on the other hand, isn't a typical cheerleader. She's a new student who recently transferred out of state. Her father bums around from job to job.

I look at the time and realize I've been immersed in Andrew and Jamie's world for almost two hours. Glancing at my page count, I see I've written 20 pages of a raw, rough draft treatment. I think I just figured out my next screenplay. Andrew and Jamie. I'll call it *Their Love*, no, scratch that. I'll call it *Our Love.*

Minutes later, I'm in the kitchen, popping open a bottle of champagne to celebrate. Thoughts and ideas flood my mind. I don't know how other writers work, but when these ideas come, I don't stop. I rush back to my computer, champagne bottle in hand, and start writing character profiles for Andrew and Jamie.

I begin with Andrew. How old is he? Where was he born? What is his favorite color? Who are his friends? Did his parents go to college? Before I know it, I've filled two pages with details about him. Once I'm comfortable with Andrew, I move on to Jamie. This style of writing works for me, this is how I get to know my characters. I can't give them a voice in the script until I know who they are, and I can't start the script until I know their story.

My phone rings. I glance at the screen and see it's

Daniel. I eye the clock, which reads 9:30 PM. Daniel's in New York, meaning it's past midnight there. He's usually not up this late. I answer.

"Hello?" I say.

"Babe!" he shouts from the other end. I hear a lot of noise in the background. It sounds like he's at a… "I'm at a bar."

I take a swig of champagne straight from the bottle. I know, classy. I was so immersed in my story that I didn't even think to grab a glass. Oh well. No one can judge me from here.

"Why are you at a bar? You hate bars."

"Not tonight," Daniel says. "Guess what?"

"What?"

"We're celebrating."

"We're?"

"Yes, my team and me. We straightened everything out with the client." I hear chatter and cheers in the background. His coworkers sound drunk. "Which means I don't have to stay in New York for two weeks. I'm coming home tomorrow. We avoided the shit hitting the fan."

I lean forward and smile. "That's great," I say. "I'm really happy for you."

I hear him take a swig of his drink. I can tell he's been drinking because his words are slurring. "What are you up to?" he asks.

"I'm working on my next screenplay. Daniel, it just came to me tonight from an article I read, and…"

"Cameron!" Daniel shouts, interrupting me. "I can't hear you that well. It's too loud in here. I'm glad you're working on a screenplay."

I roll my eyes and smirk. "I'll see you tomorrow then."

"Hey!"

"Yes?"

"I love you," he says, and I can hear him smiling from the other end. "Have a good night."

"I love you too." He genuinely sounded happy, like all that stress had disappeared.

We hang up. I lean back in my chair, taking another swig of champagne. I sigh and shake my head at my predicament, Daniel and Theo. I can't help but enjoy the attention at this very moment. I lean forward and keep writing my character profiles for *Our Love*.

An hour passes, and my phone rings again. I look down and see it's Theo. My heart sinks into my stomach, and I hesitate before answering. But I can't resist.

"Hello?" I answer.

"Hello, gorgeous," Theo says, his voice full of charm. I can practically hear his smile, and then I see his perfect teeth in my mind.

"Hi."

"Come out with me."

I take a deep breath. I can't trust myself at Theo's place, but he's asking to meet out. I can trust myself in public… well, if the club doesn't count. But that was because of the amazing energy there.

"Where?"

"Tricks. See you in thirty minutes."

The phone goes dead. Tricks is a local gay bar in West Hollywood. They pride themselves on hiring a bitchy staff of shirtless men and serving overpriced drinks. I close my laptop and leave Andrew and Jamie behind for the evening. I change into something presentable and head out to meet Theo.

The bar is packed, and loud electronic music blares the latest hits by top female pop stars. I sit at a table in the back of the bar, near the restrooms, as instructed by Theo's text. Now I understand why he chose this spot, it's poorly lit, and the tables in the back are fairly private.

I can only assume that since they're next to the bathroom, crowds tend to stay away.

Theo walks in, wearing a blue Dodgers hat pulled low to hide his face. He's dressed in ripped jeans and a blue button-up shirt to match his cap. He doesn't look like the Theo I know, the one in a leather jacket, with beautiful arms covered in tattoos. But still, he looks good. He takes a seat.

"Nice disguise," I say, just as a shirtless server wearing nothing but a lime green speedo drops off two beers.

Theo smiles at my comment. "Can never be too careful," he says, acknowledging his closeted self.

"You look good," I admit. Honestly, I want to rip open that shirt just so I can touch those amazing abs, but I snap myself out of it. "Why did you want to meet at a gay bar? Isn't that risky?"

Theo takes a long gulp of his beer and shakes his head. "I wanted to see you, and I know you live close to here. Figured it was a good shot you'd say yes when I called."

"Sneaky."

"The truth is, I've been thinking about you all day. You left my place looking worried, and I wanted to make sure you were okay."

I take a long gulp of my beer this time. "You could've just asked if I was okay on the phone," I say, playing it cool, though I'm secretly glad he called.

"Yeah, but this way, I get to have a drink with you."

I feel his foot rub my shin under the table.

"Theo…"

"How'd it go with you-know-who?" he asks, deliberately avoiding mentioning Daniel's name.

I nod. "It went fine. He's in New York, actually coming home tomorrow. I'm glad."

"You are?" He raises an eyebrow, and I feel him retract his foot.

I take a deep breath. "I need some time to think…"

"Come home with me," he says, interrupting. It's so tempting to say yes. In fact, I'd probably take him in the bathroom right now if I could. But I know that's just my lust talking.

"I can't."

"Come on."

The waiter brings by two shots of tequila, dropping them off with a smile. I eye Theo, and he says, "I told him to bring them when I walked in."

We pick up the shot glasses and toast.

"Salute," we both say before shooting the tequila.

We spend the next hour talking about my new story, *Our Love.* Theo listens intently, not interrupting once, but hanging on to every word with genuine interest.

Chapter 16

I stand in Theo's living room, facing him. He's lounging on the couch, wearing a white tank top and black pants, looking effortlessly put together.

"Okay, if we're going to do this, there need to be rules," I say firmly.

Theo raises an eyebrow. "Rules?"

"Yes, rules. I need to make sure you understand what this is."

Theo smiles. "Okay, what is this?"

I ponder the question for a moment until the realization hits me. "...An affair," I say.

He rolls his eyes. "Cameron, not everything has to be defined. You writers are so weird sometimes."

Reaching out, he grabs my hand and pulls me onto the couch beside him. He holds me close and kisses the top of my head.

"Let's call it two people fucking," he says.

I shake my head. "That's too harsh. It sounds crude."

"Screwing," he says laughing.

"I mean it's the same meaning, just less harsh," I say.

"Or how about two people connecting?"

I pause. I like that. Two people connecting. It sounds much nicer.

Theo kisses my neck and whispers, "An unstoppable connection."

I can't help but laugh. "Are you sure you're not the writer?"

His tongue slides from my neck to the back of my ear, sending goosebumps down my spine.

"Does Daniel do this?" Theo asks, his hand starting to slide down my pants.

The mention of Daniel's name snaps me out of it. I stop his hand and pull it away. "We can never talk about Daniel."

Theo senses the shift in my tone. "What's wrong? I'm sorry."

"It's not right to talk about him. It's not fair to him."

I rise from the couch and face the open balcony door, listening to the sound of the ocean waves. Theo comes up behind me, wrapping his arms around my stomach and pulling me closer to him. He's so warm.

"I like you, and you like me," he says softly. "We're two people just having fun. There's nothing more to it."

I lean my head back, resting it on Theo's shoulder. "Fair enough," I say, just as his hand slides down my waist. He begins kissing my neck again. I close my eyes and savor the moment.

Later that night, Theo and I sit on his bed, both in our boxers, eating Chinese food. Music plays from a nearby speaker on the dresser.

Theo sits cross-legged at the head of the bed, facing me. I sit in the center, cross-legged as well. We had sex twice, took a shower, and now, famished, Theo ordered Chinese food to refuel our bodies.

I ordered chicken and rice, while Theo requested beef chow mein. The takeout bag didn't include plastic forks, only chopsticks. I've never been good with chopsticks, but Theo handles them like a pro.

My chicken keeps falling back into its white carton. Why couldn't they have just included a fork?

Theo notices and laughs. "Having problems?"

"I've never been good with these things," I admit, attempting to pick up my food again. This time, I manage to grab a clump of rice, but it falls back into the carton before reaching my mouth. I sigh.

Theo demonstrates, shoving a mouthful of chow mein into his mouth first. "You have to hold the top stick like a pencil," he explains, positioning the chopstick between his fingers.

I follow his lead.

"Then, rest the other chopstick against your ring finger and hold it with your thumb," he continues. I adjust my grip.

"Now, just move the top stick with your thumb, index, and middle fingers," he says.

I mimic his movements and manage to grab a piece of chicken. Before it has a chance to fall again, I shove it into my mouth. Success. I grin in triumph, and Theo leans in for a kiss.

"It takes practice, but you'll get it," he says.

I watch him eat, unable to stop myself from smiling. He looks amazing sitting there in just his boxers, eating. With a body like a descendant of Adonis and the perfect smile of a movie star, he's everything I'm not.

I don't have big muscles or even the hint of a six-pack. Yet somehow, he's attracted to me.

It suddenly occurs to me how little I know about him. Beyond his now-confirmed sexuality and his public life, I don't know much about Theo's personal tastes or his inner world.

Theo leans in and gives me a soft kiss on the lips. "We're good, right?" he asks, his eyes looking so dough-like.

This is the point I should tell him this is a mistake, that we shouldn't take it any further. This is the point where I could end it and never do it again.

But I can't.

Because, in a way, I want this too.

I want him.

I pull him closer and kiss him back. "Yeah," I say, "we're good."

And with that, what seemed right or wrong didn't matter anymore.

Chapter 17

The morning sun shines brightly over West Hollywood as I hop on my Phantom. It's been a couple of days since I've seen Theo, but he texted me this morning to say he's at Eastgate Studios in Hollywood, doing an underwear shoot for GK by Gregory Kyle, a high-end fashion designer whose sexy underwear is currently worn by all the hottest male stars.

I knock on Theo's trailer door and hear his voice from inside: "Three seconds!"

While I wait, I glance around the bustling parking lot. Production assistants are busy moving equipment, prepping for the next shoot.

The trailer door swings open, and there's Theo, shirtless and towering over me, wearing black leather pants that are unbuttoned and unzipped, revealing a pair of white sexy boxer briefs underneath. He's been sweating, and for a second, I have to catch my breath. When he sees me, his face lights up with a big smile.

"You came," he says, stepping aside to let me in.

I step inside and take a quick look around. It's a one-bedroom, RV-style trailer with a surprisingly sleek kitchen for its size. The back bedroom door is open, revealing a large bed that's made up like something out of a boutique hotel.

Gift baskets filled with fruit and cookies sit neatly on the dining table, probably from the brands Theo is endorsing for this shoot. My eyes drift back to him, standing there in front of me, every bit the incredible underwear model.

"You look…" I begin, but he's on me too quickly for me to finish. He lifts me onto the kitchen counter, and my legs instinctively straddle his waist as his tongue slips into my mouth. I'm instantly hard as he starts unbuttoning my pants. He smells like sweat and cologne. It makes me dizzy, but only wanting him more.

"I missed you," he says between kisses.

And I've missed him. I hate being away from him. But then I remember all the production assistants I saw earlier, rushing around the parking lot to set up his next shot.

"Wait," I say, pulling back just a little. "Don't you have to get back out there?"

He keeps kissing me, shaking his head. "It's going to take them at least twenty more minutes to finish setting up," he says, sliding down my pants. "Wow." He laughs at my erection, nearly bursting out of my boxers.

I smile shyly as he drops to his knees and begins to suck me. I grip the edge of the counter, knuckles almost white, as he gives me one of the best blowjobs of my life. I'm about to…

BANG! BANG! BANG!

Three loud knocks at the door. Theo is immediately on his feet again.

"Three minutes, Mr. Diaz!" someone calls from outside.

I glance down to see that his erection is straining against his leather pants.

"We've got three minutes," Theo says, pulling down his pants. He grabs my dick and starts jerking me off, and I grab his rock-hard cock and do the same. With his free hand, he grips the back of my neck to steady himself. I mirror him, holding his neck with my own free hand.

Our grips tighten. We stare into each other's eyes, intense and locked in, as we rapidly stroke each other off. Then we kiss, hard. We both explode all over each other.

It's like electricity just jolted from my soul. My entire body goes weak, and I collapse against the standing Theo, wrapping my arms around him tightly. He hugs me back, and soon we're a sticky mess, breathing like we've just run five miles without stopping.

"That was…" I start to say.

"Intense," he responds, catching his breath. He kisses me on the forehead and pulls a towel from the kitchen drawer. He wets it in the sink and tosses it to me to clean off.

I watch him wipe himself down too. His muscles seem even tighter now than when I walked in, like he just crushed a workout. I guess, in a way, he did.

"You able to stay for the rest of the shoot?" he asks.

"Yeah, I can stay for a while," I say. I'm actually looking forward to watching Theo work. Even if he's not acting today, a photo shoot is still part of the job.

"Awesome. Maybe we can grab a bite after?" He takes both towels and tosses them into a small bathroom hamper. Then he adjusts his pants in the mirror on the back of the bathroom door, giving himself a quick tug.

"I'm gonna need another minute before I go out there," he says, winking at me. "It won't go down."

We both laugh.

Later that evening, Theo and I end up at a bar in Hollywood. It's crowded and small, but we find two seats nestled near the end of the bar. It smells like stale cigarette smoke and a hint of mildew. Definitely a dive bar, but it's packed.

The bartender immediately tosses two black cocktail napkins our way. He's in his early thirties with a nice smile, wearing a tight white shirt that shows off his chest and fitted black pants. A white towel hangs from his back pocket.

"What can I get for you two?" The place is so loud I barely hear him.

"Um…" Theo says, scanning the bottles on the shelves behind the bar.

"Two tequila shots. Whatever's top shelf," I interject. I know Theo likes tequila; he pounded those shots at The Monastery.

"Top shelf, bottom shelf, they're all the same thing here." He says with a shrug and darts away.

I glance at Theo. "It's going to be one of those nights, huh?" he says, teasing. "What kind of trouble are you looking to get into?" His eyes never leave mine.

The bartender is back in a flash, pouring two shots of tequila from a thick frosted bottle. He keeps eyeing Theo.

He slides us the shots and pours one for himself.

"Let's cheers together," the bartender says, extending his hand to Theo. "I'm Matt."

Theo awkwardly shakes his hand, his expression slightly off. Wait, is Matt hitting on him?

I glance around. There are plenty of men and women

here, so I don't think we're in a gay bar.

The three of us clink our shot glasses and throw back the tequila, immediately biting into lime wedges Matt placed on napkins in front of us. Our glasses hit the bar in unison.

"That round's on me," Matt says.

Now I'm sure he's hitting on Theo.

"Uh, thanks, man," Theo replies, shooting me a quick glance like he's trying to reassure me everything's fine. The look on his face tells me he's wondering the same thing.

Matt leans in closer to Theo's face. Seriously, what the hell?

"I'm a big fan," Matt says. "I moved out here about a year ago. I'm an actor too. Can't seem to catch a break. My agent sucks."

Theo's eyes soften. "Ah, man, thanks. And hang in there, it's a tough biz. But if it's meant to be, it'll be. Just keep doing the work."

"How long did it take you to get your big break?" Matt asks sincerely.

"A long time, dude. Just keep auditioning and find a new agent. You've gotta be an advocate for your own career. Agent shop. If they're not putting you out there one hundred percent? Fire them. Fuck them."

Matt nods reassuringly. "Fuck them. I like that."

An awkward silence grows as Matt soon takes the hint that this moment is over.

"Can I get you two anything else?"

"Yeah, two of those Cubana beers you've got," Theo says.

"Coming right up," Matt replies, then disappears into the crowd.

"Have you ever had a Cuban beer before?" Theo asks.

"No, can't say that I have. Wait, I thought the U.S.

didn't trade with Cuba?" I say, recalling some trade restriction lecture from college. No Cuban cigars, no Cuban beer.

"Ah, good for you for knowing that," Theo says, his shoulder nudging mine.

Matt returns and slides the two beers our way. "Enjoy," he says, then moves on to help other patrons.

"They're Cuban-inspired. Brewed in the States, but mimic the same flavors."

We both take a sip. It's cold and crisp.

"How do you know what real Cuban beer tastes like if you've been in the U.S. since you were a kid?"

Theo laughs. "Well, you got me there. I guess I don't. I've only ever had these Cuban-inspired ones."

We keep drinking, and I catch Theo watching Matt move behind the bar.

"I remember feeling that way," he says, gesturing toward Matt. "Wondering if this dream would ever happen."

I watch him as his eyes reflect genuine compassion. His heart melts mine.

"I think you gave him good advice. He seemed to really take it in," I say, and Theo smiles. "I like that big brother energy. It's hot."

Theo's leg brushes against mine. His eyes stay locked on me for what feels like an eternity, and somehow, I can't look away.

"Let's go back to my place tonight," he says, leaning in close. He whispers into my ear. "Let's get naked and use the jacuzzi in my master bath."

I laugh at the way he says *get naked*, like a teenage boy about to get laid for the first time.

I finish my beer quickly and nod.

"That sounds great," I say. And it does, being naked with Theo and held by him all night.

I know I should feel worse. I'm still someone's husband. But the passion in Theo's eyes, the promise in his voice…

My body already made its choice. It's like finally taking in that first deep breath after being underwater for so long.

Chapter 18

The next morning, I arrive home through the side door and enter the kitchen. I'm surprised to see Daniel sitting on a bar stool, sipping a beer straight from the bottle. He's still in his suit.

"Daniel, you're home," I say.

"Early flight," he replies.

I set my helmet on a nearby stool and open the refrigerator to grab a beer for myself. I glance back at Daniel, who is pecking away at his phone, probably sending a work email.

"Are you home for the night?" I ask.

"Yes, I thought we could go out to dinner tonight," he says. "I still owe you a date at that new Bohemian restaurant on Melrose."

"Tonight?" I take a sip of my beer.

Daniel stops typing and looks up at me, one eyebrow raised. "Yes, do you already have plans?"

I shake my head. "Okay then, I'll make a reservation." He pulls out his phone to book the table.

I take another sip of my beer as I watch him navigate through his reservation app. Deciding not to stick around, I leave the kitchen and head upstairs to the bedroom. I feel Daniel's eyes on me as I walk away.

Once in our bedroom, I quietly close the door behind me. I pull my phone from my pocket and text Theo.

Cameron: *Can't do tonight. Daniel surprised me with plans.*

I wait a few moments, hoping Theo isn't disappointed. My phone chimes with a reply.

Theo: *Okay, bummer. Will I see you tomorrow?*

Cameron: *…we'll see.*

I place the phone on the dresser and head for the bathroom to take a shower.

Daniel parks in front of Melrose Bohemian Restaurant's valet booth. A young man in his early twenties, wearing a red valet vest, rushes to the driver's side door and opens it for Daniel, taking the keys from his hand.

We approach the hostess station, located just in front of the restaurant's outdoor patio seating area. Shimmering white lights twinkle in the evening air, surrounding the patio in a soft glow.

"Hi, reservation under Nichols," Daniel says to the hostess.

"Right this way," she responds, holding two heavy menus. She wears a very short black cocktail dress and has long, straight blonde hair, nearly reaching the edge of her lower back.

We are seated at a two-top table on the patio, which is quite filled. It looks like we took the very last available table. This is one of the things I love about Los Angeles; no matter the time of year, you can always enjoy a meal outside.

We're just about to order when the waiter brings over a bottle of wine. He begins to remove the cork, but then Daniel's phone chimes. He retrieves it from his pocket, glancing at the screen.

The waiter pours a small amount of wine into my glass for a taste check. The wine is a robust red with the flavor of dark cherries dancing on my taste buds. I nod, signaling that it's perfect, and the waiter proceeds to fill Daniel's glass, then mine.

Just as I take a sip, Daniel's phone rings. His face falls.

"I'm sorry, Cameron, I have to take this," he says before rising from the table and stepping away. He begins bickering with someone on the other end of the line.

The waiter brings out a basket of warm bread and a plate of olive oil and balsamic vinegar. I pick at a piece of bread, dipping it into the mixture before taking a bite. From the other side of the twinkle-lit railing, I can overhear Daniel's conversation. He thinks he's being discreet, but I can hear the frustration in his voice.

It's clear that something's gone wrong with one of the ads his team is overseeing. The client expects the final copy tomorrow, and it sounds like the person who dropped the ball will be personally terminated by Daniel by the end of the day tomorrow.

I also know that Daniel can book a flight tonight on his company's jet and be in New York by morning to smooth over the issue in person. It's a good thing we haven't ordered yet.

The waiter returns with a notepad in hand. "Are we ready to order, or shall we wait for the gentleman?" he asks, eyeing Daniel from behind the twinkle rope.

"Actually, we'll need to go," I say. "Can you cork the

wine and bring us the check? We'll have to come back another time."

The waiter nods politely and picks up the opened bottle of wine.

Daniel returns to the table, his eyes full of apologies, the kind he always gives after a work call like this. The waiter immediately follows with the corked wine and the bill. Daniel looks momentarily confused as he sits down.

"How did you know I have to go?" he asks.

"I know that call," I reply, and I do. It seems to happen all the time.

Chapter 19

After Daniel packed his bags, I walked him to his car, where he assured me he'd be back as soon as he could. I told him to relax and save the client, that's all that matters tonight, and that we'd try the Bohemian restaurant another time. The third time's a charm, right?

Once Daniel was safely in the air, I texted Theo to let him know my plans had fallen through. He delightfully responded, asking me to come over.

I met him next to the funnel cake vendor near the middle of the Santa Monica Pier. It's a cool night in Santa Monica, so we're both wearing jeans, and each of us sports a different color hoodie. His is red and mine is gray.

Hundreds of people stroll the pier, stopping at local vendors selling hot dogs, fish tacos, burgers, and funnel cakes. I can hear the laughter and screams of children on the carnival roller coaster ride, along with the sound of the iconic Ferris wheel behind us.

We walk the pier, eating waffle cones. Theo has nearly devoured his. "I have to admit, I was kind of surprised you called me tonight," he says.

"Why is that?" I ask. The ice cream is so cold on my teeth I nearly get a brain freeze.

"I'm not sure. I just didn't know how often you wanted to see each other."

"Wait," I stop. "Is that a problem?"

Theo nudges me, and we keep walking. "Of course not. I just didn't want…" He trails off.

"What? Didn't want what?"

"I didn't know what your schedule was like with him. Daniel."

I can't help but roll my eyes. "Most times I don't know what Daniel's schedule is like."

Theo shrugs, and we enter a short silence. Then, "Production has been bumped up by a month," he says.

"Ugh, I know. Stupid investors." I hear Theo giggle.

"It's the business side of show business, and technically, I'm an investor too."

"Well, we were just lucky Grey Studios found another partner; otherwise, there'd be no movie." *Hold Up* has gone through some ups and downs with financing recently, but I'm told by my agent that it is perfectly normal.

"At least we got to meet." He nudges me again. Too closely this time. I catch a young woman eyeing us suspiciously for a brief moment. Not because we're two men walking close together, but because she seems to recognize Theo. And she probably does. I immediately turn in a different direction, with Theo cutting off all eye contact with her. She'll likely forget in about three seconds and move on. I glance back, and she's already distracted, looking into a shiny globe a street vendor is trying to sell her to read her palm.

As we continue walking, an older couple, definitely husband and wife, carry a gigantic turkey leg that that reminds me of turkey on Thanksgiving Day. Both our noses immediately take in the delicious aroma. The husband bites down on the juicy meat and my mouth waters.

"That smells so good," I say. "Dinner was rushed for me tonight because Daniel had to leave so quickly. I had one piece of bread dipped in oil."

Theo looks around and then asks, "Hey, have you ever had Cuban food?"

I think for a moment. Growing up in Collingswood, New Jersey didn't expose me to much international cuisine other than Italian, French, Mexican, and American. If I say *Mexican*, would he be offended? Wait, I do remember a small Cuban restaurant in West Hollywood that I've been to once. I think it was Cuban.

"I think so. There was this small restaurant in West Hollywood…"

Theo immediately cuts me off. "Nah, that's Americanized." He uses air quotes as he says, "What they claim to be Cuban food." He lowers his hands. "I'm talking real Cuban food, like ropa vieja and lechón asado. Cuban food like my mama makes." As he pronounces the dishes, his Cuban accent rolls off his tongue in the best way possible. The way the R's roll makes me strangely melt. This guy, *my* guy, is fluent in both Spanish and English. Wait… is Theo Cuban?

I stop. "I didn't know you were Cuban until just now."

He laughs. "What did you think I was? Mexican? Is it because I'm brown?"

"No," I respond, suddenly uncomfortable. Did I

assume he was Mexican because his skin is brown?

"Because we all look alike?" he teases.

"No, that's not what I meant."

Theo keeps laughing and places his hands on my shoulders. "Chill, Cammers. I'm messin' with ya."

Cammers. That's a nickname no one has ever called me before. Does Theo have a nickname for me now? Should I have one for him? I wouldn't even know where to start. *Thee*? Nah, that's stupid. *Teo*? Forget it. I'll just continue calling him Theo.

We pull up to a small shopping plaza in Studio City, and Theo parks. "You're going to love this place," he says, excited.

We both hop out of his car, and I look around. All the shops seem closed for the night. There's one restaurant in front of us, with bright fluorescent lights spilling out.

A bell above the door rings as Theo holds it open for me to enter. It's a small, deli-style restaurant with ten red booths and about half a dozen tables and chairs. An open kitchen sits behind a large white counter. I immediately notice a menu board hanging above the counter, featuring an array of food choices with pictures. I'm thankful for the pictures because I don't recognize any of the food names. Everything looks so delicious. My stomach growls as my eyes communicate with it through the lavish pictures.

A Cuban man sweeps the floor, and his eyes light up gleefully when he spots Theo. He's in his 60s, with gray hair and a salt-and-pepper beard.

"Alejandro!" Theo says, sporting his famous smile.

"Theo, long time no see," Alejandro says in a heavy Spanish accent. They both hug briefly. A short, plump Cuban woman, wearing a red apron, appears from the kitchen and smiles even bigger than Alejandro. Her gray hair is pulled into a bun, and she looks to be around the same age as Alejandro.

"Theo, you look so wonderful! Come and give Mami a hug," she says in a heavy accent. Theo smiles from ear to ear and embraces her, giving her a giant hug. She pulls back slightly. "You're too thin. You need to eat more."

Theo laughs. "I eat all the time, Mami. I work out a lot, and it burns the food."

She nods, but disagrees. Her eyes then slide to me, and Theo immediately notices.

"This is my friend, Cameron," he says. I step forward, and Alejandro shakes my hand. We briefly shake, and then I extend my hand to Mami. She refuses it and moves in for a hug. We embrace, and she wraps her arms around me as if I were her own child. She's a lot stronger than she looks. After a moment, she releases me and sizes me up.

"Any friend of Theo's is a friend of ours," she says with a warm smile.

Theo looks around, prompting me to do the same. All the tables are empty and appear to have been wiped down for the night.

"Are you closing?" Theo asks.

"Just about. We have one more take-out order that needs to be picked up," Mami says.

"Cameron here has never had real Cuban food."

Alejandro and Mami's faces fall in surprise. "Then you've come to the right place, my boy," Alejandro says.

"If you're closing, I don't want to…" I begin to protest, but Theo immediately cuts me off.

"Mami, I was hoping you could whip up a couple of Cuban dishes for us."

Mami, pleased, nearly leaps out of her skin. "I'd be happy to."

"Cameron said he's had Cuban food once. That place

in West Holly…"

Theo doesn't even get the words out before Mami interrupts, "That is not Cuban food. Cuban food made by gringos, maybe. I'll do a sample of empanadas, papas rellenas, tostones…" She goes on.

"Please don't go to any trouble," I say, but each of these dishes sounds incredible. I glance at Theo to reassure him that he should agree with me, but he just smiles.

"It's no trouble, my dear boy. Now you two sit. I'll be back." Mami disappears into the kitchen.

Alejandro picks up the broom again when Mami calls out, "Alejandro, get in here and help me."

He shrugs his shoulders at us and disappears into the kitchen.

"Now that's marriage," Theo says.

We sit at one of the empty booths by the window. The booth feels old, like it's been the seat for customers for decades. I catch a glimpse of Mami and Alejandro working together on what will become our dinner.

"How do you know them?" I ask.

Theo hops out of the booth and grabs two plastic cups from behind the counter. He fills them with water from a soda machine at the end of it.

"When I first moved to L.A., I had a hard time finding authentic Cuban food that reminded me of my own mama's cooking," Theo says, returning to the booth and setting the water down in front of us. "I stumbled upon this place and come as often as I can when I crave real Cuban food." Theo glances at Alejandro and Mami, who are working together effortlessly in the kitchen. "They're kind of like my adopted parents since my parents are still in Brooklyn." His eyes soften as he tells me this, and he smiles. It makes me smile, too.

"Do your parents still live in Brooklyn?" I ask.

"Yes. When we were little, they owned their own food truck and used to park it on the side of Central Park or in other touristy areas in Manhattan. *Authentic Cuban Food* they called it. I know, not exactly an original title."

I laugh. "Well, it certainly doesn't leave you guessing," I say in agreement.

"I have three older sisters, and we used to help them out. Every day after school and on weekends. It was the only way we could afford things growing up."

Mami approaches our table with a plate of empanadas. "Made these up a bit ago. Enjoy," she says, then scurries back to the kitchen. Theo slides a couple of empanadas onto my plate. They have a crispy golden color. I split one with my fork and notice beef inside. I take a bite, and the filling makes my taste buds dance.

"You know, as hard as my parents worked, they never missed one of our events growing up. My sisters' basketball tournaments, my plays… none of it." Theo stuffs half an empanada into his mouth. "One of them was always there for us, no matter how tired they were."

I'm on my second empanada. It's just as amazing as the first. Theo notices the joy on my face. "Nice, right?" he asks, and I nod, agreeing. "He loves it!" Theo shouts to the kitchen.

"Don't fill up on it! More is coming!" Mami shouts.

I watch Alejandro and Mami work together in the kitchen. They flow so well together, like a coordinated dance. Then, Alejandro wraps his arms around Mami and twirls her before she pushes him back to finish cooking. They laugh. It reminds me of Daniel and me in the early years. What we lost, Alejandro and Mami still have. After all these years together, they never lost it. I wonder how they keep it.

Minutes later, Mami returns with more plates of food. She sets them down in front of us. "Okay, boys, eat your hearts out." She pats Theo's stomach. "And fill this tummy up, will ya?

"Yes, mami. Thank you for this," Theo says, pursing his lips as they share a brief kiss. Mami looks at me and winks before leaving.

Suddenly, it dawns on me, and I can't help but wonder... "Does she know about you?" I whisper.

Theo quietly cackles. "I've never said anything, but you're the only guy I've ever brought to meet them."

"Well, that's not suspicious," I say, trying to keep my voice light.

"I've also never brought a girl," he adds. "So these are *papas rellenas*," Theo says, his Cuban accent sounding as sexy as ever when he speaks spanish.

I pick up one of the *papa rellenas*. It's a golden-brown, crispy ball. I take a bite and discover the rich flavors of mashed potatoes and seasoned ground beef inside. The hint of garlic adds a perfect touch. It's wonderful.

"Mmm," I say, savoring each bite.

"And these," Theo says, pushing more food onto my plate, "are *tostones*." I take a bite of one. "They're fried green plantains."

The *tostones* have a delightful crunch on the outside and are warm and soft on the inside. There's a subtle sweetness to it, almost like a banana. It's the perfect balance of savory and sweet. My eyes light up.

"Right?" Theo says, smiling as he takes a bite of one himself.

"I don't think I've ever had a green plantain before," I admit.

"They're very popular in Cuban cuisine."

The dishes pair so perfectly together, transporting me to what I can only imagine are the busy streets of food vendors in Havana. Mami was right, this place is authentic.

Theo is chowing down, and I can tell he's truly in heaven. It must be comforting to enjoy food that reminds him of his mom's home cooking.

As I sit here enjoying truly authentic Cuban food with Theo, I realize that in this moment, surrounded by the warmth of good food and love from Alejandro and Mami, with Theo, everything feels exactly right.

Chapter 20

The food was absolutely amazing. Alejandro and Mami were delighted to see our empty plates. Not a crumb remained. I'm so full my stomach feels like it might burst, but it was worth every bite.

"Tell me more about your parents. Do they still own the food truck?" I ask, genuinely curious about Theo's life, his real life, not the Hollywood version his publicist has created.

"Nah. About ten years ago, my papa got really sick and couldn't stand for long hours anymore, so they sold the business. Luckily, they made enough to get by," he explains.

"Is he okay now?"

"They're great now," Theo says. "They did such an amazing job raising my sisters and me. I always promised myself that if I made it in Hollywood, I'd take care of them." His voice softens, and his eyes look like they might swell with emotion. "They worked so hard their entire lives and still couldn't afford to retire after selling the food truck. Even after my mom picked up all those extra hours, while I was growing up, working for the wardrobe department in theaters off Broadway."

My heart breaks. Too many people in America face this same struggle, working themselves to the bone only to be left with little or nothing when they're too old to keep going. The thought stirs something in me. Maybe this is a story I need to write one day.

"When *Crooked Lies* made syndication, I knew they'd never have to worry about money again," Theo says, a faint smile crossing his face. "I bought them a condo they fell in love with and told them it was all theirs."

My eyes swell up too at his story, a man who truly cares for his parents. When a television show goes into syndication, it means another network licenses the rights to air it repeatedly, and everyone involved: actors, writers, directors, and producers continue to earn royalties every time it airs. Theo is essentially set for life, earning money without lifting a finger, so long as the show stays popular.

A loud thud breaks the moment, followed by Mami's voice from the kitchen: "Alejandro, be careful!" He drops a pot into the sink, producing an unpleasant clanging sound.

Theo stands, gathering our plates. "I'm going to do the dishes, so they don't have to," he says, winking at me. "Plus, it scores me mad points with Mami."

He flashes that incredible smile of his and heads toward the kitchen. I can't help but peek in after him. Alejandro is washing two large stainless-steel pots while Mami dries some pans.

"Both of you, out of the kitchen. I'm taking over,"

Theo declares playfully.

"Absolutely not," Mami insists. "You have a guest."

I laugh as Theo gently pushes Alejandro out of the way and grabs a white apron hanging on the counter. Alejandro, looking relieved, massages his lower back as Theo shooes Mami out of the kitchen with his hips.

I fly out of the booth and run into the kitchen. "I'm helping too," I announce. Mami gives me a defeated smile and hands me her apron.

"You cooked, Mami. We'll clean," Theo insists. Mami sighs and eventually gives in.

"And I'm paying for our meal too," Theo adds.

"Oh no, you're not!" Mami says as she leaves the kitchen.

I stand next to Theo as he washes one of the pots under a large pull-down faucet. Suddenly, he squirts water at me. The water is super hot, and I shriek, laughing as I playfully swat him with a dish towel. He smirks, pretending to aim again but stopping just short. I swat him with my towel.

We finish cleaning while Alejandro and Mami sit in a booth, enjoying coffee together.

"They're so in love," I say, nudging Theo.

He glances at them and nods. "I want that someday. That right there," he says softly, his gaze lingering on me for just a moment too long.

Later that night, we pull into the parking lot of Theo's condo. I step out of his car and walk to my motorcycle, grabbing my helmet. Theo comes around to stand in front of me.

"You sure you don't want to come up?" he asks.

I hesitate. My agent needs the first draft of my new screenplay in two weeks, and I've been neglecting it while spending so much time with Theo. Tonight, seeing his interactions with Alejandro and Mami shows me a different side of him, a side I really felt a gravitational pull to. But why? I can't figure out what this feeling is I'm feeling right now. It's as if I'm meeting Theo all over again, and the butterflies are fluttering in my stomach once more.

"Come on, just stay the night," he urges, gently taking my helmet and placing it back on the bike's stand.

I want to go home and work on my script. I should go home and work on my script. But… I sigh, giving in. "Why can't I say no to you?"

"Because you like me," he says with a mischievous grin.

Inside Theo's bedroom, the rest of the world melts away. Clothes come off, and before I know it, we're tangled in each other. His kisses are slower, softer this time, his touch more tender. He kisses my neck which he knows is my soft spot and I get excited. His tongue finds its way into my mouth and we kiss more as his left hand pulls on his nightstand drawer pulling out a condom.

As we continue to kiss, I feel him enter inside me and I want him more than ever. I wrap my legs tightly around his lower back as he pushes back and forth. He feels so intense inside me it makes me want to explode.

Something is different this time though. This doesn't feel like sex. I can feel his heart beating rapidly through my own chest and I know he's close. I don't want him to stop because I'm close too. His lips make their way back to my neck and I feel warmer now than I have ever before.

Again, this doesn't feel like sex. The connection is different this time. This feels like we're making… Love. No, this can't be. This is not love. This is an affair. An exciting affair of two bodies enjoying each other's company. Love cannot be here. I hear him moan and a few seconds later he falls on top of me, his head resting on my chest. I feel him breathing hard and he raises his head.

"You didn't get off," he says, surprised, more of a statement than a question. We lock eyes, but I don't see his eyes anymore, I see his soul. His gentle soul and I push him off and rise out of the bed.

Suddenly, I'm flooded with so much emotion. I feel like I can't breathe. I feel like I'm about to explode into tears. What is going on? I must get fresh air. I find my boxers on the floor and slide them on and escape outside.

I walk onto the balcony, needing the fresh air. The cool breeze hits my face as the sound of the ocean below calms my racing thoughts.

Theo follows me, wrapping his arms around me from behind. "What are you doing out here? Are you okay?" he asks, his voice filled with concern. I don't want his touch right now. It's confusing me, but I also don't ask him to stop.

I hesitate, then turn to face him. "Theo..."

"Yeah?" He asks worried.

"What are we doing?"

"Looks like we're watching the ocean," he says with a teasing smile.

I roll my eyes and turn to face him. Does he not feel what I'm feeling? Is this truly just physical to him like we originally agreed to when we decided to pursue this sexual relationship? Was I developing unwarranted and unreciprocated feelings? And if I were, it would serve me right. I have no intention of ever leaving Daniel. Daniel is the love of my life. My husband. Theo is just for fun, right? That's what Theo and I agreed to. Fun. But I have to know.

"I mean us. What is this?" I ask quickly escaping my

thoughts.

He stares at me, the silence stretching between us before he finally says, "It's whatever you want it to be, Cameron."

No, absolutely not. Theo is not going to put this on me. I needed to know if he was feeling the same thing I was feeling right now. "It's more complicated than that," I say.

"Just be in the moment," he interrupts. "I know it's your instinct to define everything, but not this time. Just be in the moment."

I just stare back at him and I start to feel my eyes swell. He wraps his arms around me and pulls me in for a hug. What exactly was I feeling? What happened tonight at that Cuban restaurant that has changed my entire perspective and feelings toward Theo? Was it his confession of wanting to always take care of his parents for being there for him his entire life? Was it the way he treated Alejandro and Mami with such grace and love? Or was it the way he made love to me tonight that was different than any time we've hooked up before?

This isn't just sex anymore.

And there it is. The realization finally dawns on me. We didn't have sex tonight, we made love.

Oh no.

I'm falling for Theo.

Chapter 21

I spend the next two weeks fully immersing myself in my screenplay. My feelings for Theo have become overwhelming, distracting me from my work in a way I can't ignore. Luckily, I have a ticking clock ringing in my ear, my agent, waiting for the first draft to be completed.

By the last day of the two weeks, the script is finally finished, 127 glorious pages. I know it will need significant trimming and probably three or four rewrites, but I've got the first draft done. More importantly, I have something I can present to my agent.

I hop on my Phantom and head over to Theo's, where he's expecting me. I haven't seen him since the night I realized my feelings for him were deeper than I wanted to admit. He understood that I needed to focus on my work and respected that. I saw Daniel a few times over the past two weeks, but he, too, has been incredibly busy, so we've become more like passing ships in the night than actual husbands.

Theo opens the door wearing a nice pair of khakis and a red polo. When he sees me, he smiles.

"Hello, handsome," he says, pulling me into his condo. He shuts the door behind me and pushes me against it. Then he kisses me, slow and deep, holding me for what feels like a lifetime. "You smell so good," he murmurs.

"Easy, tiger," I reply, gently pushing him back.

"You see what you do to me?" he teases.

I look down and notice he has a full erection bulging from his khakis. I'm beyond flattered and would like nothing more than to jump his bones right now, but we have dinner reservations, and I would very much like to talk about the movie we're about to start shooting, so I make the most practical choice and head to the bar.

I feel his footsteps behind me as I pour myself a whiskey neat. Theo immediately notices.

"Woah, when did you start drinking the hard stuff?" he asks, pulling a beer from the mini-fridge. The truth is, I've been drinking whiskey neat nearly every night for the past two weeks, just to keep my mind off Theo and focused on my script. But I don't want him to know how much he's been on my mind. He can't know. This is just fun for him, and I need to turn these feelings off.

He slides in close, wrapping his arms around my chest. He kisses my neck softly, and I feel his hips sway slowly, causing mine to follow suit.

He turns me around to face him and kisses me again. I kiss him back.

"What do you say we skip the dinner reservations tonight?" he asks, kissing me once more and leaving his tongue in my mouth for a few seconds longer than usual.

"I think we should get out of here," I say, silently begging him not to stop. "We need to talk about the movie and…"

He places a finger to my lips, silencing me. "I want you to fuck me," he says.

My heart stops. Up until this point, Theo has always been the top in this affair, and I've never really minded that. In my relationship with Daniel, he's been primarily the top. I'm fine with being the bottom, but every now and then, it's nice to top. At this point, it's probably been a few years since I topped Daniel.

Theo is masculine and he is closeted. For him to want me take on this role means he is letting his guard down. He's removing one of his walls, for me. My heart begins to race and I feel myself getting savagely excited. He slides his hand into my pants and inside my boxers and feels my hard-on. He grins and gets down to his knees. He unbuttons my pants and pulls them down with my boxers too. He takes my cock in his mouth and a warm wet sensation takes over my body.

We move to the bedroom and both get naked. I get on top of him and kiss him, then move my tongue slowly down his neck until I reach his nipples. I circle each of them with my tongue, just as Theo had done for me, causing him to buck in the bed. He arches his back in pleasure, and I see his cock is rock hard.

"I want to feel you inside me." He says pulling out a condom from the nightstand.

Just as he was gentle with me, I am gentle with him and start to give him a blowjob. As I blow him I slide one of my fingers inside him. It's very tight around my finger and after several moments I slide another. He moans.

I put the condom on and slowly slide inside him. I feel like I'm going to explode instantly, but he pulls me to down to him. As I penetrate, we kiss passionately. But it's no use. I can't control myself. Within 30 seconds, I orgasm.

I let out an incredible moan as every ounce of my body tingles as I release. Theo knows I've finished and immediately goes to work finishing himself. Moments later, we lay there, panting and completely out of breath. He kisses the top of my head.

"That was great," he says.

"I'm sorry it was so fast," I say embarrassed. He laughs and pulls me tighter to him.

"It was perfect," he says and continues to hold me. Then, "Well maybe next time we can strive for at least one minute. You know, goals?"

I hit him with the pillow, and we both laugh.

The next morning, I ride my Phantom back home. The cool morning dew hits my face, reminding me that I'm alive. The experience of topping Theo has sparked a whirlwind of questions in my mind. Mainly, is Theo falling for me too? And if we do fall for each other, what are my intentions with him? I know we're playing with fire, and we're well beyond the point of no return.

I want to get home, take a hot shower, and prepare for my meeting later today with my agent, Michael Corday. I'm also expecting Daniel to land in L.A. later tonight.

I arrive home minutes later and am surprised to see Daniel's car in the driveway. What the hell? His flight isn't supposed to land for another three hours. I park the Phantom on the side of the house and enter the kitchen through the side door. Daniel is sitting at the breakfast bar in a pair of shorts and a white T-shirt, typing away on his laptop.

"Daniel, hi," I say, somewhat shocked to see him. He stops typing and looks up at me.

"You didn't come home last night. Where were you?"

Oh no. Think fast. Where was I? I pull out my phone to buy myself some time. Did he call me and I missed it? My phone shows zero missed calls. "You didn't call me?" I ask, trying to deflect.

"I took an early flight. I was exhausted when I got home a few hours ago and just crashed on the couch."

I glance over to see the couch in disarray, with a throw blanket and cushion pillows piled into a makeshift bed. He's essentially admitting that he didn't even realize I wasn't home until just now. He never even went upstairs to check on me. Good thing I wasn't murdered and left to rot up there.

"You didn't even notice I wasn't here?" I blurt out, annoyed. Seriously?

His eyes narrow as he picks up on what I'm doing. We've been together long enough to know each other's tricks. "It was a long night," he says. "And it's been a brutal work week."

I decide to let it go. I don't want to draw any more attention to my whereabouts anyway. I grab a coffee pod and pop it into the coffee machine. Caffeine is my best friend, and right now, it's desperately needed. The machine starts brewing.

"So, why didn't you come home last night?" He asks, raising his voice slightly to be heard over the noise of the coffee machine. He repeats the question, forcing me to answer.

"I drank too much and didn't think it'd be safe to ride my Phantom home while intoxicated." Good one, I think to myself. No one's going to question a responsible motorist. He nods, buying it, at least I hope he does, and takes a sip of his coffee.

"Smart choice," he says. Then, "But you didn't call either."

Busted. He's right. I hadn't called him in two days to check in. Mostly because his work weeks are always busy, and he's never been much of a phone talker. And I, of course, have been consumed with my screenplay, and then there's Theo.

"So, where were you then? Where did you sleep?" He asks as I pour my coffee into a mug. Dammit. He's not letting this go. I figure I might as well be honest, well, to a degree.

"I crashed at Theo's," I say, telling the truth. I watch as his eyebrow arches.

"The actor?" he asks.

"Yes," I reply, now adding sugar and creamer to my coffee. His face remains emotionless. I can't read him right now.

"You two have been spending a lot of time together," he says, his voice flat. I take a sip of my coffee. Ouch. It's so hot it burns the tip of my tongue. I react, and he notices. Think fast, Cameron.

"Well, we're going into production next month, and it's been nice getting to know each other since we'll be working together. And it's not just the two of us, you know. There are others too when we hang out," I lie.

Daniel closes his laptop and shoves it into his briefcase. "I need to get a shower and catch up on some sleep," he says, rising from the stool and walking toward me. He kisses me on the lips. As he heads toward the stairs, he stops and turns toward me.

"And I never assumed it was just you and him when you hang out."

"What?" I ask, caught off guard.

"When you said you hang out with others. I never assumed it was just the two of you." His eyes rest on mine as he stands near the staircase. Shit. Why did I have to emphasize that part? "I'll see you tonight," he adds, before heading upstairs to shower and rest. If he didn't assume it was just Theo and me before, he certainly does now.

Chapter 22

Every year, Daniel's firm throws a benefit gala for charity. The event is held in one of the cities where the firm has offices, and each year, the proceeds go to a different charity. On our last year in New York City, the event was held at a hotel near our apartment. Last year, it was in London, where Daniel and I enjoyed a few days away from Los Angeles and took in the cool weather. This year, the event is in Los Angeles, at a Beverly Hills hotel, with the charity contributions directed toward addressing hunger among African children in villages desperate for aid. While the cause is admirable, the firm uses the gala as an opportunity to gather, get dressed up, drink expensive champagne, and for the executives to mingle and discuss promotions. This year, Daniel will attend as a junior executive, a promotion he received after last year's gala in London.

I picked up our tuxedos from the dry cleaners this morning. When I arrived home, I inspected them to ensure they were perfectly pressed and laid them on the bed in preparation for tonight's event. I don't get dressed up much anymore, but these charity galas are usually a lot of fun. The food is always amazing, and who doesn't enjoy endless champagne? Plus, at $2,000 a plate, all proceeds go directly to the charitable cause, with very little overhead since Daniel's firm sponsors the entire event.

I sit in the kitchen, fully dressed in my formal tuxedo, as Daniel showers upstairs. I'm usually ready before he is, but I suspect tonight he'll take longer than usual, knowing more corporate eyes will be on him, given his new role as a junior executive.

Since I know Daniel will probably be at least another 30 minutes before coming downstairs, I decide this would be a good time to call Theo. He's been on my mind all day.

I grab a wine glass and pour myself a generous amount of Chianti from a bottle I opened last night. I take a long sip and call Theo. The phone rings, and then he answers.

"Hey, gorgeous," he says. I can hear his smile through the phone.

I can't help but smile too. "What are you doing?" I ask.

"Just watched the sunset, now I'm drinking a beer." I hear him take a swig. I wish I were there with him. Watching the sunset from his balcony is absolutely beautiful. I decide now is a good time to flirt.

"Thinking of me?"

"Maybe," he replies with another swig. "Want to come over?"

I really do. "I can't," I say, glancing down at my formal

wear. I catch a glimpse of myself in the kitchen window's reflection. I do look sharp in a tuxedo, and that's not me being conceited. It's me admiring the designer. "Tonight, Daniel has a charity event I'm going to for his employer."

"Suit and tie?" he asks.

"More like a tux."

He laughs. "I hate dressing up in those monkey suits, except for the *Emmys*. That's the only time I don't mind."

The truth is, I don't really mind wearing this tuxedo. It makes me feel like I'm about to step onto the red carpet for the *Oscars*, where I've been nominated for Best Original Screenplay. I continue to stare at my reflection in the window, imagining I'm on my way to the *Oscars* when...

"I bet you look good in formal wear," he says, half laughing but half serious. "Send me a selfie."

"I will later." We stay on the line for what feels like an eternity. Neither of us says anything. I take a sip, and I hear him take one too. We just listen to each other breathe. It feels like we're so connected, like we're in the same room together, holding onto each other, holding on so we never have to let go.

"You okay?" he asks.

I nod my head, then realize he can't see me. "Yes," I manage to choke out. I know he's feeling the same connection. Suddenly, I hear Daniel whistling from upstairs. He's out of the shower and probably starting to get dressed. "I better go."

"You sure?"

No, I'm not sure. I don't want to hang up. I sigh and stay on the phone, neither of us speaking. I feel my eyes grow heavy. I swallow and blink allowing a tear to roll down my cheek. I wonder if anyone has ever felt such a connection to someone that words don't even need to be said. It's overwhelming, and I don't want to let him go.

"Have fun tonight," Theo says, finally breaking the silence.

"Thanks, I plan on drinking a lot of champagne." We both laugh to break the tension.

"Just remember, if I were there, I'd never let you go."

My heart falls into my stomach again. He's feeling the same way I am, right? I smirk. "I know, and I wouldn't let you."

"Call me tomorrow."

The line goes silent, and I gulp down the rest of my wine. The truth is, I would much rather be with Theo than at this charity gala. The whistling continues from upstairs, and I can tell Daniel's in a great mood. I shake my head, wipe away that tear, and take a deep breath. Tonight is Daniel's night, and I need to be 100% for him. No more thoughts of Theo. He needs to be forgotten tonight, and I vow to myself that he will be for the next few hours.

Minutes later, Daniel arrives downstairs. He fiddles with his silver cufflinks and enters the kitchen. He grins when he sees me. "You look great," he says, giving me a kiss on the cheek. He notices my flushed cheeks. "You okay?" he asks in the same tone Theo used minutes ago.

I nod, because Daniel can see me.

"It's the wine," I say, pointing to the empty glass with a drop of red wine still in it.

"A little early to start drinking?" he asks, stepping forward and holding out his wrist to indicate he needs help with his cufflinks. I shrug and fix them for him. We stare at each other for a moment. He places his hand under my chin subtly and leans in for a kiss. I kiss him back assuming it's going to be just a peck, but Daniel moves in further and slides his tongue in my mouth. I feel his right hand slide down my trousers and land on my crotch and he gently squeezes it. "You look so good in a tux."

What has gotten into Daniel? He hasn't been this feisty in a long time, I can't remember. I can feel his excitement on my leg and he leans down. "Daniel, what are you doing?" I ask.

He looks up at me and smiles and he unzips my pants. I look at the clock. At this rate we'll be right on time if we leave right now, but Daniel…

Then his face is back in mine. "You can look forward to that later," he says winking at me. I look down and I'm excited. I feel my heart racing. "Let's get going."

I laugh and say, "You're a tease." He smiles back and we head to the front door. I'm not sure what Daniel is feeling at this very moment, but it feels nice to see this side of Daniel. It's the side of him I fell in love with 10 years ago. The sweet, spontaneous guy that swept me off my feet. A guy I haven't seen in what feels like years.

We arrive at the hotel in Beverly Hills. A row of cars is parked outside, waiting for one of the three valet attendants, dressed in suits and red vests, to take them. Daniel and I hired a luxury car service to drive us because we both plan on drinking tonight. Daniel tips the driver, and we step out.

A giant red carpet stretches from the street curb to the hotel's enormous glass doors. I feel like I'm at a movie premiere. About two dozen press cameras and reporters greet us, snapping numerous shots as we walk the red carpet. Large banners hang along the route to the front doors, displaying images of African children opening boxes filled with food and supplies, their faces radiant with joy.

"My company doesn't do anything half-assed, huh?" Daniel says, nudging me as we walk.

"They certainly don't." Of all the charity events I've attended with Daniel and his company, this one is by far the grandest. Each year, they seem to get more elaborate.

As we approach the glass doors, I notice the lavish banner above that reads, "We Stand for Ending World Hunger," complete with Daniel's company logo. Many guests, in full formal wear, point and smile at the banner, as if it's the most charitable thing they've ever seen.

Once inside the hotel's lobby, we're escorted to the ballroom. The space is illuminated by numerous crystal chandeliers hanging from the tall ceilings, offering soft lighting. Dozens of round tables, each set for ten, are arranged across the room, with white linen tablecloths, china plates, and crystal stemware for each setting. Elaborate floral arrangements in an array of rainbow colors sit majestically at the center of each table.

A massive stage is set up at the far end of the ballroom, with a glass podium at its center. Large posters of thin African children holding fruit are displayed on easels throughout the room, each reading, "Ending World Hunger Charities."

The ballroom is packed with Daniel's co-workers and their plus-ones, presumably mostly spouses. All the men are essentially wearing the same black tuxedos, while their wives wear evening gowns in every color imaginable. The women showcase an array of jewelry, from earrings to necklaces, and their professionally groomed hairstyles are clearly meant for the occasion.

Daniel and I find our seats about six tables away from the stage. A waiter, dressed in a traditional tuxedo, carries a tray full of champagne flutes. Daniel grabs one for himself and one for me. We both take a sip but don't sit down immediately.

"I want to introduce you to Russell," he tells me. Russell Donner is Daniel's boss and a managing partner at Daniel's firm. Russell wasn't the boss who allowed Daniel's bi-coastal employment initially, but he replaced that managing partner after the firm opened its Paris office and the previous partner moved there. Daniel and Russell have spent many late nights together in the New York City office, which is Russell's home base.

As Daniel scans the room for Russell, I notice the menu at each table setting. The silver-colored engraved text pops out against the white card, which looks like it cost a fortune to print. The main course offerings tonight include chicken cordon bleu in a poblano sauce, an Atlantic salmon filet with a champagne cherry sauce, or a petite filet mignon topped with a bordelaise sauce. The menu also lists several options for appetizers and desserts. My stomach tightens with hunger. It's ironic that we're celebrating a charity dedicated to ending world hunger, yet here we are, surrounded by endless food.

"There he is," Daniel says, spotting Russell. He starts to walk toward him, and I take this as an invitation to join him, so I follow.

Russell is a tall man, around 6'4", I'd guess, with broad shoulders. He has a lot of gray in his hair, hinting that he's somewhere in his 60s. His wife, standing next to him with her arm interlocked with his, wears a stunning blue evening gown and a string of pearls around her neck. She holds a tiny dark blue purse in one hand and a glass of white wine in the other. They're engaged in conversation when we join them.

"Russell," Daniel says, beaming.

"Daniel," Russell responds happily, holding a glass of whiskey. They shake hands briefly. Daniel exchanges some pleasantries with Russell's wife, signaling to me that this is not their first meeting.

"I'd like to introduce you to my partner, Cameron," Daniel says. Partner? Why would he use that term? We haven't used that word since New York legalized same-sex marriage.

Russell grabs my hand and shakes it firmly, as I'd expect from someone with such broad shoulders. "Nice to meet you, this is my wife, Melanie." She and I shake hands too, and I notice that her hands are much more delicate than her husband's. Russell raises his now-empty glass, and a waiter quickly arrives to take it away. The waiter carries a tray with more whiskey glasses, and Russell helps himself to another.

Russell turns to Melanie. "Daniel has done an amazing job heading up our L.A. office while still managing his accounts in New York."

"Oh, that's wonderful. How do you two find time for each other?" Melanie asks, smiling. I want to say *we don't*, but I know this is mostly a rhetorical question.

"Thank you, sir," Daniel says to Russell. "It's always my pleasure."

"Good thing you two don't have any children," Melanie says, giving me a wink. "You'd never see them, Daniel." Everyone politely laughs, but I'm left wondering why she would assume we don't have children. Is it because we're two men? What if we *did* have children? Why does she automatically assume we don't? Daniel pulls me out of my thoughts.

"Children will come later," Daniel says. "Right now, Cameron and I are happy to focus on our careers." We haven't really discussed having children, except to say that it'll probably happen in our future.

"That's the way it should be for two young men," Russell says, downing half his whiskey. "Dedication. That's why our London office needs your assistance over the next couple of weeks, Daniel."

"I'm on a plane the day after tomorrow, first thing in the morning," Daniel says proudly. About three weeks ago, Daniel warned me that he'd need to spend a few months at the London office intermittently because the firm was expanding to a new market. His New York accounts were in pristine condition, so he'd be spending a lot of time with his Los Angeles accounts and assisting the London office with the expansion. I don't understand most of what Daniel does, except that he's climbing the corporate ladder quickly and efficiently.

"What do you do, Cameron?" Melanie asks, genuinely interested.

I begin to answer, but Daniel cuts me off. "He's a writer," he says. Melanie nods, impressed.

"Marvelous. Published?" I shake my head, and I notice Daniel squinting for a moment.

"Not that kind of writer," I say. "I'm a screenwriter."

An awkward silence lingers. Daniel takes a sip of his champagne, and I can't help but feel he might be a little ashamed of my profession, not writing for publishers, but for the big screen.

"Written anything we've seen?" Russell asks.

"No. I sold my first screenplay last year, but it never went into production. I actually have a script shooting next month, though."

Russell and Melanie nod, now genuinely impressed. I hear Daniel sigh with relief. Was he hoping for their approval of my career?

"I personally don't get Hollywood," Russell says. "Agents, overpaid actors, entertainment lawyers getting everyday Joe's $1 million an episode just for doing their job and calling themselves actors." Daniel nods in agreement as they both take a drink. "We're in the right business, Daniel. I couldn't handle the movie business. I don't even like Los Angeles. I only come when I have to." Russell, Melanie, and Daniel share a laugh. I fake a laugh, not wanting to be rude, but Russell is starting to annoy me. Are actors overpaid? Sure. But I could argue that Russell is too. I mean, an everyday Joe doesn't fly the company's private jet, but Russell and Melanie sure do. Now he wants to criticize actors for getting a piece of the pie they worked for? Talk about hypocritical.

We're suddenly joined by two new men and their wives, dressed in evening gowns, hanging on their arms. Introductions are made all around, and the conversation immediately turns to business, leaving the wives to casually look around at the decorations, careful not to interrupt.

I lean into Daniel once I know no one can hear me. "I don't think your boss likes Hollywood," I whisper.

Daniel giggles. "He considers it fake."

"So I guess he doesn't get creativity," I say, defending my industry.

Daniel shrugs and jumps into the conversation. Laughter erupts from the group as one of the men tells a work-related joke. I feel my phone vibrate in my pocket. I hope it's Theo texting me; I could use that right now. I glance down and see it's my...

"It's my mom," I whisper to Daniel, and he nods in understanding. I step away.

"Hi, mom," I say, noticing the time. It's 8:15 p.m. here, and since she's in Collingswood, New Jersey, that would be 11:15 p.m. My parents never stay up past 10:00 p.m. I get a pit in my stomach, knowing something is wrong.

"Cameron," my mom says on the other end. Her voice is croaky. She's been crying.

"Mom, is everything okay?"

"It's your father. He's had a heart attack," she musters out the words. I feel my knees weaken. Her voice trails off.

Chapter 23

Daniel noticed my face fall, and I felt like I had turned three shades whiter. In the five-minute call with my mother, I learned that my father had a heart attack about three hours ago while dining out with her and friends. He was immediately rushed to the hospital and is currently in surgery. The doctors advised my mother to tell my brother and me to come home immediately, as it doesn't look good at this point.

Daniel patiently waits next to Russell, Elaine, and the other two couples, who are engaged in conversation. When I hang up the phone, he approaches me.

"What's wrong?" he asks, worried. My hands are trembling.

"It's my dad. He's had a heart attack."

Daniel's face falls too. "Oh no, is he alright?" He

places his hand on my shoulder to comfort me.

"They're not sure. He's in surgery, but it doesn't look good. We have to go home, Daniel."

"Of course. I'll let our driver know to take us home." He pulls out his cell phone and opens the app for the luxury car service that brought us to the event.

"To Collingswood, Daniel," I say as he fiddles with the app. He raises an eyebrow.

"Cameron, I have to go to London the day after tomorrow."

"Are you kidding me?" I erupt. I cannot believe he's not even considering coming home with me. He's putting work over his family. My father could die, and he's not concerned about being there for him, too?

Daniel glances over his shoulder and notices Russell, who has tuned into our conversation. Daniel politely grabs my arm. "Not here, Cameron," he says. He turns to face Russell and Elaine and informs them about the family emergency concerning my father. They both nod in sympathy, and I see Daniel and Russell shake hands. With that, Daniel and I leave the ballroom.

Once we arrive home, I fly upstairs to the bedroom closet and pull out my suitcase. I toss it on the bed and begin to panic-pack. The car ride home was awful. Daniel kept making excuses about why he couldn't come with me, all while reassuring me that he believed my father would pull through.

Daniel enters the bedroom as I pull clothes out of my drawers and throw them into the suitcase. He unties his bow tie and removes his tuxedo jacket.

"You're all booked for the first flight out of LAX in the morning," he says, continuing to undress.

"I still don't understand why you can't fly to Philadelphia with me, then go to London from there."

"Cameron, I told you. I have work to finish here in L.A. before I go to London," he says, frustrated. For some reason, I just can't let this go.

"He's your father-in-law, Daniel," I scream. The truth is my emotions are all over the place right now. The terror in my mother's voice, the urgent request from the doctor for her sons to come home immediately, the fact that Daniel isn't coming home with me, and the possibility that my father could die on the operating table… Everything is too much. I feel the tears coming, and my chest tightens. I can't hold back.

"I think it's ridiculous you won't even tell your company what happened and ask for time off," I say, beginning to cry.

He stops and puts his hands on my shoulders. He looks me in the eyes as seriously as I've ever seen him. "This is how it is, Cameron," he says sternly. "You wanted to move to L.A., and in order to do that, I had to co-head the L.A. office. You knew how my work schedule would be. You knew the pressure I'd be under accepting an executive position. I don't work at a fast-food restaurant where I can just call in and get time off. My absence costs the company money."

"It's my father!" I scream, not caring what he's saying about his absence costing the company money. Does his company have no compassion for human life? Does it not value its employees enough to give them time with family when they're sick? Or is it that Daniel isn't bothering to ask for the time off because, in reality, he doesn't really want to come home with me?

I stop packing and sit on the edge of the bed. I'm flooded with emotions. Daniel sits next to me and places his hand on my leg. Theo suddenly pops into my head, and I wonder if Theo would act like this? Or would he want to be with me, to come home to be with family? I shake my head. I know I shouldn't compare Daniel and Theo, but I can't help it.

I look at Daniel and say, "How did we get here?"

"What do you mean?" he asks.

"When did work come before family?"

Daniel sighs, defeated. A defeat I've seen in his eyes before when I complain about his work schedule. "It's not, Cameron. It's just the way it is right now."

I rise from the bed, shaking my head in disbelief. I continue to pack as tears roll down my cheeks. It's not just the emotion surrounding Daniel, it's also the fear that my father might die. Daniel hugs me and holds me tight.

"Everything is going to be fine, Cameron. He'll pull through this," he says.

"You don't know that," I reply.

Later that night, I sit in the kitchen, drinking a cup of hot tea. I tried to sleep since my flight is so early, but it was no use. My mind is racing too much. Hopefully, I'll sleep on the plane. My mother contacted me again just to say there were no changes, and my father was still in surgery. I can't wait to be home so I can hold her tight and reassure her that everything will be okay, somewhat like Daniel did for me tonight.

I text Theo that I'm flying home to Collingswood, New Jersey, because of my father's medical condition. He replies right away.

Theo: Is he going to be alright?

Cameron: Don't know yet. Last I spoke to my mom, she said he was still in surgery.

Theo: I'm so sorry. Wish I could be there for you.

I half-smile at Theo's last text. *Me too*, I think to myself. *Me too*. I decide to text him back.

Cameron: Daniel can't come home with me. Work :(

Theo: What? No way!

There's a pause in the conversation. Then, I see Theo

typing again.

Theo: What time is your flight?

Cameron: 6:15 a.m.

My eyes begin to feel heavy, and I can feel the chamomile tea kicking in.

Cameron: I need to try to get some sleep. I'll call you sometime tomorrow after I land.

Theo: Have a good flight. :)

I take the last sip of my tea and put the cup in the sink. Daniel can clean it tomorrow. I turn off the light and head upstairs, hoping to get some sleep. As it stands, I'm already going to be a zombie trying to get through the airport tomorrow morning.

The morning came too soon. I barely slept overnight. Daniel was a real champ in helping me get ready this morning. Maybe he felt guilty for not coming home with me, or maybe he truly feels bad for my family's situation.

He loaded the car and drove me to the airport, and I arrived exactly an hour and a half before my flight. He held my hand during the 20-minute drive and would bring it to his lips every so often and kiss it. It was nice to feel his touch.

Upon arriving at the airport, he dropped me off in front of my terminal. He retrieved my luggage and opened the door for me. As I exited the vehicle, we hugged, and he kissed the top of my forehead.

"Send my love to your mom," he said.

"I will," I said, hugging him tighter. How I wished he would come home with me. In some ways, I feel guilty for making him feel bad by not coming home with me.

And as if reading my mind, he said, "I'm so sorry I can't come home with you. Keep me updated."

After sitting in the terminal reading the news on my phone, I board the plane when I hear my priority group being called.

As soon as I settle into my seat, a flight attendant with long, flowing red hair in a bun greets me. She wears a warm smile and a blue and green uniform. Her silver nametag reads Pamela.

"Good morning. What can I get you for a pre-flight beverage?" Pamela asks.

Oh, the benefits of flying business class. A pre-flight cocktail just enough to calm my nerves. I order a Bloody Mary, and as she walks away, I ask her to make it a double. She half-smiles and agrees, but I can sense some judgment in her tone. I glance at my phone: 5:46 a.m. Okay, Pamela, I'd judge me too at this point.

I take my seat by the window and stare out at the rising sun, casting a dark pinkish hue onto the pavement. I feel someone move into the seat behind me and nudge my back.

Pamela returns with my Bloody Mary. She offers the same warm smile and hands it to me with a cocktail napkin.

"Double for you, sir," she says, smiling, but I know she's silently judging me.

I set the Bloody Mary on the tray table, but the person behind me bumps my seat again. Twice now. What are they doing? I take a long gulp from the glass when my seat gets nudged again.

I angrily crane my neck to look behind me, and then I see a head pop into my row. A very familiar voice says, "Is this seat taken?"

I don't believe my eyes. This can't be happening. The face and the voice belong to Theo.

Chapter 24

Theo stares back at me, smiling. I still can't believe my eyes. What on earth is Theo doing on this flight? It's as if I'm living in two different worlds right now, the world in which I live in Los Angeles as a screenwriter, and the world I have back east with my family, who are in crisis right now. Theo is only supposed to be in one of those worlds, and that's in Los Angeles.

"Theo, what are you doing here?" I finally ask. He smiles and slides into the aisle seat next to me.

"It occurred to me that no one was going to be there for you during this trip home," he says.

"My family will be there."

"Well, for each other, sure, and for your dad. But no one will be there for *you*."

I can't help but smile. While I acknowledge it's a bit

creepy that Theo somehow tracked down which flight I was on and bought a ticket to accompany me, I can't help but feel wanted. Suddenly, the production of our movie pops into my head.

"Wait, you can't. We're in pre-production…"

Theo interrupts me, waving his hand. "I'll be back in L.A. in a few days." Then he places his hand on my shoulder. "Cameron, your father had a heart attack."

The realization of why I'm flying home immediately floods my mind. Theo, though it was only for a few moments, actually made me forget what I'm doing on this flight.

A woman in her late 40s approaches us with a large carry-on bag that really should have been checked. She's holding her phone, displaying her boarding pass, and looks down at Theo.

"Excuse me, sir," she says. "I believe this is my seat."

Theo looks up at the seat number printed under the baggage stowaway. He immediately rises.

"Ma'am, you are correct, but would you terribly mind switching seats so that I may sit next to my buddy here? His father just had a heart attack, and I want to make sure he's not alone as we fly to see him," Theo says, flashing her that charming smile. I can't believe he just told a complete stranger about my father's medical condition.

"Well…" She hesitates.

Theo points to the window seat directly behind me. "This seat is mine. You'd be doing us both a really big favor," he says, now with pleading eyes.

Her gaze falls on me, and I can tell she notices I've been crying, backing up Theo's claim about my need for companionship.

"I really don't like window seats," she says, and Theo places his hand on her arm, ever so gently.

"We'd really appreciate it, ma'am," he says, charming

her once again. His hand slides down just a bit, causing her to blush.

"I suppose," she says.

"Oh, thank you so much." Theo says, instantly grabbing her large carry-on. "Here, let me take that for you." He steps back up, lifts her carry-on above our heads, and slides it into the overhead compartment. His shirt rises a bit, flashing his ever-so-chiseled abs at me.

"Thank you," she says as Theo slides her bag away.

"That's a bit heavy," he says to her, and she can't help but smile. She steps toward her seat when…

"Has anyone ever told you that you look like that guy from that show? Oh, what's it called? Crooked Lies?" she asks.

He smiles from ear to ear, showing those pearly whites. "All the time," he says and turns back to me, taking his seat. We both look at each other and giggle.

Pamela returns and takes Theo's pre-flight beverage order. He glances at my drink and says, "I'll have what he's having."

"A double too, sir?" she asks.

Theo grins suspiciously at me. "But of course," he says. As she walks away, his shoulder nudges mine politely. "Hitting the hard stuff early, eh?"

"It'll help me sleep," I say, trying to convince him I'm not actually an alcoholic.

I lean back in my chair and exhale a breath of what feels like relief. I'm not sure why Theo felt compelled to come home with me, but for this very moment, I'm so glad he did. But I have no clue how I'm going to explain him to my family. I can't even imagine what they're going to think of me coming home with this complete stranger while Daniel is away on business.

Pamela drops off Theo's Bloody Mary and takes other drink orders from other passengers. Theo takes a sip and gasps, presumably at the strong taste of the vodka. I don't mind it, though. Once it kicks in, it'll quiet my mind so I can get some rest.

"I hope I'm not being too presumptuous here," Theo says. "But if something happened to my parents, I would want someone to be there with me." I smile to myself. I think the realization has just kicked in for him that he just hopped onto a plane with me to fly home to meet my family without me ever actually asking. His face seems a bit concerned. "And since Daniel won't come, I thought I'd be his replacement."

"Can't come," I say, correcting Theo.

"Nah, won't come," he says stubbornly.

I agree to disagree. Two beeps occur, and Pamela's voice blares over the P.A. system. "Attention, ladies and gentlemen, our flight to Philadelphia is scheduled for 5 hours and 12 minutes. Please take your seats and fasten your seat belts once you have been seated."

She continues with the usual pre-flight announcements. Theo and I fasten our seatbelts. He pulls out a magazine from the seat pocket in front of him and starts thumbing through the pages. I lean back in my chair, as much as my chair will allow for departure, and just watch him. As he reads through the magazine, I feel my eyelids begin to grow heavy. I blink, but they don't reopen. My head falls onto Theo's shoulder, and I drift off to sleep.

I fall into a deep slumber, my body finally relaxing from the exhaustion of the previous night. But then, I feel an ache in my bones. I sense a storm coming. I'm suddenly transported to a place right outside Theo's condo building, and it's cold. It begins to rain heavily, forming puddles on the sidewalks that resemble lime green and gray ponds.

The ocean roars as the rain intensifies, creating 50-

foot waves. They swarm onto the sand, engulfing everything in their path, dragging all the sand out to sea with them. I'm inside one of these waves, trying to free myself, but I can't. It's trapped me, binding every limb with seaweed.

The wave continues to swallow everything in its path, ebbing in and out like a rubber band. Up ahead, I see Daniel and Theo on the sidewalk, amidst the puddles of lime green and gray. They're arguing, no, fighting. Fists fly through the air. The wave is getting closer, and I try to free myself from the seaweed so I can warn them, but it's no use. My muscles sting, my bones ache. Pay attention, Daniel and Theo. There's a tsunami coming your way.

We're moving faster, closer, and closer to them, as if we're traveling at the speed of sound. The wave grows in power, becoming bigger and bigger. Daniel and Theo have their backs turned, blood dripping from their faces as they continue to fight. They must turn around. Why can't they see the wave coming?

The lime green and gray puddles are growing, forming an army of waterfalls all around them. They're drenched; their bloody faces now soaked by the rain. We're on top of them in seconds, and just as the wave is about to crash down on them, they both turn and look at me, eyes wide with horror. But it's not the wave they see, they look at me. The moment only lasts for a second because the wave crashes hard onto their bodies, crushing them and swallowing them up, and I scream, but they can't hear me anymore. It's too late. The wave releases me from its grip and my face crashes hard onto the pavement of the sidewalk that is now stained in blood.

The wave pulls them out to sea like an angry beast. I rise, my muscles barely able to move, and scream out to them. The ocean is calm now. I'm alone. It's quiet. No one is left. Daniel and Theo are gone. Ripped from my life in an instant by that violent wave. A pit forms in my stomach, loneliness, despair. What have I done? No! I cry out. Noooo!

Theo blasts me awake by shaking me. "Cameron, wake up." My eyes snap open, and I realize it was only a dream. Pamela rushes a glass of water to my tray table. Embarrassed, I begin to compose myself. The other passengers around us eye us with concern.

"It was only a dream," I say, trying to calm myself.

"Some dream," Theo mutters.

Pamela removes my two empty cocktail glasses from the tray. "Perhaps we stick to water for the rest of the flight," she suggests.

I drink the whole glass of water in less than three seconds. Sweat pours from my forehead. *Some dream* is right. Thank goodness it was only a dream, I reassure myself.

"You okay?" Theo asks.

I nod. I'm okay. But the feeling of Daniel and Theo being ripped from my life still feels so real. The crushing wave still feels real, and both of them being murdered by that 50-foot wave feels very real. I'm okay, I keep telling myself. And I am. At least for this moment.

Chapter 25

My flight lands right on time in Philadelphia. Theo and I grab our carry-on bags and race through the airport to find the quickest exit. I turned my phone on as soon as the plane landed, but there weren't any voicemails or text messages from my family. No news is good news, I'm assuming at this point. I text my mother to let her know I've landed and will be heading directly to the hospital.

We exit the doors of the airport and are greeted by the cold, frosty air. February in Philadelphia is the worst. The sun is hidden by cloud cover, and icy sidewalks stare back at us. We hop into the nearest cab waiting outside, and I instruct the driver to take us to St. Mary's Mercy Hospital, which is also located in Philadelphia. Since Collingswood, New Jersey, is just a bridge away from Philly, most Collingswood residents use the city's emergency health services.

I find myself quiet during the cab ride to the hospital. I'm worried about my father. I'm concerned I might be too late. Theo notices and gently nudges my shoulder. He does this frequently, and I like it. It reassures me that he's there, too. I half-smile at him and then continue to stare out the window, which has ice forming around its edges. Oh, the East Coast winter. How I do not miss thee.

We arrive at St. Mary's Mercy Hospital 20 minutes later. Theo tips the driver, and we grab our bags from the trunk. My mother texted me to say they're waiting in the surgical waiting room on the 1st floor.

As the automatic doors of the hospital entrance slide open, my nostrils are greeted with the smell of bleach and paint. An interesting combination, but it smells sanitary, and for that, I am grateful. It gives me peace of mind knowing my father is in the right hospital. I follow the signs through a maze of hallways to the surgical waiting room.

Moments later, although it feels like an eternity has passed as we travel through the labyrinth, we finally arrive at the surgical waiting room. It's a large room with the whitest walls and floors I've ever seen. Blue upholstered chairs fill the space, with random abstract art hanging on the walls. The décor looks like it hasn't been updated since the mid-1990s. I hear the hum of two vending machines offering sodas and coffee.

I immediately spot my family sitting on the right side of the waiting room, next to a set of very frozen shut windows. Another family waits on the left for their loved one.

My mother, Elaine, looks like she hasn't slept in days. Her brown hair hangs just above her shoulders. She normally keeps it straight, but the lack of sleep has caused it to curl at the top of her shoulders. My brother, Tyler, sits two seats away, fiddling with something on his phone. His short black hair hasn't been groomed, either. He and I have almost the exact same body build. There's no mistake that we're brothers, as we're often told. Sitting next to Tyler is his wife, the beautiful blonde-haired, blue-eyed Emily, whose hair is so long it reaches her mid-back. She's the same age as Tyler. They met in college and fell in love during an internship they both had their senior year. They married two years later, and she's always been a rock for him. I'm grateful she's here with him and my mother.

My mother's eyes scan the room and meet mine. A look of relief fills them, and her face lights up when she sees me.

"Mom," I say, and she gives me a half-smile. I race to her, and we hug tightly. I hear her exhale near my ear, and I know she's grateful I'm here. Tyler and Emily are on their feet now, and my mother releases me so we can all hug. And we do. Although I don't wish to be home under these circumstances, it is nice to be here right now, with my family. It's nice to be *home*.

"Cameron, he made it through the surgery. He's sleeping now," she says, her eyes filling with tears, tears of joy, not of pain. The whites of her eyes have disappeared, replaced by pink, which tells me she's been crying and worrying all night. But now, she can rest.

"Oh, thank God," I respond, pulling her into another tight hug.

"He's asked about you, little bro," Tyler says.

I nod and feel my own tears starting to form. Just like my mother, these are tears of joy. The release of worry is lifting from my chest. I feel like I can breathe again. I sigh in relief, but my gaze shifts, and I notice everyone's eyes have moved to Theo, who's standing directly behind me. I step aside to let him into our circle.

"Oh, I forgot," I admit, "this is my friend Theo. He flew home with me."

"We can obviously see that, Cameron," my mother says, opening her arms for Theo to come in for a hug. "Hi, Theo, I'm Elaine. Cameron's mom." They hug.

"Tyler," my brother says, extending his hand. Theo shakes it, and they exchange a firm handshake.

"I'm Emily, Tyler's wife," she says, pointing to Tyler.

"It's a pleasure to meet all of you," Theo says. "I just wish it was under better circumstances."

Everyone nods.

"Trust me, Theo," my mother says, "today is a much better day than yesterday."

My mother, Tyler, and Emily return to their seats. I sit next to my mom, and Theo takes a seat across from me.

"Can I see him?" I ask. I feel like I've been given a second chance at seeing my father again. I was so lost not knowing his health status while on the flight here.

"In a few minutes," my mother says. "They're changing his bandages right now. He's going to be so happy to see you, Cameron."

For now, everyone seems to be relaxed. I lean back in my chair and sigh. I'm glad to be home with my family, and I'm glad my father made it through surgery.

"Where's Daniel?" Emily asks, finally acknowledging the absence of my husband. I notice Theo subtly roll his eyes.

"He couldn't get off work," I explain, reinforcing Daniel's excuse. "He has to fly to London tomorrow and couldn't reschedule, but he sends his love."

"Yes, he called me this morning after you boarded your flight," my mother says. Daniel and my mother have always had a strong relationship. She was very protective of me when we first got engaged, wanting to make sure Daniel's heart had the right intentions given our age difference. This caused them to spend some quality time together, and it created a bond between them. I've always been happy that my husband has gotten along with and enjoys being with his mother-in-law.

Emily smiles at my mother's response about talking to Daniel and grabs Tyler's hand. She and Tyler's eyes then move to Theo. I know they're wondering who he is and why he's here.

"Theo is the actor casted in the movie I wrote that starts shooting next month," I explain, hoping this will ease their curiosity. "We've become good friends."

As I say the word *friends*, I notice Theo lock eyes with me. Did he not like the way that sounded? Or does he like it because we both know our little dirty secret? I can't help but smile to myself as I turn to my mother, who seems to have picked up on Theo and me locking eyes at the word *friends* too. She subtly, *and I mean very subtly,* raises an eyebrow toward me.

"Mrs. Taylor," a nurse calls from the end of the hall. My mother rises.

"Yes?" she asks.

"He's ready. But please, only one visitor at a time. We don't want to overwhelm him," the nurse says, turning back down the hall.

My mother faces me. "Room 171," she says. I beam at the chance to see my father. "No hugs, though. He's just had open heart surgery."

I leave Theo with my family and race down the hall to see my father. Room 171 is much easier to find in the surgical ward than the surgical waiting room was to find in the hospital.

When I arrive at his room, the door is wide open. I hear the sound of machines beeping as I enter. There he is: Frank Adam Taylor in the flesh, having survived a terrible heart attack that required an all-night surgery.

He's lying in his bed, sleeping. His body has been through so much, and I suspect I won't see his eyes awake for another couple of days. I quietly slide a nearby chair toward his bed and take a seat. I place my hand in his and give it a polite squeeze.

"Hey, dad," I say, hoping he can hear me while he sleeps. "It's Cameron. I'm here." I lay my head on the bed next to his hand and say a prayer to God, thanking Him for giving my father a second chance.

Later that night, we have dinner at my parents' house, the home I practically grew up in. Our house is an old-style Victorian, built in the early 1900s, and it carries with it the charm of the Victorian era. My parents turned the parlor room into the dining room when Tyler and I were in high school, so they could entertain more. The doorframes feature the original oak wood from the first homeowners. Dark blue, textured wallpaper fills the walls, dating back to the 1960s. My mother never wanted to modernize this room. She always said it's a piece of the past and should be kept that way.

My mother, Tyler, Emily, Theo, and I sit around the dining room table, eating. The table is full of food: two buckets of fried chicken, mashed potatoes, two tubs of mac and cheese (one of which is completely empty now), green beans, and coleslaw. All fried and unhealthy food from Al's Hot Chicken down on Collingswood's Main Street. Everyone eats as if they haven't eaten in days. Two empty bottles of red wine sit at the end of the table. Everyone's glasses remain half full. Emily pulls the cork from another bottle. Tyler is in the middle of a story.

"And then Cameron sat at this table, on his last day of high school, and announced he was gay," Tyler explains to Theo. "Duh, you never had a girlfriend in high school, bro." Tyler starts to laugh, and I join him. The truth is, I could probably laugh at anything right now, as my head is starting to feel lightheaded from the wine.

"Yeah, but this bozo thought, because I was gay, he was now the brother of a minority and applied for scholarships," I interject, laughing. Everyone at the table laughs too.

"What?" Tyler says, taking a healthy gulp of his wine. "You get desperate in college trying to pay tuition."

"Half of tuition," my mother says, taking a big bite of mac and cheese. "Your father and I did the best we could."

Tyler smiles, extending his hand to rub mom's shoulder. "And we appreciate it," he says. I rub her other shoulder in agreement. My parents saved enough for tuition, but with rising costs of tuition nationwide, they could only afford to send one of us to college or pay half of college for each of us. We all agreed that it was the fairest. It was up to Tyler and me to cover the other half. And we did. Through part-time jobs and some student loans, we managed. My parents have always been honest, hardworking people.

"So, how did you two meet?" Theo asks Tyler and Emily, who sit across from him, as he pours more wine into her glass.

"College sweethearts," Emily says, sliding her glass to Theo. "We're a small statistic."

"Is that like high school sweethearts? Except in college?" Theo asks sarcastically.

Tyler and Emily burst out laughing at the absurdity of saying *college sweethearts.* Clearly, the wine is affecting everyone. A moment of silence fills the room. I'm so thankful for everything right now with my family.

"I'm so glad dad pulled through," I say. Everyone nods in agreement, especially my mom, whose face wears complete relief.

"Well, there are certainly going to be some diet changes when your father gets home," she says, grabbing another fried chicken leg from the bucket.

"You know what's ironic?" Tyler asks, shoving food into his mouth, but not answering the question. We all look at him, waiting, for further explanation. "Our father just had a heart attack and open-heart surgery, and here we are, devouring fried chicken and mac and cheese."

We all stare at him for a moment. No one says a word, and then everyone laughs.

"Comfort food," Mom says, setting the chicken leg down on her plate with no intention of finishing it. "We haven't really eaten in two days."

"And if diets are going to change around here," Emily says, reaching for another piece of chicken, "we can't really eat like this in front of him anymore. So, we might as well enjoy it now."

Theo and I eye each other, then glance at the last piece of chicken in one of the buckets: a breast. The last breast. We both go for it, sticking our hands in the bucket at the exact same time and each grabbing a piece. We erupt in laughter, pulling it out together. It's slippery and lands on the table. Theo grabs it and sets it on my plate. "You had it first," he says. I smile.

"Let's split it," I offer.

"Only if you insist," he says. I cut a big chunk of skin and meat off and slide it onto his plate. He grins at me, thanking me by bringing his palms together and pressing them to his face. We lock eyes and smile.

Tyler and Emily start another story, and Theo joins in. I keep smiling until my eyes move to my mother, who's staring back at me suspiciously. Her gaze shifts toward Theo and then back to me. Uh oh. Busted.

Chapter 26

After dinner, I help my mother do the dishes. My parents have a dishwasher in the kitchen, but they rarely use it. My mother always says nothing cleans a dish better than your own two hands. I disagree, of course, as a dishwasher is much faster, but a mother is always right, so they say. She also says I come from a spoiled generation.

Tyler invited Theo out for a smoke on a Cuban cigar he picked up from a friend. Theo jumped at the opportunity since Cuban cigars are technically illegal in the United States. I had no idea my brother even knew about cigars, let alone started smoking them. He said it was only for special occasions, and since dad was going to be okay, this was warranted as a special occasion. And since Theo is Cuban, he gave Tyler the history of the

Cuban cigar and why it's banned in the United States.

From the kitchen window, my mom gazes out, watching Tyler and Theo enjoy their cigars, sitting on a wooden porch swing on the back deck. She washes the dishes and hands them to me; I dry them. One by one, we work together as a team. I can tell something's on her mind, and I don't think it's my father. She eyes Theo from the window, then me, then back to Theo.

My glass of wine sits next to the drying rack where I place the dried dishes. I take a sip when my mother suddenly asks, "So how long have you two been sleeping together?"

What? I nearly choke on my wine, feeling it trying to come out of my nose. I immediately pinch my nose, wincing as it stings. I set my glass of wine down and naturally say, "What?"

"You heard me. Your mother isn't stupid, Cameron," she says, handing me a perfectly washed plate. Unsure how to respond, I begin drying it.

"How did you know?" I ask, not bothering to lie. What's the point? I knew she was suspicious at the hospital, but then at dinner, she confirmed it.

"When you speak, he listens to every word you say, and his eyes dance at the sound of your voice." She hands me another washed plate. "I haven't seen Daniel's eyes move like that when you speak in a very long time."

I finish drying the plate and set it on the rack. "And your eyes do the same when Theo speaks," my mother adds. Do my eyes do that? I certainly haven't noticed. I set the towel down and lean against the counter. I feel like a weight has been lifted. Someone knows. I can talk about it. And if what my mother says is true about Theo's eyes dancing around when I speak, then that means he has fallen for me too. And then it dawns on me.

"Is it possible to be in love with two people at the

same time?" I ask. There. I said it. Out loud. I'm in love with Theo. The words are out, and they can't be taken back. It's almost as powerful as when I first said, "I'm gay." When you release a truth like that, your whole body feels lighter. I feel lighter now.

My mother turns off the faucet and grabs my towel to dry her hands. She leans on the counter, too.

"I suppose," she says. "But one love is going to be stronger than the other. Nothing's ever perfectly even."

I ponder this for a moment. Unequal love makes sense, but I have two different sets of feelings for Daniel and Theo. One is my husband, the other… What shall he even be called? He's not a mistress, or a mister? I decide to confess more to my mom. "It just sort of happened. He listens to me, you know? Daniel is always so busy, and…" I trail off, realizing I'm making excuses, and honestly, they don't even sound that good. 'Daniel's busy' is a lame excuse.

"Cameron, you and Daniel got together when you both were so young," she says. "You, especially. You just turned 20 and hadn't even finished college yet." She pulls out the stopper from the kitchen sink, and it begins to drain. She refills her glass of wine from a bottle sitting to the left of the sink. She makes a good point. We were young, and I was only halfway done with college. I feel more confused now than before.

"I know, but we've been together for 10 years. I always thought we'd be forever," I admit.

She nods and takes another, bigger sip of wine. "You want to know what I think?" she asks. I nod. "I think people's personalities change every seven years or so. What people think they want evolves over time, and eventually, they find themselves no longer wanting the same things anymore."

"What do you mean?" I ask, even more confused.

She places her hand on my heart for a moment. "Listen to your heart, Cameron. That's the best advice I can give you. But what you two have? It's no fling."

I decide this is a good time to finish the rest of my wine, which I do. My mom hands me the bottle, and I top off my glass.

"How do you know, though?" I ask, pondering. "I mean, you and dad have been married for 35 years. Surely, the two of you have evolved multiple times."

She nods in agreement. "And we have, *together.* It doesn't mean everyone gets it right the first time."

Hmm. What if we *do* get it wrong the first time? What if I married the love of my life but then met my soul mate?

"I don't condone infidelity, Cameron," she says, pulling me from my thoughts. "You were raised better than that. You need to make a decision on which one of them you're going to be with or end the affair." She finishes her wine in two big swallows and sets the glass in the sink. "I'm exhausted. I need to go to bed."

We hug goodnight, and she heads toward the dining room but stops to face me. "Either you or Theo can sleep on the couch, and the other in your room. But you will not be sleeping in your room together. In this house, we respect vows."

I nod, understanding. My parents weren't super religious when Tyler and I were growing up, but they always taught us the golden rule: treat others as you want to be treated and respect one another. She's calling me out for not respecting my vow to Daniel, and she's right to do so.

I finish putting away the dishes and cleaning the kitchen, so my mother won't have to deal with it tomorrow morning. I feel so relieved that someone else knows about Theo and me. It was nice to get my thoughts out and speak with my mother about my confusion. While wiping down the counter, I glance out the window to see Emily has joined Tyler and Theo. She's wearing a pink heavy coat, bouncing her legs to stay warm. Tyler hands her the cigar, and she hesitantly brings it to her lips, then erupts in a coughing fit. Tyler laughs and tells her she's not supposed to inhale. Personally, I've never understood the fascination with cigars. Tyler hands it back to Theo, who takes another puff.

Once I finish cleaning the kitchen, I grab my coat and slip it on to join them on the back deck. When I open the door, the cold air floods my lungs, and my face turns pink. I hate the winter.

I join them, and Theo immediately offers me a puff. I decline.

"Well, guys, we're heading to bed," Tyler says, rising from the swing. His nose is rosy from the cold. Tyler and Emily live in Lancaster, Pennsylvania, about a two-hour drive away, so they'll be staying at my parents' house for a while. My parents never changed our rooms after we moved out for college. It's odd, they're exactly how they were when we were in high school. Tyler teases my parents about it all the time, saying they refuse to admit they're getting old. My mother always responds that the rooms are there whenever we want to go down memory lane.

Emily gives Theo a hug. "It was so great to meet you, Theo," she says. "And I promise I'll check out your prison show."

"Streaming for the next five years, they tell me," Theo replies, hugging her back. Tyler and Emily head inside, and I take a seat next to Theo on the porch swing. "So, this is where you grew up?"

"Born and raised," I say. "Collingswood is a small town, but quaint. I'm proud to say I'm from here." I look around at my parents' small backyard, remembering all the summer cookouts. I see my dad's large red shed that housed Tyler's and my bicycles and sports equipment. It's in desperate need of a paint job after years of enduring the elements.

The kitchen light turns off as Tyler and Emily head upstairs, just as a cold wind blasts through, sending a chill down my spine. Theo notices the light turning off and my shiver, and wraps his arm around me, pulling me close.

"It was really sweet of you to come home with me, but you didn't have to," I tell him.

"Well, since your dad seems to be okay, I think I'm going to rent a car and drive to Brooklyn to see my folks tomorrow." Collingswood is about two hours from Brooklyn, so it makes sense that Theo would want to see his parents while he's close. Plus, who knows what he's feeling about his father since mine nearly died. Sometimes it takes a tragedy for us to remember how limited our time on this earth really is.

I rest my head on Theo's shoulder. He's actually starting to warm me up. "This feels nice," I say. "I wish we could stay in this exact moment forever."

"Me too," he says, taking another puff from the cigar. The cherry smell fills the air.

"I have an odd question for you," he says.

"If it's do I want to try that cigar, the answer is hell no."

Theo busts up laughing. "No, nothing like that. Do you want kids?"

I lift my head, surprised. That was a question I certainly wasn't expecting, especially since children just came up at Daniel's gala.

"Yeah, I can see myself as a father one day," I admit, saying it out loud for the first time. I've always seen children in my future. "Do you?" I ask him.

"Absolutely," he says, smiling from ear to ear. "I've always wanted to be a dad and adopt a foster kid. Give some kid a chance." I smile because I know he's sincere. "I like your family. There's a lot of love in this house. You can feel it," he adds, carefully putting out the cigar in a glass ashtray my brother left behind.

"Got you thinking about having a family of your own, huh?" I tease, and he agrees.

I decide it's time to tell him. "My mom knows about us," I say.

"What?" He responds, surprised. "Why did you tell her?" His voice shakes nervously.

"I didn't. She actually told me. She said it's written all over our faces."

"Cameron, she can't say anything..." Theo begins, and then I realize he's so nervous because he's not out of the closet.

I immediately reassure him. "Relax, Theo. She would never say anything to anyone." I pat his leg, easing his nerves. It works. He pulls me in tighter and holds me. I want to stay like this forever, but I know something has to change between us. If my mother can figure us out, we're being careless. What if someone at work notices when we start shooting our movie? Our affair could destroy Theo's career, and he'd blame me for it.

The next morning, I drive Theo to the car rental lot. I borrowed my father's SUV since he won't be using it for a while. Theo is quiet on the short drive, but once we arrive, his face lights up, clearly excited to see his parents in a couple of hours.

"Have a good trip with your folks," I say.

He smiles at me and hops out of the SUV, heading to the trunk to grab his bag. He comes back to the passenger door, leans down, and says, "I hope your dad has a quick recovery." He leans in as if to kiss me, but then pulls back, realizing we're in public. "When we get back to L.A., there's something I want to talk to you about."

"Ugh, don't do that," I say, annoyed. "Now I'm going to be wondering about that for the next few days."

He laughs. "It's no big deal. I'm flying out of New York the day after tomorrow." He explains, "Pre-production." That clears it up. Since my dad is recovering, Theo will get back to work on our movie, which starts shooting next month.

"I'm not sure when I'm flying back. It depends on my dad," I say, and Theo nods, understanding. He winks at me and subtly blows me a kiss.

"Okay, cool. I'll see you soon," he says, closing the door. I watch him throw his leather bag over his shoulder and head inside to the rental counter.

Chapter 27

Daniel

Cameron was right. I couldn't get his voice out of my head about my father-in-law having a heart attack and how I should be there for him, for the family. I love Cameron's family. They've always been supportive of me and our relationship. Well, Elaine grew to be supportive. She was very protective during the first couple of years Cameron and I were together, constantly making me feel like I was too old for her son and waiting for me to break his heart. She couldn't understand what I, a 30-year-old working professional, wanted with her 20-year-old college son. But she didn't see what I saw: a charming, charismatic young man with a heart of gold and dreams that he would shout from the mountaintops to the world. He may have only been 20, but he was, and still is, an old soul.

After Cameron left, I went to the office the next day, but I couldn't concentrate. I knew I wasn't in the right mindset to handle the London situation. So, I phoned Russell, and explained the situation, and he agreed to let me delay my London arrival by a couple of days, at least until we knew the status of Frank Taylor's situation better. I booked a flight and decided to surprise Cameron by visiting. Our marriage has been rocky for a while, so hopefully, this will be one step in the right direction for us to get back on track. He's made it abundantly clear to me that I haven't been showing up for him for quite some time. I wish I could be in two places at once, as he constantly begs for, but I just can't. Like he's thriving in his career, so am I.

My flight lands at 7:05 a.m. East Coast time. Surprisingly, I was able to get a good amount of sleep on the flight. First-class accommodations are a big plus when it comes to business travel. Though this isn't technically business, my firm insisted I book my flight through their travel department and fly to London from Philadelphia as soon as my short trip with Cameron's family is over.

I decided to rent a car to further enforce my surprise. Plus, Cameron may want to go places, and I know he doesn't have a vehicle. This way, he'll have the option to have me drive him wherever he needs to go over the next couple of days. I know his family is in limbo right now, unsure what to expect with his father's heart attack and the recovery scenario. The last time I spoke to Elaine, she informed me that he was out of the woods and beginning his long recovery.

I pull up to Frank and Elaine's house by 8:00 a.m. I

don't see either of their vehicles in the driveway, so I assume they're in the garage. Tyler's car is parked on the curb in front of their property. I didn't think everyone would be at the hospital just yet since most visiting hours are after breakfast, but I decide to chance it and ring the doorbell, hoping someone's home.

Tyler opens the door moments later. He's wearing a T-shirt and dark gray sweatpants, his hair uncombed. The smell of bacon greets me from behind him.

"Daniel," Tyler says with a big smile. "You made it." We hug, and he steps aside, allowing my entry.

I remove my long coat and hang it on the coat rack next to the door, a coat rack that's been there as long as I've known the Taylors.

"Are you hungry?" Tyler asks. I'm starving. Red-eye flights don't serve hot meals overnight, not even in first class. "Emily's making breakfast," he adds.

"Yes, that sounds great," I smile. He pats me on the back, and I follow him into the dining room. We pass through and arrive in the kitchen, where Emily stands in front of the stove, wearing a very long pink T-shirt that goes to her knees. Her eyes light up when she sees me.

"Daniel, what a surprise," she says. We hug quickly, and she returns to her sizzling bacon in the pan. They've already set up two place settings at the kitchen table in the eating area to the left of the kitchen's bar, complete with orange juice and coffee. "Cameron said you were in London," she says, then turns to Tyler, "Set him a place setting." Tyler obediently grabs a placemat and sets it on the table before pulling a plate from the cabinet.

"I was supposed to be, but he's right," I say. "This is family too, and I should have been here, so I delayed the trip by a couple of days. Probably set my career back five years." Tyler and Emily exchange a glance, looking suspicious. "I'm kidding," I add, and they both relax. Bad joke.

"Are you hungry? There's a ton of food here," she asks, flipping the bacon. She's not wrong. They've made enough scrambled eggs to feed a maternity ward: sausages, pancakes, and the bacon she's working on right now.

I move around the kitchen to grab a coffee mug from the cupboard. Fortunately, there's a quarter pot of coffee left, so I indulge. I find the dry creamer Elaine always keeps in the cabinet. This kitchen has been the exact same for the entire 10 years I've known Cameron, so I know my way around it perfectly. We've spent enough Thanksgivings and Christmases here. Elaine only uses dry creamer, which is gross. But after flying all night, I just need some caffeine in my system. I take a sip. It's perfectly hot.

Emily starts packing the bacon onto a plate with paper towels to capture the grease. I eyeball the buffet spread again. This is too much food for just the three of us, and since up until a few minutes ago it was just the two of them, I wonder where everyone else is.

"Where's your mom and Cameron?" I ask, noticing their absence. Of course, I could just assume Cameron is still in bed since he's a late riser.

"Ready," Emily says, grabbing her plate and heading to the table. Tyler does the same, loading his plate with food from their makeshift buffet.

"This looks good, babe," Tyler says, giving Emily a polite pinch on her right butt cheek. She jumps, blushes, and pinches his arm.

"Mom's already at the hospital," Tyler says. "And Cameron dropped Theo off at the rental car place so he can see his parents in Brooklyn."

I stop mid-sip of my coffee. Theo. "Theo? What?" I blurt out.

Silence. Emily sets her plate at the table, and then grabs two pieces of toast from the toaster that just popped up.

"His friend, Theo," Tyler says, sitting down. His plate is piled so high it looks like he hasn't eaten in weeks. Apparently, there isn't as much food available as I thought, if this is how he's starting his first portion. "The guy who's going to be in his movie."

"I know who Theo is," I say, but what I can't seem to understand is, "Why was Theo here?"

"Didn't Cameron tell you?" Emily asks, gesturing for me to sit. I oblige.

"No, he didn't," I reply, my face beginning to flush, my blood pressure rising. Why am I just now hearing about this? From them, and not Cameron?

"Well," Emily begins, and I can tell she's being cautious with her words, "since you weren't able to come home, Theo and Cameron flew together."

What? This makes absolutely no sense. Why would an employee of Cameron's fly home with him during a family emergency? "Why?" I ask, hoping to get some rational explanation for this absurdity.

"Not sure, bro," Tyler says, stuffing a piece of bacon into his mouth. "Cameron said Theo was his friend and wanted to be there for him."

I take another sip of my coffee. I realize Tyler probably didn't mean anything by what he said, *wanted to be there for him,* but it still stings. Sometimes, it feels like nothing is ever good enough for Cameron anymore. Emily notices my empty plate.

"Aren't you going to eat?" she asks.

A pit falls deep into my stomach. I don't understand the sudden dynamic that seems to be going on between Cameron and this actor, Theo. I shake my head in bewilderment. "I've suddenly lost my appetite," I say, and

I notice Emily shoot an apologetic look in my direction.

Chapter 28

Cameron

After dropping Theo off at the car rental agency, I drive directly to St. Mary's Mercy Hospital. My mom texted me this morning to let me know that dad has been moved to room 218.

I take the elevator to the 2nd floor and find my way to room 218. The hallways are crisp white, matching the clean white floors. The scent of bleach mixes with another cleaning product, though I can't quite put my finger on what it is.

Arriving at room 218, I notice my dad's name, Frank Taylor, written on a dry erase board posted on the doorframe. I enter and see him sitting up in his bed. It's a private room with a window overlooking another building. I'm so relieved to see him sitting up. Mom is sitting in a chair next to his bed, reading a magazine.

"Hey, dad!" I say, excited. His face lights up when he sees me, and it warms my heart.

"There's my boy," he says. "What, do I have to have a heart attack to get you to come home?"

I cautiously lean in to hug him. He winces in pain, and I immediately pull back. "Sorry," I say.

"It's these damn stitches," he mutters, his face briefly showing pain. He tries to move, but winces again.

"Frank, stay still," Mom commands. "You're just going to have to deal with it for now."

I notice a stool with wheels tucked into a built-in counter. I slide it out and take a seat next to mom, grabbing dad's hand.

"You gave us quite a scare," I say.

"Me too, Cameron. Me too," he responds, now at ease.

There's a knock at the door. I look up, and my heart sinks. It's Daniel, holding a bouquet of fresh flowers. I haven't been this surprised since Theo popped in on me on the plane.

"Daniel!" I exclaim, probably louder than I should have.

"Hey, guys," he says, smiling.

He enters the room, and mom and I stand. I give him a big hug and hold him tight. It's so good to see him. His coat smells like it's been on a plane, and I realize he probably came directly from the airport. We release our hug, and he hugs mom before handing her the flowers.

"I have a heart attack, and she gets flowers?" Dad jokes, making me giggle. Mom pats him on the shoulder.

Tyler and Emily walk in now, carrying a couple of "Get Well" balloons and a huge teddy bear. Everyone tries to hug dad, but each attempt causes him pain.

"What happened to London?" I ask Daniel as Tyler and Emily set up the balloons near the window.

"I delayed it," he says. He looks me in the eyes. "You were right. I should have been here. With family." He emphasizes *with family* and holds dad's hand. Dad returns the squeeze.

"We have nothing without family," Dad says. Daniel nods in agreement. I feel mom's eyes on me. I look toward her, and she's staring directly at me, smirking. In that moment, I can almost hear her thoughts: *What are you going to do now?* I let out a long sigh. What *am* I going to do?

Later that day, I find out Daniel didn't head straight to the hospital after the airport. He rented a vehicle and stopped by my parents' house to surprise me. The surprise was on him when Tyler and Emily told him Theo had come home with me the day before.

Daniel drives the rental car while I sit in the passenger seat. After visiting dad for three hours, we're now headed back to my parents' house. Daniel says he's desperate for a shower, and mom is picking up Italian food for dinner from a restaurant on Main Street in Collingswood. Daniel and mom even got into a polite argument over who would pay, with mom winning that battle. She insisted that everyone dropped their lives to be with dad, so this was her treat. No one was going to take that from her. Daniel shrugged, defeated, but I have a feeling he'll end up paying for the food before mom picks it up.

Daniel has not been okay with Theo flying home with me. He hasn't stopped talking about it since we left the hospital.

"You just have to imagine my surprise when they told me Theo came with you," he says as we merge onto the highway. "I mean, isn't he your employee?"

"He's not my employee," I reply. "It doesn't work that way. He's the lead actor in a movie I wrote, and he's also a producer on the film, so technically, I could be considered his employee?"

He looks at me, confused. "What?"

At this point, it's useless to explain further. I quickly take the heat off me. "You didn't even tell me you were coming," I say. "I didn't have a chance to tell you that Theo surprised me. I hadn't spoken to you since you dropped me off at the airport."

"Surprised you?" He asks, of course focusing on that part. Why did I even say *surprised me*? Sure, he did, but it sounds romantic when I put it like that.

"What?" I ask.

"It's an interesting choice of words," he says, suspicious. Indeed, it is.

A silence settles between us. Daniel focuses on driving, and I stare out the window.

"I think I'm going to see my parents tonight after dinner since I'm in town," he says. I nod in agreement. It makes sense to visit his family now that my father is doing much better. "My flight to London is first thing in the morning. Would you have morning coffee with me tomorrow before I go?"

He looks at me with pleading eyes, and it makes me blush. "Of course," I say.

He takes my left hand and gently places it in his right, bringing it to his lips and kissing it.

"I'm so glad I came," he says, almost relieved. But it makes me wonder: Is he glad he came to see *me*? Or is he glad he came to learn that Theo was here with me?

Chapter 29

I arrive back in Los Angeles a week later. My dad has been doing very well with his recovery and was able to come home. My mom said there would be dietary changes made immediately because his poor diet partially contributed to his heart attack. He's always loved fried food. Tyler and Emily said they would stick around a couple more days, so I figured that was my cue to head back home.

Daniel flew to London two days after his arrival in Collingswood. It was a sweet visit. We never spoke of Theo again after that car ride, and I made sure to avoid that name at all costs. Theo texted me twice: once to check in on how my family was doing, and the second time asking when I planned on coming back to Los Angeles.

Now, I sit at my kitchen bar, eating Chinese food that was delivered just minutes ago. I'm a sucker for chicken and vegetables in the amazing white sauce that Hunan Chinese Café uses. They've been my go-to Chinese restaurant ever since I moved to Los Angeles. My phone chimes in my pocket, and I pull it out to see that Theo is video calling me. I swallow a mouthful of food in one gulp and answer. The food burns my throat.

His face pops in and I can see he's shirtless and sweaty. Is he purposely trying to turn me on? Judging by his swollen muscles, I'm going to assume he just worked out, which is probably why he's video calling me instead of just calling.

"Hola, papi. Back in L.A. yet?" he asks.

I can't help but grin. I love his Spanish accent when he speaks Spanish to me. His charming smile beams at me, and his eyes are hopeful that I'm back.

"Next time I spend a week at home," I say. "Remind me to leave after five days. That seems to be my limit before the drama starts. Five days." He laughs. The truth is, I think we all started to get on each other's nerves after the fifth day. My mom, Tyler, Emily, and I all have fairly dominant opinions, especially when the subject of politics comes up.

"When can I see you?" Theo asks. "Wanna come over?"

I think for a moment. I really do want to see him. I've missed him, but Daniel's presence in Collingswood meant the world to me, and I know it meant a lot to my mom. I can honestly say Daniel is trying, and because of that, I shouldn't go over to Theo's. Not tonight, at least.

"I can't tonight," I say. "I'm exhausted."

Theo moves the camera down to reveal he's wearing loose-fitting gray sweats. I see his hand slide down his pants and into his black boxer briefs.

"Come on," he says flirting. "Don't you want to ride this?" He asks as I can tell he's touching himself. I get a glimpse of his abs as he pulls his hand back out and I feel myself getting excited. I bite my lower lip and decide to play along shaking my head 'no' slowly teasing him.

"Or I can ride you," he says. "We've only done that once. We can see if you can last longer this time."

"Stop it, Theo Diaz," I say smiling. He laughs again as he brings the camera back to his face. I swear I will never know how a man can have such defined abs.

"When can I see you again?" He asks.

I ponder this for what feels like hours. He patiently awaits my reply. On my flight back, I told myself I was going to think about this affair more thoroughly. But this video call has changed all of that. Everything I love about Theo is right before my eyes. Sure, his incredible body helps, but it's his glowing personality and the way he can make me smile and blush. No one has ever done that for me before. Not even Daniel.

"Tomorrow," I tell him. Screw it. I want him.

"Good," he says. "Tomorrow then. Hey, come by the studio. The sets are just about done." I was emailed by one of the producers earlier in the week that set construction started the day after I flew home for the interior house scenes we're shooting next month. This is an action movie, and because there are fire and explosions in the house scenes, the studio thought it would be better to build it as a set instead of trying to fake explosions on location and risk damaging an actual house. Oh, the magic of the movies.

"Then I'll see you at the studio tomorrow," I say.

"Can't wait to see you. Good night, papi," he says, and with that, the video call ends on his side.

I shake my head at myself, acknowledging the hold he has on me.

The next two weeks seem to fly by. My agent had requested a number of revisions for my next screenplay, which I expected since it was just the first draft he originally received. He potentially has a buyer from a new streaming service, and they've requested some changes as well.

Between making studio visits to see the sets, writing minor changes to *Hold Up*, per the director's notes, and seeing Theo on and off at his place, I am exhausted. My feet hurt, my brain hurts, and is it even possible to say that my dick hurts? Ever since I got back to L.A., Theo and I have had sex nearly every night, switching positions and trying new things. Daniel was never exploratory in the bedroom, but Theo has taught me so much about my body that I didn't even know. He takes his time with me, and he explores me.

I arrive home this evening from a writing session with *Hold Up*'s director. His notes started to become very vague, and with shooting beginning so soon, I thought it would be better if he and I sat down at the studio and hammered out his requests before the shooting draft is completed.

I notice the bedroom light on as I approach the house on my Phantom. Is Daniel home? He and I haven't talked much over the past couple of weeks because both of our schedules have been insanely busy.

I race upstairs and find Daniel, who appears to be exhausted as well, flopping his suitcase on the bed and unzipping it to unpack. He must have only beaten me home by five minutes.

"Hey, babe," he says. We hug.

"You're back," I respond. I set my phone on my nightstand and begin to undress. I know I'm due for a shower.

"Yes, it's Thursday. I told you I was coming back on Thursday," he says, throwing half of his suitcase's clothes into the hamper. In my defense, half the time he says he's coming home on a specific day of the week, it typically changes.

I throw my clothes in the hamper too and walk to the bathroom naked to turn the shower on. "How was London?" I ask from the shower.

"It was fine. Gray skies the entire time," he says from the bedroom.

I wait for the water to get hot, and once it meets my satisfaction, I'm about to enter, but I stop. I catch something in the bathroom mirror. It's Daniel's reflection from the bedroom, and I notice he has my phone in his hand.

"Oh yeah?" I say, hoping to see him look in my direction so I can catch him and ask what he's doing with my phone. But he doesn't. He pecks away at the screen.

"It's England this time of year. Rainy, gray, and cold," he says.

What is he doing with my phone? He then pulls out his own phone from his pocket and pecks away, holding my phone with his left hand and his phone with his right. Moments later, he returns my phone to the nightstand where it had originally been.

I hop in the shower, but I can't concentrate. Though the scalding hot water feels amazing on my back, I can't stop thinking about Daniel with my phone. Sure, we know each other's passcodes because we don't have secrets from one another, well, except the fact that I'm having an affair, but I always delete any non-work-related text messages from Theo. Daniel was definitely snooping. If he needed something from my phone, he would have asked.

After I wash up, I turn the shower nozzle off. I step

out of the shower, dry myself off, and then wrap the towel around my waist. I enter the bedroom, and Daniel is no longer in here. I race to my phone and unlock it. The screen pops up with Theo's contact information first. That wasn't from me, which means Daniel pulled it up and didn't realize he hadn't closed it out after using my phone. Daniel pulled up Theo's phone number. But why? Does he know?

Chapter 30

Theo

My alarm goes off at 6:00 a.m., the same time every morning when I'm alone. When Cameron spends the night, I never set an alarm. I hit the snooze button once and rise to face the day. With a mighty stretch, I wake up my muscles. I hit the floor and begin my morning routine with 75 push-ups, then 100 sit-ups. Breaking the morning's first sweat, I stretch my legs to prepare for my morning 3-mile run on the beach.

Production for *Hold Up* begins next month, and I need to be in better shape for the shooting. For the next nine weeks, I'll have to follow a strict diet and watch everything that goes into my body, especially alcohol and carbs, so I can be in the best shape of my life for this movie. There are plenty of shirtless scenes in the script, not raunchy or unnecessary, but scenes that require my character to show off his past as a kickboxer seeking revenge.

The morning run is always incredible. It begins and ends on Santa Monica Beach. The cool Pacific Ocean waves make me want to jump into the water and give my heart the shock of a lifetime. So, I do. Immediately, my feet go numb as I dunk myself into the water, reminding myself of how alive I am. The sound of the waves crashing ashore is music to my ears.

Once my run is over, I visit my kitchen and make a kale, spinach, carrot, and almond milk smoothie, complete with protein powder. It doesn't taste amazing, but it definitely gives my body the nutrients it needs. At this point, I pretty much only consume chicken, dairy products, fruits, and vegetables. No processed food whatsoever, and I extremely limit my carbs. Hollywood has a hard-on for masculine heartthrobs with perfectly chiseled bodies, and I voluntarily became a contestant of this game long ago when I found out I was going to have a shirtless scene in *Crooked Lies* in my first season.

Everyone likes to focus on the brutality Hollywood makes actresses go through, expecting them to be rail-thin and skeleton-looking. But people often overlook the expectations placed on male actors, requiring us to have muscular bodies built like Greek gods. Our bodies weren't meant to be this muscular, and I'll never be as big as some of the other leading actors, especially those in superhero movies. But I enjoy working out, and I enjoy staying fit and lean.

After breakfast, I spend the next two hours at the gym working on various parts of my upper body. The day after tomorrow is leg day, so today I focus solely on my upper body: chest, biceps, triceps, and abs. I listen to electronic music through my earphones as I lift the weights. The high-energy pump music always makes my veins feel like they're being electrocuted as I lift.

I take a shower at the gym and notice the occasional guy or two, sometimes three, check out my body. They're not necessarily gay, but they admire my work. They too have similar bodies and wish to have this kind of muscle tone. The truth is, they can have it. With the right time, work, diet, cardio, and workout regimen, any man can look like this.

Another guy enters the showers, drops his towel, and turns the shower nozzle on. His body is tighter than mine. I admire his work because it's like a piece of art. He notices and nods at me, not in a gay way, but in a "don't I look good?" way. Our workouts are long, intense, and regimented. We're proud to show each other our progress. I'm not talking about this to sound vain; it's part of my job as an actor to have a ripped and shredded body and keep myself in incredible shape. It's my investment in myself. The perk is, it's fairly easy to get laid when you look like this. And these men in the shower, checking me out, know this. Or one of them could be gay. I've had my share of secret hookups in the steam rooms in my younger days, but ever since I became a well-known actor, I'm much more discreet with hookups. My career would be over if the press found out I was gay. Not to mention, I'd probably lose my *Crooked Lies* fans, which, according to the latest demographic test, proved I was most popular among males aged 18-42. My character was a badass who eventually ran the inmates in the prison, a tough exterior that is nothing like mine in real life.

Once I arrive home, I toss my gym bag on the floor in front of the fireplace and go to the kitchen to warm up my lunch, which I prepped the night before: chicken and vegetables, including broccoli, carrots, and zucchini, tossed in Italian seasoning, salt, and pepper. While my food heats up, my phone rings. I pick it up, hoping it's Cameron. I could really go for seeing his face right now, hopefully, he's video calling me. But it's a number my caller ID doesn't recognize, a number beginning with a 212 area code. Normally, I wouldn't even answer, but it says "New York" under the display. It's possible someone's calling on behalf of my agent or manager, so I decide to answer.

"Hello?" I ask.

"Is this Theo Diaz?" a man's voice comes through the line.

Now, I'm not just going to admit to being Theo Diaz. I may not be super famous, but I'm well-known enough to get calls from various media companies, especially the tabloids. Shit. Why did I answer? They're probably wanting me to confirm some nonsense story about me that they're making up in the UK, or wanting a quote for the latest gossip trash they've created about my ex-wife, Amanda Preston.

"Who wants to know?" I ask, playing along. Fuck it, I have a few minutes to kill.

"This is Daniel Nichols," the voice says. Daniel Nichols. That name sounds vaguely familiar. Nichols. Where have I heard that last name before? Maybe this is a legit journalist contacting me after all.

"And you are?" I ask, since he doesn't give any more information. Usually, at this point, a journalist would say what media company he works for.

"I think you know my husband," he says, followed by a pause. "Cameron Taylor."

Oh. Shit. Daniel. That Daniel. Although I don't think I ever knew his last name was Nichols. Cameron's Daniel is calling me. But why? I decide to play it cool.

"Yeah, oh. Hey, man. What's up?" I couldn't think of anything better to say.

"We need to talk," he says sternly. "In person. Privately."

I swallow and take a deep breath. I'm not sure what to make of this call, but I can definitely tell he's not calling to thank me for sleeping with his husband. Cameron never mentioned that he found out, so I don't want to assume anything. Besides, would he even care? It's not like he's been around anyway.

"I know a place," I tell him, giving him the address to The Monastery. He agrees to meet in one hour.

After we hang up, the microwave dings, alerting me that my food is ready. My stomach tightens, and I'm no longer hungry. But I have to eat. My body needs the protein from the workout I did earlier. I pull out the plate and burn my finger. I lick it for a moment, and the pain eases. I debate contacting Cameron to see what's going on, but I don't want to alarm him. We could end up outing ourselves to Daniel if we're not careful. There's nothing else I can think of as to why Daniel would ask to meet with me, unless this has nothing to do with my sleeping with his husband, and maybe he's planning a surprise party or something for him. After all, Cameron and I are friends. Maybe I'm jumping to conclusions too quickly. His voice was just so stern.

I decide to call Cameron. The phone rings and rings until his voicemail picks up. I hang up and text him: *Are you there?*

After a few minutes with no response, I decide to give up. *Fuck it.* I'll go meet with Daniel and find out what he wants. Come to think of it, it could have something to do with *Hold Up*. But he's never taken an interest in Cameron's work before. Why would he choose to now?

I decide to call Cameron again on the drive from Santa Monica to West Hollywood. It's the same thing as before: rings and rings, ending in his voicemail. *Where the fuck is he?* It's not like him to ignore me. He's been busy lately with rewrites for our director and his next screenplay. Maybe he's in meetings. Maybe I'm overthinking this.

I arrive at The Monastery 15 minutes before Daniel and I agreed to meet. I told the host to seat us somewhere private, so he puts us in the back corner of the restaurant. I let him know the name of the person I'm waiting for. I know he recognizes me from the wrap party, so there's no point in trying to hide my face.

I impatiently wait for the next ten minutes, checking my phone every 30 seconds to see if Cameron has called or texted. Not that a vibration of an incoming call or text would go unnoticed by me. I bite my nails, then catch myself and place my hands on my lap. And then he enters.

The host points to where I'm sitting, and Daniel Nichols walks toward the table. He's wearing a dark blue designer suit, a pastel yellow dress shirt, and a yellow and red plaid tie. I take note that he is dressed *phenomenally*. There isn't a wrinkle in sight. He walks with confidence as he arrives at the table. I begin to stand up, but he waves his hand at me.

"Don't get up," he says dryly, so I stay seated. He unbuttons his suit jacket and takes a seat directly in front of me.

"This place isn't really known for their lunch menu, but it's private enough during lunchtime," I say, trying to ease the tension I feel building between us.

"The privacy isn't for me, Theo," he says, with no hint of a smile. "It's for you."

I eye him suspiciously. I can see a hint of rage behind his eyes, or at least anger. *Oh shit. He knows.*

"We wouldn't want your 'secret' getting out," he says. The tension thickens, filling the space between us like a cloud of doom. A male server, a young twink with dark hair, brings over two menus. Before he can even open his mouth to tell us today's specials…

"I won't be staying for lunch," Daniel says, never breaking eye contact with me. Damn, this man is intense. The server turns, and I notice he swishes away, annoyed.

"What's up, man?" I ask, leaning forward. He doesn't have to be rude to the wait staff.

"You tell me," he challenges, a slight sarcastic smirk creeping across his face.

"Look, I don't know what this is about, but you're being rude," I say. I don't have to take this.

"You don't know what this is about?" he asks, the smirk now replaced with a frown. "Really? Seriously?"

I keep my eyes locked on Daniel's not daring to look away, but careful not to look guilty.

"I'm just going to ask," he says. "Are you fucking my husband?"

Boom. There it is. My suspicions about this meeting confirmed. But he's asking, not accusing. Which means he doesn't know for sure. If I break eye contact now, it'll be a dead giveaway, but it's not my place to confirm this. It's Cameron's. Maybe that's why he's not getting back to me. Maybe he's scared because Daniel knows. But then again, he's asking, which means he doesn't truly know.

"Why don't you ask your husband?" I say. I gotta give the guy credit for having the balls to directly ask me face-to-face. You don't see that kind of confrontational courage in this town.

"I'm asking you," he replies, dead serious. The twink server returns with two glasses of water. Again, Daniel and I don't break eye contact. Out of the corner of my right eye, I notice the server picking up on the tension and disappearing, waters still on his tray.

"This isn't really appropriate, bro," I say. I mean, I guess there's no truly appropriate place to call out the guy who's having an affair with your husband.

"I'm not your bro," Daniel snaps back. "I mean, who talks like that at your age? What are you, 38?"

"36," I correct him. You know what? *Fuck this.* "I'm outta here," I say. I begin to stand up when Daniel slams his hand on the table. It's enough to startle me, but I won't give him that satisfaction, so I don't react. I notice other patrons in the restaurant have turned toward us. I wave my hands in the air, indicating we're fine at this table. I sit back down.

"Listen to me very carefully," Daniel warns, "I don't know what's going on with you and Cameron, but it ends right now. Done. Finito, hombre?"

I hate when white people start to mock Spanish. It's incredibly racist, not to mention culturally insensitive. If this guy wasn't the husband of Cameron, I'd probably punch him out right here and right now for talking to me like this. I feel my face start to turn beat red. It's taking everything I have right now not to reach over the table and slam Daniel's head onto it.

"It would take one very simple call to any media outlet or tabloid to out your closeted ass," Daniel threatens. "And that would ruin you."

I feel my blood pressure raise even more. I can do nothing more than blink at him. It has all come down to this. A decade of an acting career I built from the ground up and the idea of it being ruined by a public outing of Theo Diaz.

"I wouldn't even hesitate," he says and I know he wouldn't. "Don't fuck with me. Stay away from him."

With that Daniel rises and pushes his chair slamming it into the table. I watch him practically fly out of the restaurant. The host and server watch too, then turn their heads back to me. I am infuriated but know they want an answer. Fortunately, Daniel is dressed and just behaved like an agent so I say the most logical thing, "just fired my agent."

They both nod in understanding and laugh. Some patrons in the restaurant do too, and I feel the tension, and their concerned curiosity immediately escapes the room.

I lean back in my chair and let out an angry exhale. That Daniel is a real piece of work. Coming at me like that, threatening me over something he clearly doesn't even know is happening. But he knows enough to ask, which means Cameron and I slipped up. But how? When?

I can't stop thinking about this whole situation on the drive back to Santa Monica. One thing is for sure: the affair has to end. We can't keep sneaking around now. Daniel is too close to finding out the truth. He's not good enough for Cameron. I don't even know why Cameron is still with him. He's never around for him, doesn't take an interest in his work. Why string him along?

I've fallen hard for Cameron. I even think I may be in love with him. I've never felt this way about anyone before. He's the reason I wake up every morning so pumped and ready to face the day.

If Daniel's ultimatum is to out me if we continue our affair, then I'll change the terms of the game. It'll be as simple as that.

I'm going to take Cameron away from him.

Chapter 31

Cameron

I sit in Marc Shepard's production office, listening to his new notes for the revised script. As the director of *Hold Up*, any changes he wants are entirely up to him. I gave up all creative control when I sold the screenplay.

Marc, in his late 40s, has short, curly hair. He's wearing a blue sweater with white-washed jeans that look straight out of the 1980s. I heard white-washed denim was making a comeback, but I didn't expect to see it on a man nearly 50.

The office is a small room tucked behind the soundstage where our sets are being built. A small window lets in sunlight that illuminates his messy desk, cluttered with various drafts of the *Hold Up* script, each topped with a pink sheet of paper indicating its draft number.

Hold Up now has four producers, one of whom is Theo. Two others, Marlene and Cody, sit in the back of the office on a plush, floral-patterned couch. The furniture in here clearly came from storage, mismatched pieces likely repurposed from various Grey Studios sets. Marlene and Cody, both in their early 40s, are here solely as studio representatives, ensuring that Marc's suggestions don't exceed the already approved budget. In film school, we were taught that the director's vision is paramount, and it's the producer's job to make that vision happen. But that only holds true if you stay within budget.

I jot down all of Marc's ridiculous suggestions, concluding that he is as indecisive as a two-year-old choosing a toy from an overflowing toy box. My phone vibrates in my pocket, but I ignore it, making sure not to miss a word Marc says. When it vibrates again, I glance down, it's Theo calling.

"Do you need to take that?" Marc asks, though I can tell he'd rather I put it away.

"No, it's fine," I say, silencing my phone. Marlene and Cody are too busy pecking away at their screens to notice. They're literally here just to boost Marc's ego. Neither one of them are paying attention.

"So, what if we…" Marc flips through his script, covered in pink and orange Post-it notes. "Instead of Theo's character leaping off the roof, what if we have the house explode, catapulting him off instead?"

"Okay…" I say at this stupid idea because it makes no sense for the scene.

"Whoa, that would require bringing in a pyro unit and supervision," Cody pipes in. Ah, so he *is* listening because Marc's idea just added about $100,000 to the budget.

To be honest, *Hold Up* doesn't even feel like my script anymore. It has gone through so many rewrites and story changes that I barely recognize it. I'm not even sure if Theo knows what the latest version looks like. I think he's relying on me to ensure it stays true to itself, but I've been so distracted, between my next script, my father's heart attack, and our affair, that I don't even remember what *true to itself* means anymore in this script.

I take confidence in knowing Theo is one of the producers. Since he has money invested in the film, his say can override Marc's if he disagrees. You follow the money and those with it control the power.

My phone vibrates again. *Damn it.* I thought I silenced it. Theo is calling again. This time, Marc doesn't notice, so I hold down the power button until my phone shuts off.

"Okay, forget the catapult," Marc says, acknowledging Cody's concern. "Let's have him jump out of a plane instead."

I shake my head internally. *This guy is a real whack job.* No wonder he's never been trusted with a big-budget action film before.

Marlene is on her feet in an instant. Politely, she convinces Marc that the current script already has enough action to achieve the fireworks he wants. She's good with him. I think he likes her because he's much more receptive to her suggestions than Cody's.

I can't wait to get out of this meeting. My throat is dry, and the stuffiness of the room is making me want to sneeze.

Two hours later, the meeting finally adjourns. I toss my laptop, now filled with Marc's new notes, into my bag and sling it over my shoulder. As I leave the office, I take a quick look around the soundstage. The sounds of saws and hammers ring in my ears as I watch workers assembling sets of a house and a tavern. Both will inevitably be blown up.

I turn my phone back on and see that Theo has also texted me. Two missed calls and a message asking, *Are you there?* Something's up.

Outside Grey Studios, I head to my Phantom. I unstrap my helmet from the bike and decide to call Theo back. I'm curious. The phone rings.

"Hey," he answers. His voice sounds off.

"Hi, sorry, I was in a meeting with Marc," I say.

"Can you come over? We need to talk." He says. He sounds serious.

"Everything okay?"

"It will be. Can you?"

I think for a moment. *What could be so important?* I glance at the time: 3:02 p.m. I'll hit traffic heading to Santa Monica, but motorcycles are allowed to ride between cars when traffic is slow, which could save me 15 minutes. It's risky, but I only do it when traffic is nearly stopped, so I coast right through vehicles like a parted sea.

"Sure," I say. "Give me 40 minutes."

We hang up. He sounded serious. Also nervous. My stomach knots. *What if this is about Hold Up*? Am I getting fired? Does Theo want to tell me at his house and away from the studio? Did Marc pick up on the fact that I think he's a whack job?

I slap on my helmet, hop onto my Phantom, and head to Santa Monica.

When I arrive at Theo's building, the concierge sends me up the elevator. I walk to Theo's door and knock. He opens the door instantly as if he's been waiting for my arrival. He looks spooked. We hug, and he lets me in.

Something is definitely wrong with him.

"What's going on? You didn't sound like yourself on the phone," I say, setting my helmet on the coffee table. He looks at me with pleading eyes. "Theo, what's wrong?"

"Cameron, I didn't mean for this to happen," he says. Now I'm really concerned. "This was just supposed to be for fun, but you're so adorable…"

"Theo, are you okay?" I ask.

He grabs my hands, leading me to the couch.

"I'm in love with you," he says. I freeze. There it is. It's true. He feels the same way I do. His hands tremble in mine. "I find myself having trouble breathing when I'm not with you," he continues.

I know exactly how he feels. I feel that exact same way. "I do too," I confess. "It's not healthy. I go to bed every night thinking about you, wondering what you're doing. And when I wake up, I can't stop thinking about you." It feels good to finally say it out loud. These feelings affect me every day.

"Then be with me," he says.

Oh, how I wish it were that simple. Sure, I've just admitted to him I'm in love with him too, but I can't leave Daniel. I love Daniel too.

"Theo, I can't. I'm married to Daniel," I say. Why does he have to do this now? Why can't we just keep seeing one another as we have been doing?

"So leave him."

I pull my hands back, but Theo grabs them again and holds them.

"I love you, Cameron. I've never loved anyone like this before."

"Theo, we knew the arrangement when we started this. I can't leave him."

He stares at me, his eyes welling up. I see the emotion

in them.

"Then I can't do this anymore," he says.

"What?" I say. Why does he have to ruin this beautiful thing we have? And why now?

"Cameron, if we can't be together more than this. Then I can't do this anymore."

I feel myself starting to get upset. My heart starts beating nervously at the idea of losing him. "No, don't do that," I beg. "This is good. This arrangement works."

"For you!" He shouts and stands. "I'm going to ask you one more time. Cameron, will you be with me?"

My stomach churns, and I feel my face flush, not with anger, but with emotion. My eyes well with tears. He's serious. It's him or Daniel.

I can't choose.

How can he expect me to?

"Theo, please don't do this," I plead. "Please."

"Answer me."

"…I can't be with you," I whisper, lowering my head.

His face crumbles. He swallows hard, fighting back tears. The whites of his eyes turn a raw, pinkish hue. Then his expression shifts, anger overtaking sorrow. He shoves me onto the couch and climbs on top of me.

"I woke you up," he growls. "You were sleepwalking for ten years, and I woke you."

His hand grips my crotch, squeezing. It feels good.

"And I made you feel alive again."

He flips me onto my stomach, his grip ironclad. His weight presses down on me, his crotch against my backside.

"And I made you feel pleasure. Real pleasure, because I was inside you, and you loved it."

I buck him off and leap to my feet. He's being cruel right now, even though he's right. He did wake me up. He did make me feel alive.

My heart pounds, ready to explode from my chest.

"Stop it!" I scream. "What the hell is wrong with you?" I demand, furious at the violation of his hands on me.

He just stares at me. He hasn't lost his mind, but his face is destroyed.

"I need you to understand what you're about to give up if you won't be with me," he says.

But I do understand. I know what I'm giving up and that's what hurts the most.

He pokes my chest, right over my heart. "Does Daniel make you feel alive anymore? Does Daniel make your toes curl when he's inside you? Does Daniel come with you?"

I can't take this anymore. I've never seen Theo like this before, so raw, so desperate. I feel like a pot about to boil over.

"Theo, stop!" I yell loud enough that his neighbors probably hear. "I can't leave him. You know that," I say, my voice pleading.

"Then we're done," he says dryly, so quietly I almost don't hear him. "This is done. It's over."

My heart plummets to my stomach. I feel like I might vomit. No. He can't do this to us. No.

I glare at him in shock. "Seriously? Why?"

"Because I'm not going to do this to myself. You made your decision. Now I'm making mine."

"How would this even work, Theo?" I demand. "How would we be *together*?"

He tilts his head, confused.

"You're not even out publicly," I continue. "How would this arrangement work? Would we live together or separately? Would I watch you on TV at award shows, standing next to your next pretend wife?" I demand to know.

His face turns beet red. I hit a nerve.

He steps closer and grabs my face in his hands. His grip tightens, almost painful.

"I can't believe you just said that," he says squeezing my face tighter. "I would never make you feel the way Daniel makes you feel."

I rip his hands from my face with such force he winces, gripping his forearms.

"You need to leave," he says.

I crossed the line.

I shouldn't have thrown his secretive sexuality in his face, not when he just confessed his feelings for me. But he should have an answer. If he expects me to leave my husband, how would we be together? Would we live a hidden life, a secret marriage, like so many closeted actors before him since the beginning of Hollywood?

"Theo..." I try to reach for him, but he turns away.

"Get out!" he shouts at me.

I swallow and it feels like a bowling ball is rammed down my throat. Tears slip down my cheeks. I touch his shoulder, but he jerks away.

"Get the fuck out!" he roars so loud now his neighbors for sure have heard both of us. His voice cracked with rage and pain. I've never heard this high pitch in his voice before. Pure anger, and pain.

I grab my helmet and race out of his condo. The door slams behind me as I sprint down the hall, sobbing.

I ride my Phantom home, my helmet's shield fogging from my tears. I keep flipping it up to wipe them away, but they won't stop. My body feels numb. I don't want to feel anything. I want to crawl into a dark hole and disappear to never be seen again.

The fight replays in my head, over and over.

Why now?

Why did Theo demand this now?

What suddenly changed? Is it really that he can't love me anymore unless I'm truly his?

And how would we even be together?

Questions he wasn't able to answer.

I could carry on with my feelings for him, but the truth keeps slamming into me like a wrecking ball.

The truth that cannot be undone.

I just lost Theo.

Chapter 32

Daniel

I sit at the breakfast bar with my laptop, working on my latest travel expenditure report. Work has been grueling this week, and the last thing I needed was to deal with Theo Diaz earlier this afternoon.

I hear Cameron's Phantom pull into the side yard, and moments later, he enters through the kitchen door. I can tell he's been crying. His face is flushed, and his eyes are puffy.

"Hey," he says, setting his helmet on the side table.

"Hi, babe," I respond, but he won't make eye contact with me.

"I'm going to take a bath," he says, darting up the

stairs as quickly as he can. Though I'm not pleased to see my husband has been crying, I'm pleased to see that my conversation with Theo Diaz had some effect. I honestly didn't expect results to happen so quickly.

I go to the refrigerator and open a beer, taking a long sip. It's nice and cold. I don't want to take pride in the destruction of whatever was going on between Theo and Cameron, but something inside me feels oddly satisfied by the results. I know Theo's type. I deal with guys like him all the time in the advertising campaigns at my firm. Egotistical, arrogant, narcissistic, thinking they can have whatever they want.

Though our frustrations usually stem from overpaid models hired by their sponsors, Theo is an actor, and that's not much different from the models I'm used to dealing with.

Cameron can be naïve sometimes, and I can easily see him getting caught in a web of lies from someone like Theo, getting taken advantage of. I'm not sure exactly what was going on between the two of them, but I can guarantee Theo Diaz would have pushed it to the limit. I've always trusted Cameron, and still do, but that guy just rubs me the wrong way. I can see Cameron forming what he believes is a good friendship, while Theo takes advantage of it simply because he can, because of who he is. I'm glad I stopped it before anything more serious could happen, before anything physical.

I sit back down and finish my report. Another long sip of beer, and I realize I still don't feel happy about what happened today. Relieved, sure, but not happy. I knew threatening to expose Theo Diaz would set him straight, but I just hope Cameron doesn't suffer for it too long. He doesn't have many friends these days. But as I said, Theo Diaz was never someone to be trusted.

Chapter 33

Cameron

The sets are complete, the lighting is set up, and the casting is finished. Filming for *Hold Up* begins next week. As the writer, I've been invited to be present on set in case any last-minute changes need to be made to the shooting script during production. The producers have already told me that the writer's role is to be seen and not heard. I'll never understand why writers are always treated as the lowest on the totem pole when it's our ideas and creativity that spark these projects.

It's been four weeks since Theo ended our affair, and he hasn't made any contact with me. I just can't figure out why he gave me an ultimatum out of nowhere. When

I see him on set, he treats me like just the writer. It's as though he's completely forgotten everything we shared. He's a stranger to me now. Whatever was there, he's made sure it's gone. He's cold to me.

The nights are the worst, especially when I'm alone, which is often. I want to call or text him, but I know he's done with me and our affair. My body aches for him, for his touch, for his companionship. Most nights, I cry myself to sleep, holding myself, pretending it's Theo's arm around me.

Daniel has asked me three times if I'm okay. He said he's noticed a change in me and that I'm not my usual happy self. I tell him everything is fine, but it's not. My heart is broken, and I want Theo so badly, but I can't leave Daniel. It would destroy him if he knew about our affair. I'm so conflicted. I feel like I'm going to explode from the inside. Can a person be in love with two people at the same time? And if so, is my mother right that you'll love one more than the other? As of this very moment, I feel like I love Theo more than Daniel. But how can that be? What I thought was just a physical relationship with Theo has certainly changed. We both fell in love with each other. We crossed the line that's not supposed to be crossed in an affair. There weren't supposed to be feelings involved.

Now, I have to see him every day at work and pretend there's nothing there. It doesn't seem like much of a challenge for him, considering the way he treats me these days when we're in person. There's no way he just turned off his feelings. Four weeks ago, he was begging me to leave Daniel and be with him. He's an actor, after all, so pretending I meant nothing to him is probably easier for him than it is for me.

I sit in my living room, staring at a TV dinner I made for myself. I can't eat it. I have no appetite. In the last four weeks, I've lost 11 pounds. Daniel may have noticed my mood change, but he hasn't noticed my weight loss. I find myself drinking more, especially when I'm alone. Alcohol numbs the pain and gives me some relief. But I know I can't rely on it all the time. It's not healthy, and I know I need to wait for time to pass to heal my heart.

I try to keep busy with my writing, but even that isn't enjoyable right now. Nothing is. I've never been a depressed person, but I can't help feeling that this is what depression feels like. I have no energy, no positive attitude, and no desire to socialize. I pick up the phone and call my mom.

"Hello?" She answers right away.

"Hi, mom," I say, my voice dry.

"Cameron, sweetie, how are you?"

I sit there without responding. How am I?

"I'm a wreck," I say, and start sobbing.

"Oh no, honey. What's wrong?"

And I tell her. I tell her everything that happened with Theo, the ultimatum he gave me, the end of our affair, and his coldness on set. She reassures me that the affair had gone too far and that Theo had no choice but to end it because he fell too deep. She was a bit disappointed it was he that ended it, and not me, paying proper respect to my vows, but she only jabbed me with that opinion once.

"Let me ask you a question," she says.

I wipe my tears away, and for the first time in four weeks, I feel a bit relieved. It's nice to get this off my chest. "Go ahead," I say.

"Who do you want to be with?" The question lands on me hard. The simple answer should be Daniel because he's my husband, but I can't answer because I truly don't know.

"I don't know, mom," I say, and the tears flood my

cheeks again.

"That's okay, Cameron. You don't have to answer right now. But it's this question you have to answer for yourself in order for your heart to heal properly," she says. "Love can be quite complicated."

And it is. Or at least, in my case, when I'm choosing between Daniel and Theo. I feel more confused than ever right now, but there's a small sense of clarity. I'm so glad I have my mother to talk to. Her words of wisdom are exactly what I needed to hear tonight.

"I love you, mom," I say.

"I love you too." We're about to hang up when she adds, "And Cameron?"

"Yes?"

"Just follow your heart. It will never lead you wrong." I smile as she says this. "And make sure you're eating."

This makes me laugh. I knew my mother would know I wasn't eating, even from across the country. We hang up.

So, there it is. The ultimatum may have been Theo's that I leave Daniel or end it with him, but the decision of who to choose is mine. The question remains: Which one will my heart decide?

Chapter 34

Theo

The last four weeks have been brutal for me. I've never felt this way about another person before. Cameron rejected me and refused to leave Daniel, even though I *know* I *make* him happier than Daniel ever could. I did not see that coming.

I decided not to tell Cameron about my conversation with Daniel because I wanted Cameron's response to be genuine when I asked him to be with me. If I had warned him that Daniel and I spoke, he might have panicked. As it turns out, it didn't work out in my favor anyway. I guess the old saying is true: they never leave their wife. In my case, the uninterested husband.

I can't get him off my mind, so I've been spending most of my days working on my body even harder than before. I've never been this toned in my life. It's becoming an obsession, working out. I've doubled the number of push-ups and sit-ups I used to do before Cameron rejected my offer, and I spend more time at the gym. If I keep my body active, I don't have time to feel or think about the pit in my stomach that appears every morning when I wake up. Building more muscle means working out more, which boosts testosterone, which increases my libido, and that only intensifies my need to get laid even more powerfully.

I want Cameron. I want to feel what I felt with him. But if I can't have that, I'll settle for something else with another guy, just to keep him off my mind.

I set up a hookup with a Latin guy on a discreet gay hookup app called Dkstr. I'm not sure who comes up with these names, but the app is effective. The guy's username is Latin4YouNow, and he's agreed to bottom. I've instructed my concierge to send him up when he arrives.

The door knocks, and I know it's him, Latin4YouNow. I'm wearing jeans with holes at the knees and a gray T-shirt. I've put on my baseball cap and pulled the stiff bill down to cover most of my upper face.

I open the door, and he's hotter than his profile picture, something that *rarely* happens. He has jet-black hair combed to the left side, and when he smiles, he reveals two dimples. He's probably in his mid-twenties. I step aside to let him in, but as soon as he approaches, he goes in for a kiss. I put my hand up, stopping him.

"You need to read this and sign it," I say, closing the door. On a side table next to the door is a stack of non-disclosure agreements (NDAs) that my agent had printed for me. Latin4YouNow needs to sign one because, in about 30 seconds, he'll most likely recognize me. Since I'm not out in Hollywood, he can't share this visit with the tabloids. If he does, I'll sue him for everything he has.

Latin4YouNow gives me a strange look at first, but then starts reading the NDA. He barely skims it, by "barely," I mean he hardly notices the text, and signs it right away. He's signed one of these before, which means he knows I'm a celebrity or someone who doesn't want tonight's activities getting out.

"It's cool," he says. "I'm just down for a good time."

I remove my hat and toss it across the room. He watches me, and I can tell he's wondering if he's seen me before. But I don't care. I move in on him like a wolf, pinning him against the wall. I pull his shirt up and over his head, removing it. He has a nice, tight body. Pecks that I can tell he works on. I kiss his neck and slide my hand down his pants.

Minutes later. we head to the bedroom and he tries to kiss me again. I push his face away and throw him on the bed. We're both naked now and I go for the drawer where my condoms are.

I start topping him and I hear him moan. I don't want to hear him at all because he's not Cameron. I only want to hear Cameron moan, but he feels good right now and I need to feel good. I need to release.

He rises and rolls over to his back. "I want to see your face," he says suggesting what I think is a form of making love. Fuck that, this isn't love. It's a booty call.

"No, turn back around," I command and he does. I continue topping him until… I finish. My heart is racing and my veins feel like they're about to pop out of my muscles. I pull the condom off and toss it in the trash.

I leave and head for the bathroom to turn the shower on.

"I didn't get off yet," he says.

"Finish yourself off and then leave," I say closing the bathroom door. I know it's rude and I'm a dick for not finishing him off. But I can't. I don't even want to look at him anymore. He's not Cameron. And though I did climax, it wasn't fulfilling. It was five seconds of feeling amazing, but the loneliness immediately returned.

"You're an asshole." He shouts to me from behind the door. And he's right. I am an asshole right now.

The next night, I use the Dkstr app to find my next hookup. This guy's username is *RedUpstairs&Downstairs*. These weird names people choose. His profile picture shows that he's a ginger, a bona fide redhead. There's a hint of a five o'clock shadow, and the sunlight hits his red facial hair in the picture. He's a true ginger.

Just like the night before, my concierge sends up *RedUpstairs&Downstairs*, and I hear a knock at the door. I don't even bother putting on clothes this time. I'm only wearing my black boxer briefs and a ballcap, which I tip down, hiding most of my face.

When I open the door, he doesn't smile like *Latin4YouNow* did the night before. I feel bad for how I treated *Latin4YouNow*, and for a moment, I wish it was him at my doorstep instead. I'd return the favor he gave me last night. But it's *RedUpstairs&Downstairs* who stands before me. He's pasty white, and his red hair has been cut fairly short. The five o'clock shadow is still there. He's wearing jeans, and a plaid long-sleeve button-up over a white T-shirt. His body looks trim.

I open the door wider and point to the NDAs.

"I need you to read and sign this," I say, closing the door behind him after letting him in.

He picks up the NDA on top and reads it quickly.

"Are you a singer?" he asks.

What a random question. Why would I be a singer?

"No," I say. "Just someone who can't afford to let this

hookup get out."

He shrugs his shoulders and signs it. I remove my hat, and his eyes squint, trying to figure out if he knows me.

"Fucking Theo Diaz," he says right away. Shit. People don't usually recognize me that fast. He must be a fan of the show. His eyes survey my entire body. It's making me hard because he looks so hot in that T-shirt. I can tell he's got a body under there because it's purposely tight.

"Take off your shirt," I say, moving forward to remove his flannel button-up. He does. I raise his white T-shirt to reveal his pasty stomach and chest. He has no abs, but he definitely works out his upper body. I go in for the neck when he pushes me hard, three feet, landing me against the wall. This guy has strength and likes it rough.

"Take it easy," I say, my back stinging slightly from the force of being shoved into the wall. He moves in close, sticking out his tongue and licking the right side of my neck. His body presses hard against mine, trying to push me even further into the wall.

"Dude," I say, attempting to shove him off, but he doesn't budge. Then, I hear the sharp sound of a twitch. He raises his left forearm and pins it against my throat, pinning me against the wall. He drives it in harder, the pressure cutting off the air from my esophagus.

A silver switchblade flashes in front of my face. The twitching sound earlier must have been the blade snapping open from its holder.

I try to shove him off me, but he's too strong. He brings the blade to my right eye, forcing me to look into his eyes. They're wild, dilated. He's on something. Probably crack or meth.

"Closeted motherfucker," he sneers before driving the blade into the side of my cheek. The pain is sharp, like a bee sting, and warm blood seeps from the wound, trailing down my face.

Instinct kicks in. I thrust my right knee as hard as I can into his groin. He howls, doubling over and finally releasing my throat. I beg for air and take seize this moment to defend myself. While he's hunched over, clutching his crotch, I grab the back of his head and slam my knee into his face. A sickening crunch, like a carrot snapping, tells me I've broken his nose.

He shrieks, and with all his might and strength, I didn't know he had, he plunges the blade into my right side. It slides in effortlessly, like butter, sending a searing pain through me. Before I can react, he yanks it out and drives it in again, just inches from the first wound. He raises the blade for a third strike, but I block it. His eyes, unfocused and hazy from his broken nose, flicker with confusion.

The pain in my side is overwhelming, akin to the burning ache from running too fast for too long, but much, much worse. Gritting my teeth, I force myself to my feet and drive my fist into his nose. He lets out an agonized scream, and I'm now convinced he'll need plastic surgery. He collapses to the ground, cradling his face in his hands.

"Get up!" I shout, clutching my bleeding side. A pool of blood is forming at my feet, and my knees are beginning to weaken. I can't pass out, not yet. I need to get this psycho out of my house. "Get the fuck up!"

RedUpstairs&Downstairs slowly starts to rise. The switchblade is still in his grip. I don't hesitate, I kick it hard, sending it flying across the room. The blade slices the side of my foot in the process, and a fresh wave of pain ignites, burning like fire.

I lunge forward, gripping him by his shirt, and haul him to his feet. The moment he's upright, I shove him toward the front door. He slams into it with a thud.

"You fucking broke my nose," he spits, blood spraying with each word.

I yank him back, fling the door open, and push him outside. A couple of apartment doors are ajar, and neighbors peer into the hallway.

"Everything alright?" Tom, my neighbor to the right, asks. He's a musician in his 30s, and he wears a concerned face.

"Close and lock your doors. Call 911. This guy tried to kill me," I say, breathless.

Without hesitation, both apartment doors slam shut.

"Son of a bitch," I say and kick him one more time. He falls to the ground but slowly rises back up. With sheer desperation, he scrambles to his feet and bolts down the hallway leaving a blood-soaked trail behind. He doesn't look back. He's either running from me or from the cops that Tom is calling. Either way, he's gone.

I slam my apartment door shut and lock it. My head is woozy. I press my back against the door and slowly slide down until I'm sitting on the floor. Blood continues to seep from my side. My foot throbs. My vision blurs.

Where's my phone? I need to call for help.

Oh, right. Tom's calling.

My dizziness worsens. My eyelids grow heavy. And then I see him.

Cameron.

He stands before me, his presence soothing. His voice, though distant, reassures me that everything will be okay.

Am I hallucinating?

I don't care.

I just want to see Cameron.

Chapter 35

Cameron

I drive my motorcycle, weaving and dodging through traffic. Marlene, one of *Hold Up*'s producers, called me to tell me that Theo has been attacked and is in the emergency room. She said he's asking for me. Marc and Cody are on their way. Apparently, his injuries will delay the shooting schedule for *Hold Up*. I don't care about the schedule. I just want to make sure Theo is okay. She seemed more concerned about the production timeline than she should have. Our star, my lover, has been attacked. I don't know the extent of his injuries, except that he's been stabbed. My heart sank when I heard the news, and I raced out of my house in seconds.

I arrive at the hospital and park in the motorcycle parking. The nice thing about having a Phantom is that you can pretty much park anywhere you like. Motorcycle parking is usually just as close as handicap parking.

I fly through the hospital halls until I find the emergency room waiting area. I immediately spot Marc, Cody, and Marlene, all on their phones, pacing the room. What's happening? Did he die? I can't help but wonder. When Marlene sees me, she ends her call.

"Cameron, you made it," she says. *Of course I made it, you dense twit. He's my lover. Well, ex-lover.*

"Is he okay?" I ask, too concerned to just be a writer on this job.

"He's going to be fine," she says. My face relaxes, and I can breathe again. "He's asking for you." I hear the tail end of Marc's call when I realize he's speaking to Theo's agent. "Obviously, production is suspended…" But I don't hear anything else she has to say. I don't care.

"What room?" I blurt out, cutting her off.

She tells me to let the nurse know I'm here to see Alex Alvarez. That's the name Theo uses when his team doesn't want the press involved. Though it's typically used for things like hotel and dinner reservations, it's also used in cases like this to avoid a paparazzi storm at the hospital's entrance. He's been admitted under his real name, but for confidentiality reasons, and to avoid a media circus, he's listed as Alex Alvarez.

The nurse sitting behind the waiting room desk opens the doors for me to enter the emergency room. It's a long hallway with rooms on either side. Most rooms have two beds, separated by curtains. I pass a nurse's station where four nurses are typing away at computers until I arrive at the end of the hall, at ER24. I enter the room.

This is a private room with only one bed. Theo is lying in the bed, looking straight at me when I enter. He's wearing a blue and white hospital gown. My heart flutters when he smiles. I notice a large bandage over his cheek.

"Hey, you," he says.

I feel my eyes begin to swell. He's okay. He's right in front of me, and he's going to be okay. I rush to his bed and give him a hug, but he gasps in pain.

"Oh, I'm so sorry," I say, releasing him. He grabs his left side.

"It's okay, I've only been stabbed a couple of times," he says, easing his pain but smirking. I smirk too. I grab a nearby chair and drag it to the side of his bed. He offers his hand for me to hold, and I grab it. Daniel or no Daniel, affair or no affair, nothing else matters right now. It's just him and me.

"What happened?" I ask.

He shrugs, then his face falls, embarrassed. "Hookup gone wrong?" His voice rises at the end of *wrong*, then he bursts out laughing, but immediately winces in pain. The tension eases. I laugh too.

"Seriously?" I ask.

"I missed you. Like, really missed you," he says, squeezing my hand. And that's when it hits me. The truth finally slaps me in the face. It's Theo. I choose Theo.

"I love you," I say. "And the thought of losing you…"

He holds a finger to my lips to silence me. "I actually thought I was going to die. The amount of blood I lost caused me to hallucinate, and all I wanted to see was your face one last time. And I did," he says. "When I woke up, I was here. They told me the police busted down my door after Tom said I was attacked by a meth head."

"Wait, you hooked up with a meth head?" I say. What?

"Well, he was on something, that's for sure. But Cameron, stay with me here," he says, trying to distract me from the image of Theo with a meth head. "It made me realize that none of this matters if I'm not with you. The career, Hollywood, the money, I only want to be with you. And if coming out is what it takes, then it's done." He stares at me with doe eyes, waiting for me to respond. But it doesn't matter if he's closeted or not to me anymore. I decided moments ago that he's the one.

"I don't care about the Hollywood thing, Theo. I only want to be with you too," I confess.

His eyes light up like a child's on Christmas morning. "Are you serious?" he says, flashing that amazing smile of his. He adjusts his back and grabs his side in pain.

"I'm serious."

He leans forward to give me a kiss, but the pain returns. I decide to lean down to kiss him but stop when there's a knock at the doorframe.

We turn to see Marc. That was close. We were almost caught.

"Hey, buddy. We're all gonna take off," he says, indicating that he, Marlene, and Cody are leaving.

"Alright, man. Thanks for checking in on me," Theo says.

"Sure thing. Your agent and Marlene and Cody are working out a schedule," Marc says, waving goodbye.

I stare at Theo, and he stares back into my eyes. This is it. We're a team.

"I love you," he says.

"I love you too," I reply. My heart feels like I've made the right choice for the first time in my entire life.

"So what's next?" he asks.

"Daniel," I say, swallowing a lump in my throat.

Chapter 36

They call it Miracle March. It's the hope that when Southern California doesn't receive the rainfall it needs in January and February, March will bring monsoon-like rains to prevent a drought for the remainder of the year. Miracle March has been in full effect for the last two weeks. Buckets and buckets of rain have plagued the city of Los Angeles, causing flooding in the streets and mudslides in the Hollywood Hills. But it always ends in the same statement: "Well, we needed the rain."

It's been three weeks since Theo's attack, and he's recovered very well. Daniel has been out on business most of the time, constantly flying between New York and London. He checks in on me nearly every day to make sure I'm okay. My mood has definitely changed. Ever since I made the decision to choose Theo, I feel like a giant weight has been lifted off my shoulders.

I've been staying with Theo nearly every night, nursing him back to health. His wounds have healed nicely, and his doctor even thinks he can begin running again in another month or two. He's not in the finest shape of his life anymore, and that bothers him. But since *Hold Up's* production shooting dates have been pushed back another six weeks, I assured him he'll have time to get back into his proper physique. Trust me, his body is still in perfect shape to me.

We lay shirtless in his bed on a lazy afternoon. Storm clouds have formed over the Pacific Ocean. I lightly rub my fingers over his bandages covering his stab wounds.

"Does it hurt anymore?" I ask.

"A little, only when I get up. Mainly just itches now," he responds.

The man who attacked Theo is Chadwick Alexander. He's a drifter, as the police called him, and targeted Theo because of the address he lived at. Theo's team managed to avoid notifying the police about how Theo and Chadwick met, on a gay hookup app, and instead said that Chadwick just happened to stumble into the building and target Theo. This also excused the concierge from getting into trouble since he let the man up per Theo's request.

Chadwick was arrested two hours after attacking Theo. He checked into an emergency room because of his broken nose and was arrested after receiving medical treatment. Theo didn't want to press charges because he didn't want to draw any further attention to the matter, but the police charged him with assault with a deadly weapon.

Daniel is to arrive home this evening. I still haven't figured out how I'm going to tell him about my decision to be with Theo. I decided not to take Theo up on his offer for him to come out of the closet publicly. I don't need it. Theo's worked his whole life to get to this point in his career, and I know he'll never make me feel like I'm in the shadows. But when he makes the decision to come out publicly, it will be his decision, and his alone.

"Daniel comes home tonight," I say, if he's not back already. "I have to find a way to tell him about us without being cruel. He deserves that. This is going to crush him."

Theo rises from the bed and doesn't wince in pain for the first time since the stabbing. "Oh shit," he says.

"What?" I ask, sitting up.

"With everything that happened, I didn't realize I didn't tell you," he says.

I rise from the bed now, too. Lightning flashes in the sky outside. "Tell me what?" I ask nervously. "Theo, what are you talking about?"

"Daniel knows. About us," he says.

I fly off the bed as if I'm a superhero. How can this be? "What? How?"

"He confronted me about it. That's why I told you that you had to choose. He threatened to out me publicly if I didn't end it."

I feel my face fall, and my cheeks start to feel warm as blood rushes to them. Daniel never said a word to me about it. Is Theo crazy?

"Are you kidding me?" I ask, bewildered.

"I assumed he told you," he says. "And since you didn't choose me, I thought that was why you and I were over."

"What does he know?"

"I don't know."

I turn to the window and stare for a moment, in complete shock. Daniel confronted Theo weeks ago, and I'm just now hearing about it. Why wouldn't Daniel have called me out on our affair? It does explain why he's checked on me so often since Theo and I broke up. My entire mood shifted. The rain starts to patter against the window.

"I better get going. My Phantom doesn't do well when the roads are wet." It rains so little in Southern California that when it does rain, the roads become slick as snot from months-old oil being rinsed off.

I find my blue T-shirt and put it on. Theo stands at the foot of the bed.

"What are you going to do about Daniel?" he asks.

I shake my head, confused. "I don't know why he didn't confront me," I say. "And you don't know what he knows?" I ask again, just to be sure.

"No, but he assumed something. Enough to threaten my career," he says.

And there it was. If I ever needed a sign of when the right time to tell Daniel was, it was now. For weeks, we have coexisted in the same house. Well, when he's home from work, and nothing about Theo has been brought up. For weeks, he witnessed me fall into a sad state of heartbreak and oppression, and he checked on me nearly every day. But he never asked about my relationship with Theo. But I can't stop asking myself, what exactly does he know?

By the time I get home, the rain is coming down so hard that my helmet shield isn't even visible anymore. I really should have left Theo's 30 minutes sooner. The roads were so slippery, I nearly slid off my Phantom twice.

I hit the button on my keychain, and the garage door opens. As I pull in, I park my Phantom next to Daniel's car. I hop off the Phantom and remove my helmet. I'm soaked from head to toe from the rain. I slide off my leather jacket and give it a few shakes. Water droplets splash onto the concrete floor. My eyes land on Daniel's front left tire. It's completely flat. That's strange, I think to myself. The car hasn't been taken out of the garage in the last three weeks while Daniel's been traveling. He takes a car service to and from the airport. Of course, the tire could have been flat this whole time, considering I usually park my Phantom in the side yard, but not when it's raining.

I enter the foyer from the garage and set my helmet on the side table. I hear Daniel pecking away on his laptop in the kitchen.

"Cameron, is that you?" he shouts.

"Yes," I say. Who else would it be? An intruder certainly wouldn't answer.

I enter the kitchen and find him sitting at the breakfast bar, working. I pull out a small towel from the kitchen drawer, where we keep the towels, and wipe my hands and face.

"Did you know your car has a flat?" I ask him.

"Yes, I noticed that when I got home," he says. "Forgot to call AAA."

Thunder blasts outside, sounding like the roof is about to cave in. Daniel peers out the kitchen window.

"Wow, it's really coming down out there," he says.

I look down at my soaked jeans. Clearly. I move to the other side of the bar to face Daniel. I stare directly at him. This is it. This is the moment of truth. Daniel looks up, then stops typing.

"Cameron, what's wrong?"

I can't hide the emotion from my face. It wears heavy on me. "You know," I blurt out.

"Know what?" he asks.

We continue to stare at each other, daring the other to make a move. Checkmate. We both probably think, who's going to blink first? I decide it will be me.

"About Theo."

Daniel stares back at me for what feels like an eternity. He calmly replies, "I do."

"How?" I ask. I have to know. What weren't we careful of?

He raises his eyebrows and closes his laptop. "I didn't really know until you chose not to tell me he went home with you," he says.

That's it. When Theo surprised me when I went home to see my father in the hospital. I knew Daniel suspected something then, when we fought about it in the car. But then I remember Theo telling me Daniel threatened to out him publicly, and this bothers me.

"You threatened him with his career?" I ask.

He tilts his head and looks at me strangely. Almost like a tribal chief. "I was protecting mine," he says.

"Mine?" I ask. Is he serious right now?

"Yes, you are mine. He was threatening that."

I take a deep breath. It's time he knows the truth. It's time he knows I'm leaving him.

"Daniel, I don't know how to tell you this…" I begin, but he cuts me off, waving his hands in the air and then smirking.

"Cameron, don't. It's over. He won't be bothering you anymore."

"Bothering me? You don't get it." In all the years I've known Daniel, I've never seen him this arrogant before. Like he won a wrestling match with a state champion.

"What don't I get?" he asks sarcastically.

I'm not sure if it's his pompous attitude right now or the fact that I've been wanting to come clean so desperately these past few weeks, but the words escape my mouth before I can even edit them. "I'm in love with him."

A cold chill grows in the room as Daniel's smirk immediately disappears.

"No, you're not. Cameron, you had an emotional affair. Sometimes they happen. It's going to pass," he says in complete denial. An emotional affair. What? And then the realization hits me like a ton of bricks. Daniel doesn't really know about Theo and me. He thinks we had an emotional affair. This explains so much to me right now. For one, why he never confronted me about it. He thought he stopped an affair from happening. He thought he beat Theo.

I close my eyes, ashamed. I never wanted to hurt Daniel, but this is going to do it. It's going to crush him, but he must know. "It was physical too," I confess.

Another thunderclap blasts in the sky, shaking the windows. I watch as Daniel's face literally crushes before my eyes. He sits staring back at me in disbelief, words unable to escape his tongue. His eyes transform from hurt to scorned in the matter of moments.

"You let another man touch you?" he asks, as cold as ice. His tone has definitely changed to something darker. I tense up.

"Daniel…" I say as he rises from the stool and stands on his feet.

"How long?" he demands to know. I swallow hard but notice Daniel never taking his eyes off me. He walks around the counter toward me. "How long have you been fucking?" he screams at me. I jump at the level of his voice. His scream startled me.

"A few months," I blurt out. He comes to me and stands face to face. Our noses are only an inch or two apart. He grabs me by my shoulders, and I flinch. There is pure rage in his eyes. A rage I have never seen before. His face screams anger, and I can tell he's restraining himself from doing something worse right now, like headbutting me for causing him this pain.

"Where is he?" he asks, tightening his grip on my

shoulders. I shake my head.

"Daniel, you need to calm down."

"Where the fuck is he?" he asks again, but this time, deadly serious.

"He's at his home," I say, hoping that by answering his question, he will calm down. I look into his eyes again, and they stare back at me, revealing not only rage but also scorn and betrayal.

Without a moment of further hesitation, Daniel pushes my shoulders back, knocking my hips into the kitchen counter. I stumble back to my feet and watch Daniel race out of the kitchen.

"He's mine!" he screams, heading toward the garage.

Oh no. What have I done? What have Theo and I done? And what is Daniel about to do?

Chapter 37

Daniel

There have been only two times in my entire life when I was so angry that I literally saw red. The first was in high school, when I was on the basketball team. My coach benched me so a transfer student could get some game time because that transfer student had two scouts in the audience. The same scouts I had spent the entire season working to impress for a scholarship to college. When I was pulled from the game, rage consumed me, and suddenly, the entire court turned red. Every single person in the audience took on a pinkish hue, and my coach's face burned as bright as an apple.

As I calmed down over the next several minutes, the

red faded. But it was a color I would never forget.

The second time I saw red was today.

Right after Cameron told me he had been having a sexual affair with that little prick, Theo Diaz.

I always knew Theo was untrustworthy. I just didn't know Cameron was too.

The moment he confessed, my blood pressure skyrocketed, and the world shifted.

Red.

All I see is red.

And as for Theo Diaz. He's mine.

My warnings to out him clearly weren't enough. He must have thought I was bluffing. But that's fine. Because when I'm done with Theo Diaz, he'll wish he had never crossed paths with me. I'm going to destroy him. First, his reputation. Then, his career. He is mine.

I've never been a fighter, but I grew up in the suburbs of Philadelphia, where disagreements were settled with fists. Once you learn how to throw a punch, or block one for that matter, you never forget that skill. It stays with you like muscle memory, like a reflex buried deep in your bones.

I pushed Cameron, hard, to get him out of my way.

He stumbled backward, crashing into the kitchen counter with a sickening pop. His hip, probably. I didn't mean to push him so forcefully, but I can't help it. The anger inside me is unbearable.

I race to the foyer, snatching my car keys from the side table. I hear Cameron's footsteps behind me, his voice desperate as he pleads with me to stop, to listen.

I don't care what he has to say.

I'm so livid, I might hurt him too. Just like I'm going to hurt Theo.

The red haze refuses to lift.

I can't even stand the sight of Cameron right now. He

disgusts me.

I fling open the garage door, only to be greeted by the mocking sight of my car's flat tire.

"Fuck!" I roar, my voice shaking with fury. The veins in my neck and forehead feel like they're about to burst.

Slamming the garage door shut, I turn back to Cameron, who stands there with pleading eyes.

"Daniel, stop. Please, let's talk about this."

He looks so dirty to me right now. Like a filthy rat.

I did everything for him, and this is how he repays me?

The betrayal churns inside me, turning my stomach into knots. I want to vomit. I gave him everything he went and cheated on me. Destroyed our beautiful marriage. And to confess to me that he's in love with another man.

"Daniel…" He pleads again.

"Fuck you!" I snap.

I don't know what's come over me, but right now, I feel like the villain in some overbudgeted superhero movie. I feel like I have the strength of ten men, and I need to release it.

Then, I see Theo's smug face in my mind. That arrogant, nonchalant expression he wore when I warned him to stay away from my husband at The Monastery.

I turn away from Cameron. His guilt, his tears, they mean nothing to me.

My eyes land on his Phantom helmet.

In an instant, I grab the keys, snatch the helmet, and dash through the side garage door.

"Daniel, no," Cameron calls after me. "It's raining."

But I don't care.

I'm the one who taught Cameron how to ride the Phantom. My father had a motorcycle when I was growing up, and he taught me everything. During the summers, we'd ride for hours, the Pennsylvania air rushing past us.

If anything, I'm a better rider than Cameron.

And since he made it home in the rain just fine, so will I.

In the garage, I throw on the helmet and hit the button to open the large door. The Phantom roars to life beneath me just as Cameron rushes out, blocking my path.

"Daniel, get off the bike. It's dangerous," he says.

I don't listen.

The rain pounds against the pavement behind him. I grab his black leather jacket, slide it on to cover my upper body from the storm, and glare at him.

"Move aside, Cameron," I command.

I'm not sure if I'm capable of running him over at this point, but God help him if he tests me.

He doesn't move.

I shrug, and peel away.

Cameron flies out of the way, landing on the wet grass.

I wasn't really going to hit him… was I?

I zoom down the street, watching him get back to his feet in the side mirror.

Left behind.

The rain pounds harder, making it difficult to see, but I don't care. My rage fuels me. The adrenaline rushes through my veins.

I merge onto the 10 Freeway, weaving between cars. Water sprays against my helmet visor, lowering my visibility. The front tire slips, and for a split second, I think I'm going to slide beneath a semi-truck.

But the tire holds.

Good.

More speed, then.

I haven't been this reckless since high school, and it feels good. Anything feels better than picturing Theo's body on top of Cameron's.

The image flashes in my mind, and I nearly slam into the trunk of a slowing car.

I swerve at the last second, riding between lanes at 45 miles per hour in the pouring rain.

I know where Theo lives because I transferred all his contact info from Cameron's phone before he even agreed to meet with me. I hope Cameron doesn't warn him of my arrival. I want to see the surprise on his face when I confront him and announce to the world that Theo Diaz is a gay man who has been having an affair with my husband.

A car honks, snapping me back to reality. I veered into its lane. Nearly crashed into me.

Minutes later, I finally arrive at Theo's condo building, a sleek, ten-story high-rise. The storm clouds cast a dark gray over Santa Monica, making the lobby lights glow from within. Through the floor-to-ceiling windows, I see the lavish interior of marble floors, granite walls, and chandeliers.

Several occupied metered parking spaces sit before it in front of the sidewalk. I zoom into a spot that the vehicle has left enough room for me to park the Phantom sideways in. I nearly drop the bike to the curb as I hop off it and race up the stairs to the lobby.

A woman bundled in ski gear exits the lobby. I grab the door before it swings shut and step inside.

A few residents lounge on plush white couches, watching the rain. Their conversations fade as I storm past them.

I charge to the enormous concierge desk that sits in the back of the lobby. Its marble finish is gray, black, and white. The concierge, a man in his late 50's, with white balding hair, wears a red and gold uniform with a navy-blue blazer. His name tag reads *Carl.*

He finishes a phone call and offers me a polite smile. "How may I help you, sir?"

"Theo Diaz," I say, my voice sharp. "What's his unit number?" I was able to get Theo's phone number and address from Cameron's phone, but his actual unit number wasn't listed in Cameron's address book.

"I'm terribly sorry, sir, but I can't give out that information."

I slam my hand on the counter. The sound echoes through the lobby.

"Then get him down here."

Carl stares at me, unmoved. He's probably seen plenty of entitled brats throw tantrums in this building.

Fine.

I step back and bellow, "*Theo Diaz! Theo Diaz! Come down here, you coward!*"

I'm not proud of myself right now, but I know the commotion will definitely get his attention.

Carl picks up the phone. I don't know if he's calling Theo or the police.

Everyone in the lobby has stopped their conversations. All eyes are on me.

Now I wait.

Either I get escorted out in handcuffs or Theo faces me like a man.

Either way, a scene will be made today and hopefully a tabloid will make a story of it.

Chapter 38

Theo

I sit in my living room, nursing a beer, watching the rain pour outside. It rarely rains in L.A., and when it does, it reminds me of being back East. The dark gray and purple storm clouds turn the ocean into an ugly, almost black, menacing stretch. The waves crash onto shore violently, whipped by the storm.

My phone rings. I glance down, Cameron. I smile.

"I was just thinking about you," I say as I answer.

"Theo," he responds, his voice shaking. My stomach tightens, and I sit up. "Daniel knows about us."

"I know…" We discussed this earlier today.

"No, he didn't know before. He thought it was just an

emotional affair." Cameron pauses. "But I told him the truth. I told him I loved you."

I take a swig of my beer, unable to stop the smile forming on my lips. Cameron loves me. And I love him. We're finally going to be together.

"He's enraged. I've never seen him like this before."

"Are you okay?" I ask. His voice is so unsteady. Did Daniel do something to him? Did he hurt him?

"It's not me," Cameron says. "He's coming for you."

I frown. I don't exactly know what to make of that statement. "Coming for me? What do you mean?"

Cameron's breath is shaky. "He took my Phantom. He's on his way to you." A heavy silence, then, "Theo… he's lost it."

Lost it? What does that even mean?

"Okay…" My mind races. I'm at a loss for words. He's coming for me and he's lost it?

"I have to go. My Lyft is here. I'm on my way to you." Cameron hangs up.

I exhale sharply and get dressed, swapping my sweats for dark blue jeans and a light green T-shirt. Then I wait.

The minutes drag. It's been almost half an hour since Cameron called, and nothing has happened. Maybe Daniel just needed time to cool off.

Then my phone rings again. The concierge of my building.

"This is Theo."

"Mr. Diaz, I'm so sorry to bother you," Carl, my concierge, says. I hear yelling in the background. "There appears to be a mad man here screaming your name."

"Theo Diaz! Theo Diaz! Come down here, you coward!" I hear the man screaming in the background.

"I am going to call the police, but I thought you should know first."

Cameron was right. Daniel is here. And from the

sound of it, he's lost it. But I can't let the police get involved. Who knows what he'd tell them? And in this town, no one keeps a damn secret. After the cover-up my team had to pull off after that hookup-turned-attack, the last thing I need is another scandal.

"There's no need to call the police," I say. "He's a friend of a friend. I pissed him off."

"Apparently," Carl says with a hint of judgment in his voice. "I'm sure you understand this man's behavior is simply unacceptable."

"I'll be right down."

"Sir? Are you sure? He's extremely upset. I really think it would be safer if we contact the authorities."

"No cops." I say sternly. Dammit Carl. Just listen to me. "I'm coming down."

I hang up, lock my door, and head for the elevator. I'll talk Daniel down. He's pissed because I slept with his husband, and now we're in love. If I were in his shoes, I'd be furious too. Hell, if punching me will make him feel better, I'll let him.

The elevator ride feels endless. My feet fidget and my stomach turns sour. I have no idea what's about to happen, but I know this much: this is my punishment for taking another man's husband.

The doors slide open.

Carl stands at the concierge desk to my right. His eyes meet mine, then flick toward the lobby. I follow his gaze.

Daniel is pacing in the middle of the room, soaked from the rain, his leather jacket dripping onto the marble floor. His face is flushed red. Then his eyes lock onto mine.

"Daniel," I say, cautiously approaching him.

His fists clench. His expression hardens. "How could you?" His voice is loud, too loud.

I notice three residents, or their guests, sit on the

couch about ten feet from us. Their eyes and ears fully engaged into this conversation.

"I…" I don't know what to say. But I don't have to because in the matter of two seconds Daniel's fist connects with my left cheek.

Pain explodes through my face as I stumble back. The three people on the couch jump to their feet.

"It's okay," I raise a hand to them. "I'm fine."

"He's everything to me," Daniel says, cradling his fist.

"I deserved that," I admit. "Do it again." If punching me makes him feel better, then go for it. Or does it make me feel better?

"What?" He blinks.

"Hit me again. I deserve it."

Daniel hesitates, then swings. Harder this time. My cheek feels like it's about to explode.

"Don't stop. Let it out, dude." I barely register that two people are now filming us with their phones. Carl has picked up the phone. He's calling the cops. Shit.

"You're crazy," Daniel mutters, shaking his injured fist from the pain of meeting my cheekbone twice.

"Look, unless you want us both to get arrested, we have to leave this building," I tell him. Daniel just stares at me in disbelief. "Let's go outside."

I turn toward the lobby doors. After a moment, he follows.

We step onto the sidewalk, the rain hammering down. My cheek burns, blood trickling down where the skin split. Damn, just when it had finally healed from the knife wound. Who knew a businessman could have such a swing?

"You're a son of a bitch!" Daniel screams at me.

And now I've had enough. Daniel got two good punches in on me. Not that that excuses my actions, but he seems to be unwilling to understand he let this happen too.

"You don't deserve him," I confess. "You aren't there for him."

I have to shout to drown out the sound of bustling cars and trucks zooming by on the wet road. Several people with umbrellas breeze by us.

"What are you talking about?" Daniel asks. "I have given him everything we always wanted. His career is because of me." As Daniel says this, he pushes his fingers into my chest hard pushing me back a couple steps.

"No!" I shout back. "His career is because of HIM. He did it. You were on the sidelines putting your career first. You don't even know who he is anymore." Daniel's eyes scream fury back at me. "Ask yourself, Daniel, when was the last time you asked how he was. How he truly was?"

Daniel stiffens. I said something that struck him because his eyes are transitioning from that fury to sadness.

"You don't get to judge my marriage," he seethes. "You're the one who destroyed it. You had an affair with my husband. My *everything*!" He screams at me with spit flying out of his mouth after every word.

The rain pours harder. It beats on my now swelling my left cheek, causing pain. My heart breaks at the way he said *his everything.* It's almost as if he knows he's responsible too. Not for the infidelity, but for the marriage sinking.

A car screeches to a halt in the distance. Cameron flies out of the back seat.

"If he really is your everything," I say, "then ask yourself, *is he happy*?"

Daniel stares at me, frozen.

"Are *you* happy?" I ask.

Cameron is now running to us from the street. Daniel

tilts his head almost confused. He's considering what I said.

"Daniel!" Cameron races to him and immediately notices his bloody hand. Daniel just stands there staring like a deer in headlights. "Theo, your face," Cameron says pointing to me. Guess Daniel busted me up pretty good on that last swing.

I hear sirens in the distance. Daniel looks at Cameron and then at me. Even without touching, he sees it, our body language, the way we *fit*.

His breath shudders. He shakes his wet hair and turns away.

"Daniel?" Cameron grabs his arm, but Daniel yanks it free.

"You two deserve each other," he mutters, heading toward the Phantom.

Cameron rushes to me, fingers ghosting over my face. "Theo, are you okay?"

"I'll be fine," I say, watching Daniel.

He reaches the bike, grabs the helmet lying beside it, and puts it on. Then he swings onto the seat, gripping the handlebars. He flinches. His right fist is still raw from hitting me.

He turns the handlebars to the left and quickly pulls out. He doesn't check for traffic. Just pulls out. This was a mistake.

A car screeches. Tires burn against the wet pavement.

Then, impact.

The car slams into him without breaking. Daniel and the bike are smashed into the car's front grille. The car skids several feet before coming to a stop. Daniel is catapulted into the air.

He hits the pavement with a sickening crack.

The sound of a melon falling from a 2nd story building is the same sound I hear in that instant as Daniel's head, secured in the helmet, slams onto the pavement.

And then, I hear Cameron scream.

Chapter 39

Cameron

My heart sinks deep into my stomach, and my body freezes in shock as I watch Daniel's body hit the wet pavement with a loud thud. I can hardly believe my eyes for the first two seconds. I know the image of him soaring through the air will be permanently etched into my memory.

I stare in shock for what feels like hours, but I know it's only been a few seconds. Without thinking, my mouth opens and a scream erupts, loud enough to pierce anyone's ears.

Theo turns to me, his mouth open, just as shocked as I am. His face has gone three shades paler, and then he looks back at Daniel, lying on the street. His feet move lightning-fast, and he races to Daniel.

The screeching of tires on the pavement fills the air. I look to see a white box truck skidding through the street, heading right for Theo. Theo immediately leaps back onto the sidewalk as the box truck skids out of control, specifically avoiding the lying Daniel and the Phantom. It veers to the left and crashes into a traffic pole with a loud smashing sound. Glass shatters everywhere.

People begin to swarm the accident site within seconds. Daniel and the Phantom lie in the street, the car that hit Daniel skidded onto a grassy area, and the white box truck has smashed into a traffic pole.

The driver of the vehicle that hit Daniel exits her car. She wears jeans and a purple coat. Her stringy blonde hair flutters in the wind as she cries over what happened. She seems uninjured.

A door creaks open, and the driver of the box truck hops out of the front cab. He's an overweight man in his 50s, Latin. His eyes are wide in shock, probably from the accident, and he, too, seems uninjured.

By the time I look to Theo again, he's gone. He's already with Daniel, and another man has joined them, claiming to be a doctor. The man wears a green raincoat and black slacks. All I can think is, *What have I done?* None of this would have happened if I hadn't told Daniel tonight. I stand frozen in place, staring.

"Don't move him!" the doctor yells at Theo. Theo's already on the phone, presumably calling 911. He looks panicked. He glances back at me, his eyes as wide as saucers. I still can't believe my own eyes. I can tell he can't believe his either.

Refusing to be a statue anymore, I force my feet to move and sprint to Theo and the doctor standing over Daniel.

"Cameron, no!" Theo screams at me as I get closer. He blocks me from coming any closer. I can't see anything on Daniel. His helmet is still on, the visor covered in blood from the inside.

"Oh, no…" I look at Theo. "Is he… dead?"

Theo pulls me in close and holds me tight. I look at the doctor in civilian clothes, carefully assessing Daniel, being cautious not to move him, checking for a pulse.

Fifteen minutes.

That's how long it took for the ambulance to arrive at the scene. It was the longest fifteen minutes of my life. It felt like fifteen hours. The doctor on the scene was able to confirm Daniel had a pulse and was still breathing and assisted him until the EMTs arrived.

I rode in the back of the ambulance with Daniel and two EMTs, one man and one woman, while they worked on him. They told me they couldn't be sure, but they think the helmet may have saved his life. I thanked God Daniel put that helmet on right before getting on the Phantom. *Dammit, Daniel. Why didn't you check before pulling out of that spot?*

They also advised me that he probably has several broken bones, but we won't know for sure until X-rays are conducted at the hospital. He's lucky he didn't get run over by that box truck, I keep telling myself.

Once we arrived at the emergency room, a team of doctors and nurses was already waiting for us. Daniel, still unconscious, was rushed to the operating room right away. I followed the running doctors and nurses until we reached the double operating room doors, where one of the nurses stopped me. She wore a warm smile as she said, "You can't go any further. He's in the best hands right now." She then directed me to the waiting room.

I've been sitting in the waiting room for the past three

hours. I hear the news blasting from a flat-screen TV on the wall. My head aches from the sobbing I've done since the accident. I can feel my bloodshot eyes throbbing, and my headache intensifies. I find myself rocking back and forth in the chair when Theo walks in, wearing a worried face.

"Any news?" he asks, taking a seat next to me and handing me a paper cup of black coffee. It steams from the heat. He looks as bad as I feel. I shake my head.

Theo stayed behind to speak with the police officers, who are now investigating the accident. Amid the commotion, no one reported Daniel assaulting Theo. When the officers asked about his injuries to his face, he simply said he'd been in a fight with another actor while rehearsing scenes for his new movie *Hold Up*. Within seconds, the officers recognized him as they were fans of *Crooked Lies*. No one knew about the fight Daniel and Theo had, except Carl and the witnesses, but no one has come forward, at least not yet.

I glance at Theo, and he glares back at me with so much worry in his eyes. His left cheek is swollen, black and blue, from Daniel's punches. I feel my eyes begin to swell once again.

"This is all my fault," I say, as the tears escape and roll down my cheeks.

"Cameron, stop," Theo says.

I take a sip of the scalding coffee, and it instantly burns my lips and tongue. "This is too hot," I bark, setting it on the floor. Theo touches my hand, but I pull it away. "This would have never happened if I'd told him in a different way."

"Cameron, you can't blame yourself," he says.

"Why? Why not? It's my fault."

A family of three enters the waiting room: a mother, father, and their six-year-old son. The mother and father have been crying. They take a seat on the opposite side of Theo and me.

"Then it's *our* fault," Theo says. "The burden isn't only yours."

I roll my eyes. "He's my husband, Theo. I'm the one who cheated and broke our vows. That's all on me." His eyes soften with comfort. "But thank you for trying."

Theo touches his face and winces in pain. "I'm hoping these painkillers will kick in," he says, shaking a bottle of pills from his pocket.

"Where did you get those?" I ask.

"I have my ways," he says, putting them back.

I eye his left cheek again. "Theo, why did you let him hit you like that?"

He sighs. "Because it's what I would have done to the man who took you away from me," he says. "He needed to."

A doctor, in his early 40s and wearing blue scrubs, steps out from a restricted hallway into the waiting room.

"Cameron Taylor?" he asks.

I rise to my feet instantly and walk toward him. His face is warm.

"That's me," I say. Theo stands behind me.

The doctor smiles, and I feel my heart jolt. "He's going to be fine."

I exhale a long breath of relief. I can't help but smile myself. In that moment, it feels like a 300-pound weight has been lifted from my chest. "Oh, thank God," I say, reassured.

"It was a nasty little wreck, but fortunately, since he was wearing a helmet, it prevented any brain trauma," he says. "There's no internal bleeding, but we had to remove his spleen. We'll keep him for a couple of nights for observation. He does, however, have a broken leg and a couple of cracked ribs, but that appears to be the worst of it. We'll need to put a cast on the leg once the swelling goes down."

I let out another sigh of relief. I smile and turn to Theo, who is smiling too.

"Can I see him? Please? Can I see him?" I ask.

"He's heavily sedated right now, so he won't notice you're there, but for a few minutes, I think it'll be fine."

I feel like jumping up and down with joy. Daniel is going to be fine. "Thank you, doctor. Thank you so much."

I lunge at the doctor and hug him. He jumps, startled, meaning I caught him completely by surprise. He half-hugs me back, and we release. He notices Theo's face.

"Looks like you took a nasty beating," the doctor says. I see Theo nod proudly.

I slowly tiptoe into Daniel's hospital room, not wanting to disturb him. The moon shines through the window, casting a blue glow over him. He's hooked up to the same machines my father was, making the same beeping sounds. His broken leg is propped up and wrapped in mounds of beige bandages.

I take a seat next to his bed and watch him sleep. He looks so peaceful, nothing like the rage I pulled out of him hours ago. My eyes fill with tears as I'm so grateful he's alive.

"I'm so sorry. I never meant for anything like this to happen," I whisper to him. I touch his hand and hold it in mine. "I'm so sorry, baby."

And I sob, not just from easing my own guilt, but from a deep, compassionate sorrow. It's my fault he's in this bed, and I will have to face him when he wakes up.

Chapter 40

Two days later, I head straight to the hospital. I don't even make time to stop for a coffee. The doctor called and informed me that he's awake. I asked if I could see him, fully expecting the staff to tell me no because Daniel refuses to see his cheating husband. But they didn't. They said I was welcome to come see him during visiting hours and that he'd probably be thrilled to see me. They obviously don't know about the affair I've been having, which ended with my husband nearly being killed in a motorcycle accident, leaving the site of my lover, after beating his face.

Daniel has been moved to room 218 as his injuries are healing to the doctor's satisfaction. When I enter, I see Daniel sitting up, awake, picking at a plastic container of orange Jell-O on a tray table over his bed. His leg is still propped up, now encased in a large white cast. I suppose the swelling has gone down since they casted it. I smile wide when our eyes meet.

"Hey, you're awake," I say.

He half-smiles. "The nurse told me you've been here the past two days."

"Of course I have," I say, eagerly sitting in the chair next to his bed. "How are you feeling?"

He shrugs. His eyes fall to his casted leg. "This is going to be a bitch," he says.

I politely grin and grab his hand. "I'm so glad you're okay," I say.

We sit there silently for a few minutes. The room feels thick with things to say, but neither of us attempts to speak. Until…

"I was out of my mind," he says. "I've never lost control like that. I can't even believe I punched him." Daniel looks at me with apology in his eyes. But he doesn't owe either of us an apology. He did what he should have done. We deserved it. Our eyes meet, and then I see the reality of the situation fall upon us. "Cameron, we have to talk about this."

I shake my head. "Daniel, no, we don't. You just survived a motorcycle accident, and…"

He holds a finger to my lips. Funny, Theo does the same thing to me to hush me. How odd.

"Theo said something that made me think," he says.

What did Theo say to him? And when has he had time to think? He's practically been unconscious for the past two days as his body heals.

"We haven't been happy for a long time," he says.

This silences my thoughts. "I know," I admit. "But we try."

Daniel never takes his eyes off mine. I see them begin to fill like puddles of water. He blinks, but doesn't let a tear fall.

"Does he take an interest in you? In everything you do and everything you love?"

My head feels as heavy as stone as the truth will now come out. No more lies. I nod to him, and I feel my eyes beginning to fill too.

"He does," I admit. "He loves to read my work, to hear my ideas."

Daniel half-smiles, a half-smile of regret. "I wish I read more of your stuff too," he admits. "The whole Hollywood thing and movies, and plays, and all that just doesn't interest me."

"I know," I say, nodding in agreement. "I could have done better at listening to your work stories, but your business is just so repetitive and always about making profits."

We continue to stare at each other, both of our eyes as full as an ocean.

"Do you really love him?" Daniel nearly chokes on the word *love*. My eyes are too full, and I release my ocean. I feel warm tears streaming down my cheeks.

"I really do," I concede. It's time to tell Daniel the whole truth. He needs to know this. "I don't know how to tell you this, but while I was falling in love with him, I was falling out of love with you."

He closes his eyes, and the tears are released, now streaming down his cheeks. I hope this moment of honesty isn't hurting him more, but it's time he knows. I owe it to him.

"I want to talk to him," he says.

"Oh, Daniel, that's not a good idea," I protest. The last time Daniel saw Theo, there was so much anger in his eyes I didn't even recognize him. We cannot have Daniel going through that frenzy again.

"I don't care," he says.

"Why do you want to talk to him?" I ask, confused.

"Because it's my right in this. I want to talk to him."

I glance at the bandages over his hands that I hadn't noticed before.

"Cameron, do you really think I'm in any condition to fight him?" he asks, as if reading my mind glancing at his bandaged hands. I chuckle at his statement.

"I suppose not," I say. "I'll see if he's here yet."

"Here?" Daniel asks, surprised.

"Yes, he's been here with me the past two days," I say. The truth is, Theo has refused to leave my side this entire time. He's also been concerned about Daniel's well-being. We may have snuck around Daniel's back and had an affair, but both of us were fully aware that our actions caused all this to happen. But each night, we've gone our separate ways, me to my house, him to his condo.

"Bring him to me," Daniel says.

I find Theo in the waiting room, playing with his phone. I tell him Daniel wants to speak to him. He gives me a confused look, but I assure him it's going to be alright.

I return with Theo. Daniel doesn't smile when we enter the room.

"I want to talk to him alone," he instructs me.

"Daniel…" I say. This cannot be good.

"Cameron, alone."

I glare at Theo, whose eyes reassure me that everything is okay. I step into the hallway, but make sure I'm within earshot. An altercation cannot happen. I hear Theo slide a chair next to Daniel's bed.

"I'm glad you're okay, man," Theo says. I peek into the room and catch Daniel surveying his handiwork on Theo's face.

"I'm not sorry for doing that," Daniel says, and Theo nods.

"I understand."

"What you did was awful. You are responsible for breaking up a marriage," Daniel says.

"I know. I'm sorry," Theo replies.

A quiet grows in the room, and I almost think Daniel has caught me eavesdropping when he asks, "Do you love him?"

"I do. Very much," Theo responds without a moment of hesitation.

Daniel swallows hard. His eyes turn towards the window and gaze at the sun shining on his face. Then they slide back to Theo.

"Then you should be with him."

I see Theo's head pop up, surprised. "What?"

"I'm not going to stand in the way of this. Cameron deserves to be happy, and so do I. What I once thought was going to be forever changed when I realized we were too busy living other lives than sharing the one we had," Daniel says. This realization hits me hard. He's never been more right. He truly has been thinking.

"He's a good guy," Theo says.

"He is, and don't you dare break his heart. If you do… I'll do more than that to your face."

I can see Theo smiling. "I would never."

"Now please leave," Daniel says, looking away again. Theo gets up and offers to shake Daniel's bandaged hand, but Daniel refuses.

Theo approaches the door, meeting my eyes, now knowing I've been listening the whole time. Not to be nosy, but to ensure another fight doesn't break out, I assure myself. Well, maybe a little to be nosy. Theo stops and turns back to Daniel.

"Why are you letting him go so easily?"

I see tears roll from Daniel's face, and he turns to us, now seeing me too.

"Because I almost died protecting something that didn't belong to me anymore," he says. "Life is too short."

Theo nods in agreement and leaves the room. I begin to sit in the chair Theo was in when Daniel looks at me and says, "I don't want you here anymore."

"Daniel…" I protest.

"I need to be alone right now, Cameron. You owe me that."

And I do. "I'll probably be in here a couple more days, and I'll call you when I'm ready to come home." Daniel says.

I rise from the chair. He looks so sad. I begin to head for the door when, "Cameron?" he says. I turn, hoping he's changed his mind. "One more thing, can you bring me my work laptop?"

I shake my head. "Sure," I say. Typical Daniel, always working.

I step into the hallway and glance back at Daniel, whose eyes are staring out the window now. It is in this moment that I realize he and I will never be the same.

Chapter 41

After four days, Daniel calls me to tell me he's being released today. I drive his car to pick him up from the hospital, where he's sitting in a wheelchair with two crutches on his lap, accompanied by a nurse, waiting for my arrival. Once Daniel told me he didn't want me visiting him at the hospital anymore, I contacted a repair service to replace his flat tire.

I hop out of the driver's seat, and by the time I reach the passenger side, the nurse has already helped Daniel inside.

"Thank you," he says. She hands him a brown paper bag. I eye it suspiciously. "Meds," he tells me. I thank the nurse as well and get back into the driver's seat.

The drive home is quiet. Daniel mainly stares out the window. His color has returned to his face, but his right leg, casted up, looks uncomfortable.

Once we arrive home, Daniel and I decide to have lunch. He says he's sick of hospital food. I have him sit at the eat-in kitchen area while I make us two turkey sandwiches. The last time we were in this kitchen together, I told Daniel I was in love with Theo. But I don't dare mention his name today.

I set the plates of turkey sandwiches and potato chips before us on the kitchen table and take a seat across from him.

"Cameron, I'm moving back to New York," he says as I'm mid-bite into my sandwich. I spit my food out. I wasn't expecting that. Daniel just pokes at his sandwich.

"Okay," I say, unsure of what else to say. I'm surprised, but should I really be? Los Angeles has never been his home.

"You can buy me out of the house," he says. "I've already spoken to my boss, and I'm going to be permanently re-assigned to the New York office. I may even get promoted to a VP position by next year."

I nod, trying to be happy for him, but I can't help but feel a pit in my stomach. I've spent my entire adult life with Daniel. Am I really ready to give him up? But I love Theo.

"Daniel, I'm..." I go to apologize for the hundredth time. He's going to completely uproot his life again because of me.

"Don't," he says, interrupting me. "I can't hear apologies anymore. It is what it is." He pauses. "Cameron, I was never happy in L.A. anyway. This is your home, your city, and now you can be happy." He slides his plate back. If he was hungry before, he's not anymore.

"When are you moving?" I ask.

He stares at me in silence, then says, "I have a flight

out tomorrow."

"What?" This is too soon. Daniel just got home. His cast is going to be on for at least another four weeks.

"I probably won't be back. My company is going to pay for my belongings to be relocated back to New York. I don't want any of the furniture." He looks around the room and into the living room. "Too many memories anyway."

I look away, ashamed. "So it really is over?"

"It is," he says. "You'll need to get a divorce lawyer. But it'll be a smooth process."

I look at Daniel's full plate. "Not hungry?"

"Nah," he says. "It's going to be a while before I get my appetite back." We stare at each other for a few moments. Flashbacks flood my memory of meeting him that night at Donna's party, our visits to New York, the winery, our wedding, and moving to Los Angeles.

"I'm going to pack for my flight tomorrow," he says.

Daniel grabs a crutch that had been leaning on the countertop and lifts himself to his feet. I hop out of my chair to assist.

"Don't help me," he snarls. "I need to manage on my own."

Shut down, I slowly take my seat again. I know it must be frustrating to be injured. I know it's the right thing for him to do, go back to New York, but I will miss him dearly. He hops away with the crutch, leaving the kitchen.

"You can come back and visit. Or when I'm in New York, we can have dinner," I say, hoping to secure a future friendship. But he stops.

"You can't have it both ways, Cameron," he says. "You can't have Theo and *me* in your life. It's too hard."

I swallow hard. Daniel doesn't even look back as he speaks. "Maybe one day... but not for a very long time."

And with that, he hops toward the foyer to make his

journey up the stairs, to say goodbye to his life in Los Angeles, and to say goodbye to me.

Forever.

One Year Later

Chapter 42

I wake up to the smell of fresh sausage greeting my nose. Slowly, I rise and stretch from my master bedroom. The morning sun shines in, welcoming the day. I hear Cuban music coming from the kitchen downstairs, and then I remember this is our Sunday morning routine. I smile and hop out of bed, getting dressed.

The music blares louder as I strut down the stairs, stretching one last time. Now, the smell of strong coffee wafts up to meet me.

As I enter the kitchen, I find Theo, wearing his typical Sunday morning outfit, basketball shorts, and a blue tank top that always highlights his great arms. He's wearing a red apron and shaking his hips to the Cuban-themed music, a salsa of some sort.

"Morning, Papi," he says, his glowing smile making

my heart skip, just like when I first fell in love with him. "Café con leche." He slides a small cup of strong black coffee with milk onto the breakfast bar.

The music continues to blare as he grabs my hips, and we dance together. My hips flow ever so delicately with his. We end our dance with a kiss.

Theo stands over the hot stove, continuing to cook the sausages that woke me up. I notice he has already cooked the sunny-side-up eggs, and rice and beans are waiting for us to devour, a Cuban brunch, as he likes to call it.

I take a sip of my hot coffee and lean back, watching my man cook our brunch. I've never seen him so happy before. And I've never been happier, either.

After Daniel moved out, I lived in this great house alone for about three months. Theo and I stayed together and ultimately decided that the house was way too big for just me. I contemplated selling it, but Theo insisted we take the next big step in our relationship and move in together. And we did. He sold his condo in Santa Monica and moved in with me.

"How's the coffee?" he asks, placing the sausages on a hot plate.

"Delicious," I reply, smiling.

I open my phone to check the news, and the first story that pops up is from *The Business Journal*, a New York business magazine that Daniel used to always read and that I find myself reading from time to time. My jaw drops when I see a stunning photo of Daniel, dressed in a complete three-piece designer suit, staring out the window of an enormous corner office facing Central Park. The headline reads: *VPs & 40s: Meet the New Bachelors in Their 40s*. The sub headline says: *Daniel Nichols to Be Named Youngest VP at Mantron & Parks, Corp.*

I can't help but smile as I read the article about the

company's newest and youngest Vice President of their East Coast division. Daniel Nichols finally did it. He earned the job title he'd been working toward his entire adult career. Plus, it mentions a very healthy seven-figure salary that comes with his new digs. I lean back in my chair, proud as I read the article.

"Brunch is served," Theo says, setting the plate in front of me.

Later that day, we both lay out by the pool. I turn to him and ask, "Any regrets?"

He turns to face me. "Not a one, because I love you." And I know he does.

About six months ago, Theo made the decision that it was time to come out. I told him to only do it if he felt it was absolutely necessary, and he said we couldn't move forward until he finally embraced his true self. Against the advice of his management team, he publicly came out, sitting down with a highly rated television journalist.

The ratings were through the roof, and he mostly received public support from the community. The real challenge came when *Hold Up* opened in theaters last month. Gray Studios was furious with Theo for coming out before the movie's release. But to everyone's surprise, the film did rather well, hitting all the anticipated box office numbers. In fact, some reporters claimed it was Theo's coming out that attracted a whole new fan base, the gay community.

Hollywood only cares about numbers and money. Since Theo's film surpassed box office expectations, job offers have kept pouring in. I'm happy to report his career hasn't been affected negatively whatsoever since coming out. We got lucky.

"What do you want to do tonight?" he asks. "We could check out that new restaurant on Santa Monica Blvd, the one with the dancing servers."

I laugh at the thought of dancing servers. Oh, the crazy, cheeky things Los Angeles businesses come up with to stay posh.

"Or…" I say, "we could stay home and…" Before I even finish my thought, Theo is on his feet, pulling me toward him. "Whoa," I laugh as he slings me over his shoulder and slaps my butt.

"You're mine," he says, carrying me to the bedroom, where we make love the rest of the afternoon.

And there it is. Everyone got what they wanted. Daniel finally got the promotion he worked so hard for and longed to achieve, without the nagging spouse demanding more of his time. I finally realized he and I were never meant to go in the same direction. And I think he did too. My mother and Daniel still speak, and she told me she hasn't heard this kind of happiness in his voice in a very long time, which warms my heart.

Theo and I got what we wanted. We finally get to be together and share our love. Ultimately, I got what I wanted too because Theo came out publicly. We would never have to hide our relationship again. It's funny how well life can work out, and it did. What once was considered a risqué love affair between two men has blossomed into a beautiful relationship, and I'm sure we'll be hearing wedding bells soon.

The End

Acknowledgments

To my beta readers, Jose Guerrero, Linda Stiverson, Melissa Stepanian, and Nik Johansen, thank you for lending your time, eyes, and honest feedback on early drafts. Your insights were invaluable.

To Gregory Loizzo and Trystan Colburn, your anticipation for new pages kept me going more than you probably realize. Knowing you were waiting made me sit down and *finish*, again and again.

To my incredible writers' groups, Nick Henry Jackson, Ember Condron, Nikki VanBroekhuizen, Sean Michael Conway, and Mike Warnecke, thank you for your creative notes, thoughtful questions, encouragement, and the occasional brutal honesty. Your input shaped this story in ways I'll always be grateful for.

Every book is a collaboration, no matter how private the writing process may feel. I'm lucky to have had such talented, supportive, and amazing people in my writing circle.

About the Author

Kyle Coffman is an award-winning filmmaker, writer, and the host of *Dark Corner,* a horror podcast. He has a knack for storytelling that spans genres and platforms.

Under his production company, *Sebastian Films Unlimited*, Kyle has written, produced, and directed a range of acclaimed short films. His work has screened at numerous film festivals, with his short film *Groomsday* earning multiple awards at LGBTQ+ festivals. He also directed and co-produced the popular LGBTQ+ first season of *Guys Like You.*

Kyle's storytelling extends to fiction literature as well. His debut novella, *Hell's Road* (2016), is a chilling survival-the-night teen thriller that showcases his horror roots. His novel, *Falling for Theo*, is a poignant gay romance that asks: what happens when you marry the love of your life, then meet your soulmate? This novel explores the complexity of love, timing, and the choices that define our fate.

Whether he's behind the camera or at the keyboard, Kyle's ability to connect with audiences and readers through emotionally meaningful and genre-blending stories continues to define his voice as a dynamic writer in today's entertainment landscape.

www.KyleCoffman.com

www.ingramcontent.com/pod-product-compliance
Lightning Source LLC
La Vergne TN
LVHW090556110826
845146LV00001B/144

* 9 7 9 8 2 1 8 9 3 4 1 4 9 *